OPERATION DIMWIT

Yellow Shoe Fiction

Michael Griffith, Series Editor

Also by Inman Majors

Penelope Lemon: Game On!
Love's Winning Plays
The Millionaires
Wonderdog
Swimming in Sky

OPERATION DIMWIT

A *PENELOPE LEMON* NOVEL

INMAN MAJORS

LOUISIANA STATE UNIVERSITY PRESS   BATON ROUGE

Published by Louisiana State University Press
Copyright © 2020 by Inman Majors
All rights reserved
Manufactured in the United States of America
First printing

DESIGNER: Michelle A. Neustrom
TYPEFACE: Whitman
PRINTER AND BINDER: Sheridan Books, Inc.

LIBRARY OF CONGRESS CATALOGING-IN-PUBLICATION DATA

Names: Majors, Inman, author.

Title: Operation dimwit : a Penelope Lemon novel / Inman Majors.

Description: Baton Rouge : Louisiana State University Press, [2020] | Series: Yellow
shoe fiction

Identifiers: LCCN 2019040504 (print) | LCCN 2019040505 (ebook) | ISBN 978-
0-8071-7267-4 (cloth) | ISBN 978-0-8071-7316-9 (pdf) | ISBN 978-0-8071-7317-6
(epub)

Subjects: GSAFD: Humorous fiction.

Classification: LCC PS3563.A3927 O64 2020 (print) | LCC PS3563.A3927 (ebook) |
DDC 813/.54—dc23

LC record available at https://lccn.loc.gov/2019040504

LC ebook record available at https://lccn.loc.gov/2019040505

To Michael Griffith,
King Moonracer on the Island of Misfit Writers

Whatever is funny is subversive.

—GEORGE ORWELL

OPERATION DIMWIT

1

It was Thursday afternoon after work and Penelope was stalking around her friend Sandy's den, holding a refreshing glass of chardonnay in one hand and gesturing with the other. She was mimicking her son with his face in a cell phone searching for PlinkyMo characters. In her wanderings around the den, she was bumping into floor lamps, chairs, the couch and TV, sloshing a bit of the divine nectar here and there. She was demonstrating the extreme focus Theo exhibited while on the hunt for Plinkies.

Her friends at the kitchen table found this amusing. They both had kids addicted to PlinkyMo, the latest gaming fad, and had been driven out of their minds by it. This is how their get-togethers generally got started—making sport of their children's foibles, quirks, and assorted psychological vulnerabilities—before moving on to other topics. Penelope assumed they'd eventually get around to her ex-husband James. His obsessions and escapades were always comedic gold, and the audience before her was like bees to honey when the subject came up. She had a few decent-size nuggets to drop on them when the time was right.

"I think you missed a spot," Sandy said, pointing to an old recliner that her husband sat in on fall days to watch football. "Pour a little wine on that one and I think you'll have watered the whole room."

Grinning, Penelope returned to the table. Her performance of entranced Theo had been nuanced and subdued, even down to his cute little frown of concentration as he bungled around the room. If some furniture had taken it on the chin in the process, well, that was the price of art.

"Do you want me to clean up?" she asked. "I'll get a rag out of the kitchen."

Sandy waved her off with a look of disgust. "Are you kidding? Slosh away. No telling what my kids have spilled on that furniture. It's like one big petri dish in there."

Penelope nodded and filled her glass from the bottle on the counter. Her offer to clean up had been perfunctory to the max. That wasn't how they rolled when the wine was flowing, no matter whose house it was. This was doubly true if one was the guest of honor, as she was today. Staring at the glimmering presents on the bookcase, she could almost forget the long months in her mother's basement. Things were finally moving in the right direction, and this housewarming party was a celebration of that inarguable fact.

"So I think James and Ms. Dunleavy, the teacher, are no more," Penelope said, diving right into ex-husband dirt, though she'd planned to build a bit of suspense first. But why wait? When was there ever a wrong moment?

This caused a minor uproar.

"Good for her," Rachel said. "Good for her. Hopefully she got out before James put a stopwatch to her showers."

"He wanted her to split the water bill, and that was all she wrote," said Sandy.

Penelope sat back at the table, smiling. It was true. James and water bills were a volatile combination. In fact, any utility invoice could work him into a froth. On the other hand, charges for his kayak, which went unpaddled in the garage, his archery arrows never fired, or his model volcano that resided so snugly in the hall closet all those years left him unfazed. He was a complicated man.

"I feel better about the young minds of Hillsboro," Sandy said, "just knowing that James and his crackpot ideas on whale calls and nursing babies won't somehow make it onto Ms. Dunleavy's curriculum."

"Whale calls?" said Rachel, smiling her falsely earnest cheerleader smile. "Are you two keeping secrets from me?"

"You have to tell her," Sandy said. "It's time she knew."

Penelope took a long sip. The wine was even more delicious today than usual and that was saying something. There were days she thought she could marry Mr. Chardonnay.

"When Theo was a baby," Penelope said, grinning over her glass, "he used to make this really strange noise after he finished nursing that sounded like a whale call."

Her friends grinned and exchanged glances, which indicated that Penelope was coming through as usual in the story department. This was no surprise. She was totally clutch at cocktail hour.

"You laugh, but that's what it sounded like. Kind of mournful and satisfied at the same time, like Shamu at the end of a show. He'd doze off like four seconds afterward, with a little baby smile on his face. Anyway, the first few times James heard it, he freaked out. He thought something was wrong with Theo."

"Yeah," said Sandy, "nothing that putting him on a toddler leash in a few years wouldn't cure."

"He never did that," Penelope said, feeling duty bound to stick to the facts.

"Yeah, but he talked about it."

This was true. Only an online quiz that determined that the *Harry Potter* character James most resembled was Dumbledore had saved Theo from being leashed like an uncoordinated dog. Dumbledore, said James, would never leash Harry, and neither would he tether young Theo.

Like she would have let him.

"Anyway," said Penelope, looking pointedly at her friends to stop interrupting, "James got used to the sound. In fact, he decided to turn it into a scientific study. Every night he'd record Theo's postnursing moans, and then he'd play those recordings alongside this set of whale call CDs he bought. Which cost like sixty bucks, by the way. So I'm out of my mind—like you always are when you're nursing—and don't remember all the details, other than a microphone hovering around my breasts and James using the word *primordial* a lot. He was sure there was some evolutionary link between Theo's moan and whale calls. He was saying stuff like *You know, our aquatic cousins nurse their young for even longer than humans do.*"

"James is an aquatic cousin himself," Sandy said, and this caused something of a minor laughing jag. Eventually they calmed themselves and Penelope continued.

"So one day I jokingly said we ought to call the song "Ode to Boobie"— which I thought was pretty funny. James didn't. He got so upset. It was like he was an anthropologist and I was undermining the seriousness of his work. I said, *Hey, it's my boob he's gnawing on. I can call it whatever I damn well please.*"

This line did the trick and the lid came completely off the party. They were in full swing now. You could always count on James. He was clutch at story time too.

"By the way," Sandy said once they'd calmed themselves, "how do you know that James and Ms. Dunleavy are Splitsville?"

"Easy. He took down all the references to teachers on his Facebook page."

Her friends cut eyes at each other now, as they did when they thought she'd done something ill advised but oh-so-expected. It was their patented look.

"I'm not checking his Facebook all the time like I was," Penelope said, letting out a sigh. "Seriously, I'm not. And don't act like it's not normal, because it is. Everyone checks up on their ex now and then. It's human nature."

The veracity of this pacified them. If they were divorced, they'd do the same and more. Sandy for sure. Sandy had restraining order written all over her. It dawned on Penelope what was going on, namely that her friends were so habituated to giving her advice that they didn't know how to act when she had her life in order. A drama-free move from her mother's basement and a regular paycheck had flummoxed them. They were now desperate for subjects on which to counsel her. She felt a little guilty for depriving them—for not having any problems that needed their immediate, expert opinion—so she threw out this bone as a kind of peace offering:

"I think James is dating someone else."

This elicited the predicted howls of protest, as well as sympathetic murmurs for the single women in their community who were relegated to dating junior Dumbledores and amateur marine biologists.

"Okay," said Penelope, rubbing her hands together like a game show host when it's time to start the first round. "Let's see who can guess the occupation of James's new mystery gal. I figured it out in one visit to his page, but I was married to him. Let's see how well you know my ex."

Rachel and Sandy settled in now by taking a dose of chardonnay. They were competitive about who the true James expert was. Penelope felt a twinge of guilt—she'd visited his Facebook page three times during the week, not once—but that seemed an irrelevant detail at this point. The game was afoot.

"First off," said Penelope, "his status is now listed as *single-ish*."

"No it is not!" Sandy said, instantly irritated and frowning in her funny way. Nothing got her going like James and his Facebook-as-grand-riddle ways.

"Of course it is," said Rachel, shaking her head knowingly. "He's fourteen and Snapchatting away with his middle school friends. Why wouldn't he be *single-ish*?"

"By the way," Penelope said, "the first one to guess the occupation gets an orange Tic-Tac. The clues will all come from the Likes section. The first one is filed under Movies. The movie is *Rocky*."

"He's dating a boxer," Sandy blurted out.

"No," said Rachel, rushing in. "A judo partner from his dojo. And they will soon be wearing matching little judo robes."

"Damn it, that's it," said Sandy. "Plus you got to say *dojo,* which everyone knows is James's favorite word."

"Sorry," said Penelope, "but we don't have a winner yet. The next clue comes from the Books section. The book is *How to Train Your Dragon.*"

"He's dating Hermione," shouted Sandy, banging her fist on the table for emphasis. "His latest Internet quiz declared him Ron Weasley."

They laughed for a bit about this, though it made no sense. The clue had stumped them.

"*Rocky* and *How to Train Your Dragon,*" Penelope said. "Do you have any guesses?"

"She does something physical," Rachel said. "She's a badass of some sort."

"Maybe," said Penelope, trying to tease it out as long as possible. She felt sure the next clue would clinch the deal. "Okay, here's the last one. It's a song from the eighties."

"'Tainted Love'!" Rachel shouted.

"'Super Freak,'" said Sandy. "Oh wait, he's not talking about himself. Still, I stick with 'Super Freak.'"

Penelope shook her head to both of these. "'Let's Get Physical,' by Olivia Newton John."

"He's dating a trainer at the fitness center," Rachel said, smiling and nodding in a satisfied way to aggravate Sandy. "Case closed. Fork over the Tic-Tac."

"*Rocky,* 'Let's Get Physical,' and *How to Train Your Dragon,*" Sandy said trying to make it all add up. "OMG. Is *train* a pun on *trainer*? Tell me it's not. Because if it is, James has named his penis Dragon."

Penelope frowned at this. During their marriage James had often referred to his junior partner by a pet name. The *frisky cowpoke* was one she'd heard a lot. And during the *Sopranos* she'd grown accustomed to talk of the *little gangster.* But nothing as grand as Dragon. James thought highly of himself as a lovemaker, but this might be a stretch, even for him.

"I think it's just a play on words with *train, trainer,*" Penelope said. "But yeah, I think that's what she does. You guys know I joined Fitness Plus last week? I think James has too. How weird will it be to see him down there?"

"Not as weird as his new girlfriend leading your aerobics group," Rachel said, looking at Sandy, who said, "Oh, yeah. That has awkward written all over it."

Penelope didn't care for the sound of this. She'd yet to attend a class but was considering either Zumba or Dance Fusion, mainly because they were the most fun to say. Maybe her ex's new lady was just a personal trainer. If that were the case, she'd be easy enough to avoid. Fitness Plus was huge.

"Okay, I'm sorry," Sandy said. "But I just can't think anymore about Dragon. I think I'm permanently scarred as it is. Why don't you tell us what your crazy new boss is into now? I know she's got something cooking."

"Nothing much," Penelope said. "Still trying to get that permit from the city so we can move the trailer park somewhere else and get away from the whacker who comes to visit every day."

As intended, this got the conversation onto Dewitt—he was a favorite of the gals—and away from Missy. Penelope wasn't sure why she felt uncomfortable talking about her boss with them, other than it felt a little like betraying one friend to another. Didn't everyone have a quirky pal? And didn't she fulfill that role for Sandy and Rachel? There was also the sisterhood of the single woman. At any rate, she felt no qualms about picking and choosing what she'd divulge about her employer at Rolling Acres Estates, the upscale manufactured home subdivision where she'd recently started working as a receptionist.

Instead, she regaled the ladies with tales of Dewitt, who owned the land that Rolling Acres occupied. Missy and her father leased the property from him, then collected rent from their residents. Rolling Acres was one of forty mobile home communities that father/daughter ran throughout the Southeast. In short, Missy was a trailer park heiress, a duchess of the mobile home. Suitable land was scarce in Hillsboro, so they'd agreed to an unusual stipulation in the contract: Dewitt could use the office bathroom during working hours.

The fact that Dewitt's trailer had a functioning toilet of its own added intrigue to his visits. All signs pointed to a serial wanker, one who liked to do his business in ballpark range of actual women, as gross as that thought was. The women in this case being Missy and Penelope herself.

One of Sandy's kids came in now, complaining of hunger and heat exhaustion, but was quickly hustled out the door with a handful of Popsicles for himself and any other children who might think they were allowed in the house while the ladies were having wine time. While this bum's rush was going on, it dawned on Penelope that her friends were studiously, earnestly, trying not to bring up the subject of her love life. Their avoidance of the topic couldn't have been more obvious. This didn't sit well. It smelled like one of those things they'd decided before she arrived.

When the room was free of youngsters, Penelope blurted out: "So, I've got a date Saturday with my older gentleman friend."

"That's nice," said Sandy, smiling insincerely. "But let's get back to your resident masturbator."

Penelope knew a subject being avoided when she saw one and said: "That's it. Nothing else really to report. It's been pretty quiet at work lately."

"Well, that's good," said Sandy, failing to meet her eye. "Now, who's ready to open some presents?"

So saying, she cleared the plates and floral arrangement while Rachel moved the gifts from bookcase to table.

"Our last date was okay," said Penelope stubbornly. "I think we were both nervous. We'd written each other so much, it felt a little weird to talk face-to-face. I bet it's a lot better this time though."

"Uh-huh," said Rachel, arranging the presents biggest to smallest behind Penelope's wineglass.

"That's great, sweetie," said Sandy, going to the kitchen for a second bottle of wine.

Her instincts had been right. They definitely didn't want to talk about Fitzwilliam, the man she'd met on LoveSynch, her Internet dating service. She hadn't told them much about that date, other than that when she arrived at Starbucks, he was already there and reading the London *Times*. She'd found his outfit—blue blazer, white pants, boating shoes, and a sailing cap on the table—pretty cute, but her friends had hooted considerably when she described it.

"Fitzwilliam is cooking dinner for me at his place," Penelope said, loudly and provocatively, as her friends tried to appear busier than they were. It was obvious they still thought it was too early for her to be dating and that she'd be better off reading self-improvement books and learning to knit.

A long silence ensued.

"I have no idea what his place is going to be like. I thought about Google Mapping it, but that seemed kind of creepy."

Justin Timberlake came over the speakers, and Sandy reentered the room, clapping her hands and saying: "Presents! Presents for Penelope's wonderful new home! Yay! Yay! No more basement. Hurray! Hurray!"

Penelope smiled. "Are you guys refusing to talk about my first real date since the divorce? It kind of seems like a big deal to me."

An even more uncomfortable silence followed, with the friends looking neither at her nor at each other.

"I'll talk about him," Rachel said. "But do you care if I call him *the Admiral* while we do? It just seems to fit an older gentleman in a sailor's cap."

"I'm guessing you guys eat an early bird supper around four thirty," said Sandy, sitting at the table and yanking the stubborn cork out with her teeth. "Then a nice stroll to feed the ducks at the park, followed by a few hands of pinochle. You'll be home by sundown."

Penelope grinned but said no more. Now that the gifts were on the table, she felt less inclined to force a conversation no one else wanted to have. It was business time, and Sandy pushed a package her way. She grabbed it, shook it a little as one does for dramatic effect, then delicately peeled off the wrapping as her friends rained smiles upon her. It was a new coffeemaker. James had gotten theirs in the divorce. The next box contained four plush bath towels. This gift brought her to tears, as she'd been making due with her mom's leftovers, ancient relics originally intended for tiny circus people. The towels were a godsend. As were the toaster oven, three bottles of bubble bath, and some darling oven mitts.

"Wow," Penelope said. "You all did too much."

She was rising to dole out hugs when Rachel put a hand on her shoulder. "Keep your seat, honey. We found one more little gift for you. And it might be the best one yet. It's monogrammed and every-thing." She looked at Sandy. "Is the coast clear?"

Sandy went to the front door and took a peek, then to the bay window that looked out on the backyard. "I think so," she said, "but let's hustle. My kids always know the worst time to bust in."

Rachel nodded in a hurried, furtive way and reached behind her to the cabinet where Sandy kept her place mats, tablecloths, and things of that sort. She pulled out a thin package wrapped in brilliant gold paper. When placed on the table, it landed with a hollow thump and rolled toward Penelope. She picked up the gift by one end and held it straight up. She glanced at the expectant faces of her friends with what she knew was a quizzical look.

"You're going to like that one," Rachel said, nodding and smiling.

"Definitely," said Sandy, leaning over the table for a closer look. "It's just what your house needs right now."

<hr/>

On her way home, she kept looking in the rearview at the bounty in the backseat. She felt like she'd won a showcase on the old *Wheel of*

Fortune. It was a ton of stuff she needed, and she couldn't wait to get home and start finding places for everything.

The exception was the last gift, which she found not as everyday utilitarian as the rest. Would it be ungrateful to throw it out? It was personalized, after all, though that was weird in its own way. Gag gifts weren't supposed to be complicated. But was it even a gag? Her friends had been a little hard to read on that front.

Considering the last, complicated present led to thoughts of Theo and the unpredictable searches he went on when looking for batteries for a Wii controller. When electronics went dead, he was truly a madman, rampaging through drawers and rifling closets in his quest for renewed gaming power.

These indoor explorations reminded her that in two days' time he would be making explorations of the outdoor variety at Camp Sycamore. It was his first ever summer camp and she worried that she'd been hasty in agreeing to let him go. What if they had feather pillows in the cabin and his asthma kicked in? There wasn't an inhaler big enough to handle that scenario. He'd need a scuba tank of albuterol.

She made a mental note to remind James about the inhaler and the foam pillow when he dropped Theo off after karate. Then she punched the gas. She had less than an hour to hide the very complicated gift. It wasn't the sort of thing a nine-year-old boy would want on his mind when roasting wienies around the campfire.

2

The next morning at work Penelope paid a few Rolling Acres bills then made a phone call to the recycling place to confirm that the new pickup day was Friday. Afterward, as often happened at the end of the week, she found herself with little to do, and her thoughts drifted to Theo. Wasn't two weeks an awfully long time for a nine-year-old to be away from home? Of course, the camp was in North Carolina, so that made everything awesome, according to James. He was a staunch Tarheel, a proud Tarheel, a Tarheel from head to toe, and he was determined that his deprived Virginia son would know every plaintive lyric to "Carolina in My Mind" before the next school bell rang.

She realized she was working herself into a solid case of parental anxiety, partly to distract herself from what Dewitt was doing in the office bathroom ten feet away.

Maybe a new ringtone would distract her. As kickass as it was, "Crazy Train" was getting stale. She needed a song that said *Single* and *Independent* and *Not a mom for two weeks*. She was looking at no parental duties for the longest stretch in more than nine years. Talk about footloose and fancy-free. What tune encompassed all that?

Definitely not "Footloose." That song bit the big one, even if the movie was pretty good. She needed a song that still rocked Ozzy hard.

While she looked for that perfect tune, she was not—repeat, *not*—imagining Dewitt's grimy Yosemite Sam baseball cap or what lotions, farm animals, or WD-40 he might now be pulling out of his coveralls to assist him in his daily round of rustic self-abuse.

Wait, yes she was. She definitely was. She couldn't not imagine it. The silence from the bathroom was deafening. How could he be doing what she was sure he was doing, yet make no sound?

She didn't know. What she did know was that she was spending too much time thinking about Dewitt and his silent closet of doom. To pep herself up, she reached into her top drawer for lip gloss. The gloss was flavored like lemon bubblegum and had medically proven therapeutic benefits. With just two quick swipes, the world seemed a friendlier, more benign place.

But where was it? Her desk was neat and there were only a few decent hiding places for a tricky tube of gloss—behind the stapler and in the deep mystery corners where mischievous paper clips often went to roam. She rifled this way and that, moving the same stapler three times and running her finger up and down both corners. She was licking her lips at the thought of the shiny sweetness to come, but the gloss was nowhere to be found. Deciding to be thorough in her search, she dumped the whole of her purse onto the desk and was searching madly when her boss was hurled through the door by what could only be a massive catapult in the parking lot.

"Well, we're screwed for sure," Missy said, circling round Penelope's desk as if riding a superfast conveyer belt and unable to get off. "Seriously. Totally screwed. So we finally get the okay from the idiot mayor for our move, and now it turns out we can't get out of our contract with Dimwit for another year and a half. How that clown has a better lawyer than I do is beyond me, but apparently he does."

During all this, Penelope had been motioning toward the bathroom to warn Missy that the subject of her diatribe was on the premises, but Missy paid no heed. Desperate, Penelope snagged a legal pad from the desk and wrote:

Dewitt is here.

She thrust the pad and pen into Missy's midsection during one of her circumnavigations of the desk. Without pausing in her orbit, Missy stabbed at the pad a few times then handed it back to Penelope:

Dimwit it is and Dimwit it will always be. I don't know any Dewitt.

Penelope replied:

Have you seen my lip gloss?

Missy stopped now and sat down on the desk, scowling.

No. But I'm missing lipstick, a pair of hose, and a fresh pack of gum.

Penelope:

I'm missing a pair of socks I had in the drawer when I was planning on working out last week.

The two women were staring intently at each other when the toilet flushed and Dimwit exited. He passed by them at the desk with a formal nod of Yosemite Sam then exited the modular office trailer. That he was humming "Zip-a-Dee-Doo-Dah" seemed symbolic and right.

They watched him through the back window as he made his way to the haunted trailer on the hill, past the handwritten sign at the pitted gravel driveway that said, "Forget the Dog, Beware the Owner!" Then past the Confederate flag that hung limply from one forgotten bird feeder and the *Don't Tread on Me* sign affixed to another.

They observed him in silence, a begrimed goblin en route to his lair, walking with a lively bounce to the step. The bathroom adventure seemed just what the doctor ordered, for at his trailer door he leaped in the air like a merry leprechaun and clicked his boots together at his side. It was a joyous leap, a roguish clicking of heels. The human world had been successfully breached again, the pot of gold safe as ever.

The contemplative silence in the office lasted for several moments after Dewitt's trailer door closed behind him. Eventually Missy spoke: "Did that clodhopper freak just click his heels together? Or did someone roofie me at lunch?"

"He clicked," Penelope said. "I was wondering if you saw it too."

They stayed as they were, Penelope in her chair, Missy leaning against the desk, staring up at the mysterious dwelling on the hill, so rusted and run-down and out of place above the tidy lots of Rolling Acres, which sat like a nursery of cherubic innocents below.

This was the longest Penelope had ever witnessed her boss go without speaking or moving and she feared a minor case of shock. She was reaching for the bottle beside her to fling water in Missy's face, which is what they always did in movies, when Missy spoke: "Dimwit's stealing our shit."

"You think?"

"I know," said Missy, popping off the desk and racing to her office. She returned with the main drawer of her office desk. This she dumped on the floor at Penelope's feet.

"I had two canisters of lipstick, those hose, and half a pack of Dentyne," Missy said, her skinny tan legs pacing around the junk on the floor. "All mysteriously disappeared in the last two weeks. You tell me what happened to them."

Her employer was glaring at Penelope as if she might be the culprit and Penelope couldn't help but smile. How could anyone be this intense? It was mesmerizing.

"Okay," said Missy, poking through the contents of the drawer with the toe of a Neiman Marcus. "What else are you missing? And what kind of socks were they?"

"You know," said Penelope, "those little ankle ones like you wear with tennis shoes. They were pale yellow."

"Oh, those *are* cute socks. I'd bet a million dollars Dimwit wears them on his hand in the bathroom like an erotic puppet. Ooh, what if he drew a face on it that looked like you?"

At this, Missy began talking to her hand in a weird backwoods accent meant to be Dimwit's. Actually, she employed two voices. The hand, which would presumably be encased in Penelope's adorable little yellow sock, spoke in the voice of an ingenue, both frightened and intrigued by Dimwit:

Missy as Dimwit, talking to her hand: *You got a purty mouth.*
Hand/sock: *I like your hat. But I'm shy.*
Missy/Dimwit: *I got puppies in my pockets.*
Hand/sock: *Oh, I love puppies!*

Missy/Dimwit and hand/sock now met over the clutter at Missy's feet. The chemical attraction was clear when they began to make out. The ingenue sock—all wily veteran now—was going at Missy/Dimwit's neck, shoulders, and breasts. Penelope thought the sock was perhaps moving too fast, but Dimwit/Missy moaned in ecstasy. The sock was just making its way to points south of the border, murmuring *Oh Dimwit, oh Dimwit,* when Penelope put a stop to the pantomime before her: "You are grossing me out."

Missy cackled her high, hoarse, coughing laugh. "You think that's gross? Wait till I tell you what he's doing with your lip gloss."

Penelope found this thought unappealing and decided to get back on point.

"I was thinking about how his routine has recently changed," she said. "Lately he comes when I've been out of the office for a while. He used to always pop in right after lunch. I thought he just wanted to do his thing when one of us was here. But lately, whenever I get back from an errand, the bathroom is already occupied."

"When did he come today?"

"Right after the UPS guy."

Missy renewed her pacing, hand to chin in the classic detective-pondering-clues pose. "Does he always sneak in when you're doling out the UPS deliveries?"

"UPS comes at different times each day. Sometimes it takes me ten minutes to hand out the packages, other times half an hour. Twice I've come back from lunch and he was here. Oh, and on Monday, it was after I had to run over to my mom's to give Theo his inhaler."

Missy frowned thoughtfully at this. "So. It's been established that he no longer has to have us in the office while doing his hoedown with grubby Dimwit Junior?"

"I think so."

"And it's further established that he is now materializing at all hours of the working day?"

"Yes."

"The one consistency is that he only comes when both of us are out of the office, even briefly?"

"Yes."

Missy pounded her tiny fist on the desk and said: "Then that troll is spying on us from his gloom factory on the hill!"

Penelope considered for a moment: "He'd have to be watching all the time. Because sometimes I pop out, then pop right back in, and he's already here."

"He's spying night and day," Missy said, stalking around the office. "With a telescope trained right at the window like a hickass Galileo."

Penelope grimaced, but Missy held out a hand to stem any threat of rebuttal.

"Here's the thing, homegirl. It's all systems go now with the city. That place behind the old Food Lion is ours. I just have to get out of my current contract. And if I can catch that little pud thumper stealing from us, I'm out. We have a morals clause or an extenuating circumstance or something like that. This is just the ticket we're looking for. I can feel it in my bones. We just have to catch the thief in the act."

So saying, Missy did several rotations around Penelope's desk, her tan brow furrowed for all it was worth. Her skinny little brain was getting quite the workout, and she'd need a snack soon.

"By Jove, I've got it," Missy said, snapping her fingers.

Penelope didn't like the sound of that snap, nor the *by Jove*, which felt way too Sherlock Holmes for her liking. Sure, Dimwit weirded her out, and yes, that lip gloss was both delicious and luminescent. Her lips had never looked or tasted better. But was it worth being dragged into a scheme of Missy's hatching?

She thought not. And was ready to give voice to her concerns when Missy said: "I know exactly what we'll do."

3

Before Missy could dive into her foolproof plan, there came a knock. It was Carl Junior, the only person within Rolling Acres who didn't take the sign on the door—*Open, Come In*—at face value.

Missy hollered, "Please do come in, Carl Junior."

The maintenance man entered the cool of the office and removed his Virginia Tech Hokies baseball cap, checked that his work boots weren't tracking in dirt, then softly eased the door closed behind him.

"Good morning, Carl Junior," Penelope said, smiling.

"Mornin', Miss Penelope. Mornin', Miss Missy."

Penelope smiled broadly at this, anticipating what was coming. She'd seen this routine a dozen times and it never failed to entertain.

"Carl Junior," said Missy, turning to the door, where the ruggedly handsome older man had made no further entry than his original two feet across the threshold. Just enough to shut the door behind him and allow no further escape of the costly cool air. "I thought we'd agreed that the term *Miss Missy* is ridiculous. It makes me sound like a character on a Saturday morning show for slow children. Please just call me Missy."

Carl Jr. offered a sheepish smile and said: "All right, I'll try."

He ran a large calloused hand across his sweating brow and fiddled for a second with a Band-Aid on his head. He'd just come from weed-eating the curbs on Elm Tree Lane and Penelope knew the air-conditioning felt good. She also knew that he never spoke in the presence of his boss unless asked a direct question. That question came now: "Everything all right out there, Carl Junior? Are you staying hydrated? I don't want you overdoing it. This isn't the Biltmore Estate, you know. A weed here or there won't kill anyone. This place already looks like a country club. No need to overdo it."

"I drink half a thermos of water every day, so I ain't going to fall out on you. Not anytime soon at least, Lord willing."

"Carl Junior, that thermos of yours is tiny. Half of it is like two cups of water. You need to drink more than that."

"Don't need more. Just drink when I'm thirsty."

This went on a few more rounds, as was customary, Penelope smiling all the way through. The maintenance man was one of the few people that Missy spoke to affectionately, and their interactions were always riveting. It was like watching a lion tamer sooth the beast without even trying. This trait obviously ran in the family. Her first husband, the huge huge redneck (HHR), was Carl Jr.'s nephew, and he shared this ability to relax those in his company, and not just because of the primo weed that grew on his back forty. It was this feeling of being casually hypnotized—more than the sex or anything else—that had compelled Penelope into her early redneck marriage at nineteen. But that was another story.

"I just wanted to tell you," the maintenance man said, "that Mr. Burke is still complaining about the grass. I told him we have to keep all the yards the same length so it looks nice and neat, but he wants his at two inches, not three like everyone else."

Missy frowned at this, then scowled, then her mouth twitched a few spasmodic times. She was struggling with the torrent of profanities that were vying to foul the air.

"Carl Junior," she said, rubbing her face in a painful-looking way that showed the self-restraint she was employing. "How many times do I have to tell you that I don't give a rat's . . . patooey . . . about what that old sack of . . . something . . . wants done with his lawn. He's been a pain in my . . . tush . . . since we got this place."

"All right, Miss Missy. I figured you'd feel that way, but I wanted to let you know in case he came in complaining. He's particular, but that's just how some people are."

Missy scrunched her face so hard about the particularity of Mr. Burke that Penelope thought her ears might blow off.

"Thank you for letting me know," Missy said, sighing massively. "I will add it to the list. Now I need to ask you something, Carl Junior. Do you ever see Dimwit leave his place? He has to get food and necessities at some point, but I've never seen that rusty heap of his in actual motion."

"Who?"

"Dimwit, Carl Junior, Dimwit."

The maintenance man frowned until Penelope said, "She means Dewitt."

"I said Dimwit and I meant Dimwit," Missy said, rounding dramatically on Penelope. "If ever a wit was dim, it is his."

Carl Jr. worked his tongue artfully in his lower lip for a spell. He was deep in thought. "Ain't never seen him leave during the day."

"I knew it," Missy said. "He's growing his own food and raising chickens in that trailer. He probably has solar panels and is fertilizing with his own waste. I knew it all along."

Carl Jr. took in this theory. He hadn't finished talking when Missy interrupted him. Waiting a full five seconds to ensure the floor was indeed his, he continued: "When we had that one break-in back in December and you had me on night security, I saw him leave. Every night in fact. Right around midnight."

"Walmart stays open twenty-four hours," Penelope said, her innate detective skills kicking in. When she wasn't racing through raunchy romance novels, a hard-boiled mystery often called her name. She felt well trained in the arts of observation and hers was a gut that could be trusted. That gut was presently telling her that she was about to be embroiled in something stupid.

"Every night, Carl Junior?" Missy stated. "Every. Single. Night."

She'd said this last part in the manner of a TV attorney to show that the wheels of justice were in motion. Penelope blanched at this intonation, Newtonian laws of motion being what they are.

The maintenance man popped his Hokies cap against his leg and nodded once, as was his way when confirming something he'd already confirmed.

"Thank you, Carl Junior."

Carl Jr. nodded and said *Ma'am* to Penelope, then nodded and said *Ma'am* to Missy, then departed the office as quietly as he'd entered.

"I swear to God I'm going to marry Carl Junior," Missy said as soon as the door nicked shut.

This was a familiar claim.

"Seriously," said Missy. "You think I'm kidding, but I love him. I'd do him on your desk right now. You and Dimwit could watch. You could film it, I don't care. I love me some Carl Junior."

Ignoring this, Penelope rose and went to the window to gaze up at Dewitt's bulbous trailer on the hill, a patch of land void of trees or plant life, where only a few lank brown weeds swayed sadly in the breeze. Penelope had seen scarier-looking houses—they'd gone looking for them in high school—but none so warty. She felt sure dengue fever grew on the premises, likely in crusty Beenee Weenee cans. Ringworm for sure. And tapeworm. Both of which Theo would definitely catch at Camp Sycamore.

"We don't know for sure that Dimwit took our stuff," Penelope said, turning to Missy, who was lying on the couch in the reception area, her feet resting on an end table, crumpling that month's crisp new periodicals.

"Of course we do. He used to always come in after lunch when we were here."

"Okay, that proves my point. Why would he change his habits if he needs us in the office to do his business?"

Missy shrugged. "Maybe Dimwit needs a little romance. His powers of concentration aren't what they once were, so he needs a little totem from his ladies in his life to remind him of the good old days when love was fresh and new. You can't blame him. I couldn't tell you the last time I had sex with a man when I wasn't imagining someone else. It's been years. Am I alone in this?"

It had been so long since she'd had sex that Penelope judged the question moot. With a gun to her head, she'd admit that her boss wasn't alone in carnal imaginative wanderings. She wouldn't have survived the last year of her marriage without a few Jedi mind tricks. How else to negotiate James and his tiny kimono? During these outings, often with the yellow geisha robe above or below her and whishing this way and that, she'd envisioned she was the protagonist from her latest naughty book. In those instances, the material she kept feeling about her was not a shorty robe but an expensive silk shirt, left on in their hurry to turn the executive's office into a nasty boudoir. Other times, the kimono became the satiny touch of a sail as she and Dmitri tumbled about on deck en route to Morocco. There they would meet the mystery man in the red hat, but in the meantime Dmitri worked the rudder, and her too.

Of course if she was tired, and her imagination wasn't firing on all cylinders, she'd just picture a boy she knew from high school, one who knew his way around the inside of a Mazda RX-7. On these occasions it was difficult to account for the satiny swish that kept intruding on her trip down memory lane, and she'd have to remove the kimono in order to fully enjoy the leather passenger seat, the mag wheels, the kickass spoiler.

"So," said Missy. "I'll take that as a *No, you are not alone in this.*"

Penelope smiled but didn't respond. Winston Hackler and his RX-7 were still parked out by the lake in her mind and she felt no real hurry to depart.

"Listen," Missy said, popping off the couch like a submerged pool toy breaking the surface. "We're going up there and finding our stuff. He's probably eaten the candy and gum. But those socks of yours? They're hanging in a Hello Kitty frame in the sex dungeon beneath his trailer. We find those tee-tiny socks and presto-bango—he's busted and I'm out of the lease."

Penelope didn't care for this vision of the ill-fated anklets. They were new and still smelling of fabric softener when they'd gone missing. In fact, they'd freshened the whole bottom drawer of her desk with their lemony-fresh scent and brightened her day every time she saw them. Truly, they were cheerful socks. She hated the thought of them being utilized in an indecent fashion. Now these old panties she was wearing? That was a different story. Dimwit would be a mere babe in the woods in their presence. They'd seen plenty.

"There would be no way to prove those were my socks even if we found them."

"He could have swiped anything," said Missy. "I have no idea at any given moment what's in my purse or desk. He could have stolen my son's bronzed baby booties and I wouldn't know." Missy checked her watch. "Anyway, details about Operation Dimwit to follow. Right now, those ultraviolets are calling my name down at Tammy's Tanning Shack."

"You know . . ." Penelope began.

Missy raised a hand. "I know, I know. And I have one word for you: *Whatever*. I'm addicted. And now Carl Junior's got me all riled up. Unless you can get him in here right now to show me all the tools in his belt, I'm going to have to strip down in a booth and get tropical."

"It's so bad for your skin."

"Correct. I'm going to end up looking like one of those shriveled-up raisiny ladies you see at the beach. I'll be pulling bread crumbs out of my wrinkles and tossing them to the gulls every morning when the sun comes up. But don't you worry about ole Missy. She can always get a man if she needs one. And some fellows like that beat-up shoe look. A lot, in fact. So ta-ta, doll, I'm off for some radiation love down at Tammy's. I do some of my best concentrating down there. I'll have our Dimwit plan formulated by tonight, guaranteed."

4

As Friday quitting time approached, Penelope vacillated between anticipation of the wide-open weekend before her and continued worry about Theo. The poor kid had just survived a year of school bullying and now they were packing him off for an extended spell with strangers? How much supervision did Camp Sycamore offer? And what was the counselor/camper ratio? Theo was as sweet as they came, but perhaps a little odd to some boys. Not everyone wanted to hear long discourses on PlinkyMo and trilobites. Would counselors pick up on this?

And could James be trusted to pack properly, especially in the preventive care department? She'd offered to gather toiletries and medicine and let her ex handle the rest, but he'd insisted on the whole enchilada. He had the official Camp Sycamore list of provisions, after all, and Penelope knew he'd been checking those items off with a well-sharpened pencil for weeks now, reliving a cherished part of his Tarheel upbringing when all angels looked homeward. It would be mean-spirited to deprive him of that.

Still. Theo would be loaded up with knives, canteens, flashlights, headlamps, compasses, and other doodads from James's suburban survivalist collection. But would James remember the underwear? The soap? The toothbrush and nonallergenic pillow? And most importantly, the Benadryl, itch cream, and inhaler? If ever there was a living, breathing histamine magnet, it was Theo. Even looking at a mosquito on TV would cause fiery red bumps to explode on his leg. These bulbous reminders of the dangers of Anglo-Saxon inbreeding would then be scratched to bleeding, scab over, the scab picked, in an infinite cycle of bloody, crusty summer grossness.

Penelope would take any odds given about Theo and his future date with impetigo. She could practically see his iodine-stained legs from here.

She was brooding about how to ask James about his packing without getting him on his commonsensical high horse, where he spent most of his day, when Carl Jr. knocked lightly to interrupt all this mulling.

"Come in, Carl Junior," she yelled. "It's just me in here."

He entered, taking off his cap, and stood just beyond the door, a rolled-up newspaper in his hand, a sly smile on his face.

"Come on in and cool off, Carl Junior," Penelope said. "It's burning up out there."

"Not too bad," said the maintenance man. "Getting a little breeze off the mountain."

"Take a seat. Rest them dogs a bit."

He nodded and tentatively made his way over to the least nice chair in the waiting room. He checked the back side of his pants legs to make sure no grass particles had managed to escape his eagle eye, then sat down with the satisfied sigh of a hardworking man.

"What did you do to your forehead?" Penelope asked, pointing at the Band-Aid.

"The old lady finally had enough."

"I've been waiting for Lorraine to do that. You've had it coming for a while."

"Naw," said Carl Jr., grinning. "Dr. Hagood just froze off one of them pre-melanomas. Nothing to worry about. And if Miss Missy inquires, I'm putting on sunscreen three times a day."

Penelope nodded, pleased with the answer.

"Did you hear Hagi made the paper again?" Carl Jr. said with a smile. It was the sly grin that accompanied any comment he voiced about his nephew, the HHR.

"No I didn't," said Penelope, returning the smile.

Carl Jr. got up, shaking his head, and made his way over to the desk. As he did, Penelope tried to catalog all the nicknames she'd heard for the HHR. To his mother's side of the family, he was Hagi. To his father's side, Zeke. The following groups also had their pet names: bowling buddies (Clacker), fastpitch buddies (Cha-Cha), fishing pals (Otis), friends on the police force (El Duque), friends on the herbal enthusiast side of things (Ziggy). How many of these nicknames had marijuana as their etymological prompt, she didn't know, though she guessed quite a few. *Otis* and *Ziggy* for sure. She'd been there when those were coined beneath mushroom clouds of smoke.

As Carl Jr. stood beside her, grinning expectantly, Penelope took the paper. That day's headline in the *Hillsboro Daily Record* read:

LOCAL MAN RESCUES BEAR CUB

Below it was a photo of a handsome, athletic, shirtless man point-ing up at a tree. According to the story, the HHR had found the cub by a creek bed, bawling for its mother. After waiting an hour for the mother to return, he'd decided to take the lost waif's cause as his own and had carried the cub—fireman style—in an eastbound direction for reasons known only to himself. His instincts were proven correct, however, for bear and man soon met in a clearing near an electrical tower. He placed the cub down "as lightly as I could and said, *Here you go, Momma. Your little baby's safe and sound.*"

The mother bear had thanked him warmly by giving chase "for a mile or better," an adventure which ended only when the HHR had shimmied a large oak to approximately forty feet. The bear, weary from the chase, had only made it twenty feet up before calling it quits.

Penelope now read out loud for Carl Jr.'s amusement: "*I don't mean to boast, but they've yet to build a tree I can't climb.*"

27

"He's a mess," said Carl Jr., shaking his head fondly.

"He slept all night in the tree?"

"Yep. He'd probably still be up there if that park ranger hadn't come and woke him up. You know how he is. He'll sleep through Judgment Day, you just watch him."

Penelope continued to read, thinking that for someone who claimed to live off the grid, he sure got his picture in the paper a lot. Bowling three hundred at Twilight Lanes, pitching a no-hitter in the fastpitch county championship, catching a fifty-pound catfish down by the dam, finding a well-preserved Civil War pistol during another trek through the woods. He was in the paper every other week, now that she thought about it.

And still he refused a cell phone for fear of government surveillance. Or was it concern about a low sperm count? Sometimes one, sometimes the other, depending on what exposé he'd recently read on the Internet.

She read aloud again: "*The local man claims to be an avid hiker.*"

She and Carl Jr. exchanged smiles at this one but said no more, for the only hiking the HHR did was to check on the assorted pot plants he cultivated in George Washington State Park, which abutted his property. That he was stoned out of his mind while negotiating with the mother bear, and while sleeping in the tree, and even when talking with the park ranger and the newspaper reporter went without saying. He went nowhere out of doors without Otis Jr., his trusty one-hitter.

Penelope finished the article then looked back at the photo.

She thought: *I was married to that man. The one who slept overnight in a tree.*

It was like a fact from a dusty history book.

⁓

Penelope was in the Kroger parking lot after work, a cold bottle of chardonnay at her side, loading her groceries into the trunk. The pendulum had swung and she was again excited by the child-free zone that awaited her. She'd miss her son, sure—the little survivalist, the brave Histamine Boy—but she was about to live for two weeks as an unfettered, badass single gal, as often depicted on television shows set in New York City. She planned to make hay in the home decoration department, namely by painting her new den. While she worked, she'd play music as loudly as she wanted without Theo asking her to change to some lame pop song that was the latest elementary school rage. How she could be raising a child with such bad musical taste, she had no idea. But there it was: Imagine Dragons.

If so inclined, she could spend the night with a man or have a man spend the night with her. Who would know? Who would wake up, as Theo did as toddler, and complain of sounds coming from his parents' bedroom *like people walking around in wet flip-flops*? The thought of an intimate adult sleepover—the first since her divorce—was foreign, exotic, and also a little tiring, so she decided to give it a rest. She closed the trunk, pondering her date with Fitzwilliam Darcy the following evening. She noted that it was possible to force thoughts of sex from her mind while still contemplating Fitzwilliam. That likely said something right there.

She'd met the older gentleman on the dating service her mother gifted her with on her fortieth birthday, a few months back. He didn't really share his name with the love interest in *Pride and Prejudice,* but that was his online moniker and she couldn't think of him by anything else. She'd even called him that on their coffee date at Starbucks a couple weeks back, first in a joking way, then later because he really did seem to act and talk like a nineteenth-century aristocrat. Or at least the ones Penelope had seen on TV. Penelope had heard quite a bit about his cat, Algernon Moncrieff, that day and felt sure that he'd be as particular about his scones and jam as Fitzwilliam himself.

Anyway, for now he was Fitzwilliam. A name change would require a performance a lot less Fitzwilliamish than the first.

She got in the car, started the engine, and checked the oil light as was her paranoid habit. Another problem with the car would spell financial doom, and she still hadn't paid back her stepfather, George, for fixing her head gasket the last time. But no lights—oil, temperature, or factory-issue dashboard middle finger—appeared and she breathed a sigh of relief. As she did, her phone buzzed with a text from Missy:

Master plan begins with you pretending to seduce Dimwit.

Okay. I'll be right over.

Seriously?

Yes. Just need to run home and get my sexiest outfit.

Awesome. I knew I could count on you. Wait, are you messing with me?

Not at all.

Yes you are. And now you're going to send me one of those stupid winky emoticons.

Penelope sent the winky face. Seduce Dimwit? Give her a break.

I guess I'll do it myself then. Even though it's your sock he's getting married to. But whatever. Meet tonight for recon action?

Can't do it.

Why?

Beg pardon. Don't WANT to do it. Have house to myself. Talk later.

Bye.

Now that she had the phone out, it seemed a good time to check on her junior camper and see how the packing was coming along. She dialed James's number, hoping, as happened about half the time, that Theo would answer instead of his father. The phone rang and rang until James answered, sounding a little breathless.

"Sorry it took me so long," he said, laughing wryly. "I was down in the den reading about William Wallace. You know, the guy from *Braveheart*. I must have tuned out the phone."

Penelope didn't take the bait. They were no longer married and she didn't have to listen to mini history lessons based on that week's biography. She also no longer had to listen to him apology-brag about his incredible powers of concentration, powers which made it impossible for him to hear anything Penelope said while he was absorbing facts about heroic men of European descent.

She had noticed, of course, that his reading-tune-out superpowers waned greatly when she was on the phone kibitzing with her friends. His questions afterward were always informed and thorough, showing that he'd well followed the conversational gist while his cranium was supposedly riding the dusty trail with Theodore Roosevelt. One such question he posed after a conversation with Sandy was *What were you laughing about right after you mentioned our trip to North Carolina?*

"How's the packing going?" Penelope said, before James could begin his top ten countdown of brave Scotsmen and their haggis of choice.

"The packing is all wrapped up," James said. "I told Theo we'd be hitting the road at oh seven hundred, so I want to get him off to bed as soon as possible."

This military time thing was a running joke from their marriage. She'd started calling him Sarge one morning, irritated at his chop-chopping her before a trip to the Outer Banks, and he'd spent the week at the beach saying, *I plan on having my first beer at fourteen hundred hours, Penelope*, and other such nonsense. It was funny then and it was funny now, and she found that she was smiling despite herself.

Coming back to the present, she quizzed James about the things she was worried about being forgotten. Per tradition, James pooh-poohed her concern. Her ex was a proud packer and hated to have his abilities questioned. And don't even think about making a suggestion about how to arrange the suitcases. You might as well tell him Thomas Wolfe was a one-book wonder.

He'd yelled out for Theo a moment before and was now apparently walking around the house looking for him. She heard Theo say, "Tell

Mom I'll call her back. I've got a cool Plinky that's about to launch." Then the muffled sound of James snapping at him to get on the phone now. They did have that in common, she and James. Neither would let Theo avoid a parental call for a stupid video game.

"Hi Mom," Theo said, sounding a little sullen.

"Hold on, Theo," Penelope said. "Can't talk right now. I've got my own Plinky about to launch. I've been walking round and round the couch for about three hours now. I have to see how this turns out."

Theo laughed. He wasn't a natural sulker and could never keep up the front of being put out for long. And then—despite just being made fun of for being obsessed with PlinkyMo—he blasted into his nightly recitation of captured Plinkies. This catalog was precise and invigorating, at least to the narrator, and Penelope could feel the rush of adrenaline coursing through the little tracker's blood as he spoke. It was reminiscent of James's triumphant summation of how he'd managed—through native engineering skills and careful study of plane geometry—to pack the cooler in the trunk after all.

"Dad says I can play on the drive down," Theo said. "But after that, it's no Plinkies for a whole two weeks. Camp Sycamore doesn't allow electronics. Dad's saying it's time for bed."

"Okay, honey. I'm going to miss you. You've got the stationery and envelopes, right?"

"Yeah," Theo said, sounding furtive, as if he hoped this topic wouldn't come up before he'd made a clean exit from the conversation. He generally preferred a mic drop after a PlinkyMo soliloquy.

"Sweetie, I'm going to miss you like crazy, so you have to keep me in the loop. Will you promise to write?"

"Okay, but not every day. Like every other day. Otherwise it's like homework."

"Fine. Every other day. And take your inhaler wherever you go. And put on sunscreen. And don't scratch your bites. Seriously, you'll get impetigo."

"Love you too. But it's impossible not to scratch mosquito bites."

5

After unloading the groceries, Penelope stood in her new kitchen, trying to decide what to eat for supper. She wasn't that hungry so settled on an apple. She wouldn't mention this in mixed company, but fruit kind of bored her, other than as a flavoring for gum, Slurpees, and Starburst. But it was rumored to keep the doctor away, so with a big loud crunch she entered her den and flopped backwards onto the couch, wishing already that she'd taken the time to peel this bad boy before she got skin stuck in her teeth and had to floss before she was ready.

She turned on the TV. The news was on. She turned off the TV. It was a total shit show out there.

Munching away on the apple, she looked around her little place, a rented cottage on the back of a hundred-acre farm, which she got to by traveling half a mile down a dusty gravel road. Her landlords were a hippie-ish couple from out West who had vague and flexible jobs, which indicated there was family money and that they'd soon be raising alpacas for their Internet fleece consortium. Her mother had befriended the woman while shrewdly evaluating azaleas at the Mennonite nursery. They'd struck up a horticultural conversation, and her mother was delighted to learn that the newcomer was not a subversive who wanted to install the *native dandelion flower* alongside the classic iris. None of this fiddle-faddle about *blooming weeds*. By responding thusly, the woman had come down on the right side of the civil war currently raging in the Hillsboro Garden Club. And when the botanically correct neohippie mentioned she had a place to rent, Penelope's mom sprang into action. Already the grand matriarch was salivating about what she'd do along the cottage walkway, and soon the trowels would fly.

Honestly, Penelope felt lucky to have the place. The 1960s-era bathroom she shared with Theo was not the greatest, but the screened-in porch that allowed her to watch the deer gambol was cute as pie. Of course, her preference was to own, not rent, but it would be a long time before that was feasible. She was currently the very definition of living paycheck to paycheck, and one emergency away from financial calamity. What would it take to get ahead? Fifty thousand dollars a year? And what did *get ahead* mean? Other than the Xbox Theo wanted because none of the good games were on Wii anymore.

Then again, nothing was accomplished by worrying about money on a Friday night. She was broke, sure, but not as broke as before, and a steady paycheck was coming in. She looked around, eyeing the walls in the den she'd primed the weekend before, more sure than ever that the turquoise paint waiting for her on the front stoop was the right color. Yes, turquoise.

James and his earth hues could kiss her sweet ass.

~

Penelope was about finished with one wall and was enjoying playing music as loud as she wanted. Or at least as loud as her phone would play, as that was the only sound system she currently had. She'd been getting seriously funky with Beyoncé. In fact, she had bonded pretty heavily with her on "Single Ladies" and thought the two of them would make a pretty good duet if ever they got the chance. She was doing this—synchronizing perfectly with Beyoncé and dancing a bit as she used the big roller on the wall—when her phone lit up with a message.

It was a nearly midnight, which was late for a text in her world. Apparently teens were now texting the night away. And sexting too. Even middle schoolers! And politicians—local, state, and national. Was she the only one who had to get up in the morning?

She was not currently receiving a sext but a question from her employer.

How do you turn the flashlight thing off on a phone?

Why?

Cause I'm about to start Operation Dimwit and it's glowing like a mother. I had it on so I didn't bust my ass walking around.

Where are you?

Somebody's yard. Starting to think we're not handicap friendly. There's booby traps all over the place here. Pretty sure I slipped a disc already.

Go home.

No way. How do you get the flashlight off? Dimwit's probably already seen me.

Penelope picked up the roller to touch up a spot she'd missed while doing a little spin move during her duet with Beyoncé.

Flick your phone up from the bottom then hit the flashlight button.

Damien usually shows me how, but I got it now.

Penelope considered, for the umpteenth time, why anyone would name an innocent child Damien. Hadn't everyone their age seen *The Omen*? She'd watched it at her friend Debbie's house during a sleepover and it had freaked her all the way out.

Where's your car?

Down by Mr. Burke's. The old fart's yard does look nice. Almost feel guilty for throwing a huge hunk of gum in it. He'll shit himself.

Are you drunk?

Not that much. Come hang out.

I need to paint.

Come on. It's exciting as hell.

Go home.

Not happening. Doing surveillance. It's completely dark up at Dimwit's. Sock Penelope wore him out. Maybe I can get a photo of something incriminating through the window.

I don't like you stomping around all by yourself at night.

Stop worrying.

You're really loud. He'll hear you.

You may be right. I overdid it at Tammy's. I'm crunching like a walking stick of bacon.

Go home and put some lotion on.

No can do. Dimwit's going down. Will report back later. Keep your phone on.

6

She was pooped but satisfied as she lay in bed, preparing to check LoveSynch for the bevy of messages she was sure to have received from the thousands of men within her dating radius. She laughed at herself. Had she really become this cynical? She'd have at least one message from a nice, sophisticated local man. So he was a touch older than was ideal. Who cared? More than likely that nose whistle he had working at Starbucks was a one-time thing. Whose nose whistled all the time?

She yawned and closed her eyes for a moment, listening to the tree frogs outside. She liked sleeping in the country and come fall she'd leave her window open and feel far away from the hustle and bustle of life. This new place was going to work out nicely. The paint job was moving right along and she'd found just the right spot for all her housewarming gifts from Sandy and Rachel, save one.

That one was going to take some consideration. For the moment, it looked back at her—Cheekily? Guiltily? Forbiddingly?—from atop her dresser.

Or was it boredly?

She had no idea, only that she and the gift had entered minute two of their staring contest and all she could think of was her mother. She crossed the room, obtained the gift, and examined it once more. Why had they put her name on it? And why had they chosen an orange font when the inscribed item was green? It was a lurid combination, but maybe that was the point. Feeling more than ever that her friends were perverts, she tucked the orange and green **PENELOPE LEMON** into the bottom drawer where she kept her cold weather garments. *Out of sight, out of mind* was a motto she trusted and she dove into bed, clear of conscience and ready for LoveSynch.

As always, she compulsively read over her **Portnal** (Portrait + Journal) to see if kind Internet fairies had managed to improve, or at least freshen up, all the lame stuff she'd written about herself when she joined the site and had never bothered to change. Unfortunately, it showed the same list of last year's hot TV shows and a bunch of hooey about traveling, wine tasting, and outdoor adventure. In short, TheosMom75 liked to sniff a rich burgundy while hiking strenuous Costa Rican trails or shooting rapids in her kayak.

All right, all right, it wasn't that bad. Harmless insinuations and white lies like everyone else posted on dating sites. Plus, her answer to the Exercise Frequency question—a bald-faced *Very frequent*—was creeping closer to accurate. Or soon would be once she popped into Fitness Plus in the morning. And she could update her Enthusiasms section as well. There were some new shows she liked and she'd read several of the good books that everyone was talking about. She wouldn't mention *Carnal Liaisons,* which was loudly calling her name from the bedside table, because that might give the wrong impression. Plenty of time for that later if some naughty boy proved himself worthy.

She was smiling at her frisky self when her phone buzzed. Missy again.

I think Dimwit's got pet skunks.

Penelope laughed out loud and replied.

What?

I made it about fifty feet up the hill before they started in on me.
I'm in the office right now with the ac cranking and I'm spraying
OFF everywhere and I can STILL smell them. I think they're sneaking
in through Dimwit's bathroom. The whole office has gone feral.

Go home.

Can you just come down here?

Why?

They've got me surrounded. I need a bodyguard to the car.

Penelope smiled and glanced at her LoveSynch messages, a disappointing haul. She return-texted.

It's like one skunk who's probably already gone. They have a really
strong scent.

That's impossible. I'm choking on skunk. Dimwit's breeding them
up there in his laboratory. Are you coming or not?

Penelope realized she was thirsty and headed to the kitchen. En route she paused for a moment to savor her paint job. Even with just one coat on a single wall, the wood paneling looked better and brighter. She and Beyoncé had done good and speedy work. She was totally sold on the turquoise but was beginning to second-guess the Soft Linen trim. What else though? The only other sample she'd taped to the wall was Daisy White. Might that be too dramatic? Too bold? Turquoise + Daisy White would be quite the statement.

Remembering her skunk-addled friend, she wrote:

Just hold your nose and run to the car.

Oh thank god. I thought you'd forsaken me. Listen, I can't feel my
nose. What is toxic shock syndrome again?

Penelope went to the fridge and got half a glass of cranberry juice, then filled the rest of the glass with water. It was what her stepfather

George did and she agreed it was just the nighttime ticket. Missy had texted again.

> **Because I definitely have it.**
>> You don't have toxic shock syndrome. Hillsboro is always skunky this time of year. You're just not used to it.
>
> **I tell you Dimwit has trained skunks guarding his place. These are super skunks. It's like the Island of Dr. Moreau. They may be his own offspring.**
>> You can't train skunks.
>
> **That's what I thought. But these were definitely organized. They were on me before I was halfway up the hill. Hold on, I hear something.**

While her boss did God knew what, Penelope stood at the sink, perusing that day's LoveSynch contacts from the poignantly single men who lived within her forty-mile dating perimeter. But why just forty miles? Was that perimeter enough? Why not a hundred? Why not the whole of the eastern seaboard?

Smiling at her hyperbole, she headed back to the bedroom, tallying LoveSynch icons as she went. Cupid's mailroom had brought her three *flirts*, two computer-generated *blends*, but only one *Eiffel Tower*, which was the jackpot of icons. She didn't know what the Parisian landmark signified, exactly, other than earnest Internet love with perhaps a side baguette. Only one person had messaged her, and that was Fitzwilliam. She hopped back into bed, on top of the covers, and started the message.

```
My Dearest TheosMom75,


Or might I call you Penelope now? (I was tempted by
the melodious sound of My Dearest Lemon Sorbet but
```

thought that presumptuous). Anyway, a rose by any
other name . . .

I have been counting the days until our appointed
tête à tête and can hardly conceive that the time is
nigh!

Penelope's phone buzzed again.

**First it was a scratching at the front door. Then scurrying in the
bushes. Now nothing. Like dead silent. Dimwit's army is playing
with my mind.**

A raccoon and/or wind. You're like a person in a scary movie—like The
Omen—slowly freaking herself out.

Penelope wasn't sure about using that specific movie reference. She
erased *like The Omen* and pressed Send. Then returned to Fitzwilliam's
message.

Like Mary, Mary, Quite Contrary, *I've pretty
maids all in a row* dusting and cleaning so that fair
Pemberley will be just so for your arrival. And it is
only by summoning my strongest resolve that I refrain
from telling you what delectables the menu has in
store for fair Penelope (one hint: *fromage* and more
fromage!).

Oh, I pray that I do not sound too stuffy, for I
want this evening to be as breezy and casual as our
enchanting conversation over coffee a fortnight
ago. I look so forward to hearing more about that
winning young scamp, Theo, and how your charming new
domicile is coming along. Delightfully, I'm sure!
And I promise to limit my stories about my own scamp,

Algernon Moncrieff, to one hand (if the other hand has its fingers crossed behind my back).

Missy was texting again so Penelope paused once more.

Seriously, these are GMO skunks. And there's literally hundreds of them.

One skunk. Half a mile away.

Why are they stalking me? Am I emitting something? Tammy dosed the hell out of me today down at the Shack. Is that it?

Have you ever been outside at night before?

Probably not.

Because it smells like that all over town every night.

Maybe in Skunk Town, USA.

I'm not coming to get you.

I'm breathing into a bag now.

Go home.

My gag reflex has stopped working.

Hitting the sack.

Dimwit's smarter than he looks.

Suggest you do the same.

And with that, she muted the incoming text alert and returned to LoveSynch:

Though longing to break out the black tail for our evening together, I shall refrain for now. Hopefully, in the not too distant future, we will attend a proper gala, but for now I will stick to the modern trend of casual-is-better (oh why was I fated to be born a century too late? Were there ever a natural Edwardian, it is I!). Now be gone, non sequiters! And do stay on task, Fitzwilliam, old boy. What I am

taking unforgivingly long to convey is this: please
wear whatever you like. I want you to be comfortable
and happy in my home.

    If you'll forgive another literary allusion before
I close my modest epistle, please know that I shall
wait anxiously and faithfully for your arrival, as
your mythic namesake did for heroic Odysseus.

    Until tomorrow, alas—

Fitz. Darcy

Penelope finished reading and let out an audible sigh. Fitzwilliam's missives often had this effect. She appreciated the time, effort, and apparent sincerity he put into them, but how was she supposed to reply? She didn't write epistles. In fact, the only other person she knew besides Fitzwilliam who did was Paul from the Bible. And no one seemed to respond to him either. It was just too much pressure.

Perhaps she should check her Facebook page before replying, just to clear her head. She did that now, and found—as usual—a pastiche of the following on her timeline:

1. Inspirational quotes from the devout among her friends

2. Photos of old ladies with comedic captions about drinking and/ or sex from her more libertine acquaintances

3. Vacation photos; children photos; flattering portraits of the posters themselves

4. Political articles of both persuasions marked *READ THIS*

5. Dessert recipes

Was that all Facebook was good for, making you feel vaguely dissatisfied with your life, your friends, and your experiences? She felt like she was missing something. Maybe she should post a shot of her new place to advertise that the door was open and the party about to begin. Or even a short video of her belting "Single Ladies"? She was weighing possibilities when a friend request popped up from someone named Megan Scott.

She racked her brains but couldn't think of even a single Megan. Maybe it was someone from elementary school who'd moved after first grade or something. Or another of cousin Becky's soccer mom friends from Richmond. Every day on Facebook she received about ten thousand photos of smiling, sweaty kids holding trophies, none of whom she knew. But she'd never refused a friend request and saw no reason to start now. The travel girls from soccer—champions all— had her blessing as well. Then the request vanished. She scrolled up and down her page to see if it had moved elsewhere—Facebook was always shuffling stuff around—but former/future friend Megan Scott had vamoosed. Maybe she'd decided Penelope's page was boring and reconsidered the friend request. If that were the case, Penelope could appreciate her discernment.

It was mysterious, to say the least, but she'd stalled long enough. It was time to bite the epistle bullet. She went back to LoveSynch and wrote the following:

```
Dear Fitzwilliam,

I'm looking forward to it as well. Let me know if I
can bring anything. You originally said not to, but I
hate to arrive empty handed. I'm glad to make a salad
or dessert or something. Just let me know. I've got
the directions in my phone, but just in case I get
lost, you might want to give me your number. I thought
I knew every street in Hillsboro, but I've never
heard of yours. Is Pemberley a fictitious wonderland
or something? ☺
```

See you tomorrow and do let me know what I can
bring.

Penelope

Her teeth felt weird after the cranberry juice so she went to brush
them again, her mother's familiar voice ringing in her ears about cavi-
ties and future root canals should she ever go to bed without perfectly
scraped canines. Thoughts of her mother reminded her again of the
housewarming present hiding in the dresser. Why was she associating
the two? Did it stem from that time in high school when she'd snuck
Winston Hackler in the house one winter afternoon, only to have her
mother bust them in the basement just as Winston was starting to get
familiar with that cute fluffy sweater of junior year?

It was truly a case for Freud.

She grinned at her paranoia, thinking how different she was from
Esmeralda, the protagonist of *Carnal Liaisons.* Speaking of which, it
was time for a heavy dose of erotica and then lights out. She was near
the end of the book, and things were really starting to heat up in the
Hollywood office where studio boss Esmeralda Duvall took absolutely
no prisoners, business or otherwise. All those handsome, insecure
men trying to make it big in the movies were like putty in her hands
when the hosiery turned to bondage materials. When last Penelope
read, the young intern from Nebraska—the one with such high hopes
for his ska band—had never seen it coming when Esmeralda pinned
him against the microwave in the snack area. Needless to say, that was
one tofu burrito that never got eaten.

7

Bright and early Saturday morning, Penelope was sweating away on a stationary bike, lamenting that she'd only had enough coffee for one smallish pot. She felt groggy with exercise and lack of caffeine. The gym was swarming with oldsters, third-shifters pumping free weights through bloodshot eyes, and an assortment of women torturing themselves as Penelope was now doing. Why she'd chosen Ultra Alpine as her setting she'd never know. But she was, by God, going to haul her ass up Von Trapp Glacier for the full twenty minutes even if it killed her.

She'd be feeling less at death's door if she'd hadn't botched her audio choice. Like some academic rube, she'd chosen an educational podcast instead of hard-charging rock-and-roll. It was a ludicrous decision. Who gave a rat's ass about that Dutch man and his long-lost identical twin, separated by two continents, a language barrier, and fighting on opposing sides of a war, when your heart was about to fly out of your chest? With AC/DC or something she could have battled this bike to the bloody end. These old fart twins on the podcast were wheezing worse than she was. She was sorry for the trials, glad for their reunion, but could they not speak a little faster or more forcefully? It was like biking the Alps with double Methuselahs on her back.

There. She was done. Muttering apologies to the Van Slyck brothers of Amsterdam and feeling happy—after the fact—that they'd gather once more around the yuletide goose as they'd done as boys, she disembarked. She paused for a moment, legs quavering, to give the bike a hard stare. She'd be ready for its ass next time, and Ultra Alpine as well. *Back in Black* would make sure of that.

At the water fountain, she stood slurping away, kicking herself for forgetting a water bottle. Speaking of that, she needed some new ones. All hers were nasty from their months spent cavorting under the car seat. That, or the plastic straw had been chewed to a stub by Theo's weird oral fixation, likely an evolutionary remnant from his days as a member of the beluga clan eating nothing but plankton. All the other women had cute, clean receptacles that fit neatly under the fancy spigot designed for filling such vessels. She, on the other hand, was left gulping away at the same nozzle all the sweaty guys used. No telling what was falling out of their mouths as they bent to drink while still huffing from their dead lift grunting sessions.

Okay, now she was grossing herself out just for the heck of it. Why did she do that? It was a bad habit. She was thinking all this—water bottles, whale boys, guys sweating into the fountain—while casually drinking, breaking for air, then drinking again, working on the assumption that no one was waiting for a turn at the fountain.

This assumption proved faulty when a female behind her *harrumphed.*

Penelope stopped slurping immediately and turned, water dripping off the side of her face like a dog recently gone to town on a toilet, to offer an apologetic smile. No one liked a fountain hog, herself included. The waiting woman had a pink water bottle with a decal from a local winery. She was a fit oenophile, much like TheosMom75 advertised on LoveSynch. Penelope offered a *Sorry about that,* but this didn't seem to appease the wine-loving workout lady, who stood there glaring even after Penelope had moved hurriedly to the side to clear the lane for hydration.

Penelope now stood next to the elliptical chin-up machine, thinking the woman meant to strike up a conversation. She had this notion because the thirsty throat-clearer had made no further movement toward the fountain but simply stood gazing at her with an unsparing eye. She seemed mesmerized by all things Penelope Lemon. Was it her ensemble that caused such frank appraisal? Her one good workout outfit, the sassy fuchsia spandexy thing like all the cool-looking women wore, was dirty, so she'd grabbed what was clean: ratty shorts, mismatched anklet socks, and a T-shirt that said "Team Mom," which she'd bought as a joke at the thrift store a few years back.

The woman gawking at her wore a name tag. This tag indicated that she was not just fit but professionally fit, and an official staff member of Fitness Plus. The name on the tag was Megan.

After what felt like an unusually long time for a smiling, apologetic person to be stared at, Penelope nodded and moved on. She was discombobulated and wondered if perhaps she was misinterpreting things after battling the stationary bike tooth and nail over the Matterhorn. A cup of coffee from the fitness bistro would clear her mind and she raced toward the energy beans like one long-lost Van Slyck twin toward the other.

She got her coffee and sat down in the little café area that divided the front lobby from the fitness center proper, a position that allowed her to see all the people huffing and puffing on the main floor.

Suckers.

Rejuvenated by the steaming mug before her, she checked the barrage of texts she'd ignored from Missy the night before.

It's like my entire face is a skunk's butt.
Like where my nose should be is just straight ass.
Hello? Are you there? Why aren't you responding?
You're kidding right? No way you'd abandon me now.
I am literally choking to death.
My death is on your hands. Tell Damien I love him. Do Not Ask For Whom The Bell Tolls!

Penelope was chuckling from the enjoyable morning read when

she felt eyes upon her. Looking up, she found Fitness Megan working away at a machine and giving her the stink eye. WTH? Who was this Fitness Megan person and why was she so strict about water fountain etiquette? Hillsboro wasn't in a drought or anything. Shouldn't she be demonstrating proper lunge techniques with a kettlebell about now?

She went back to her texts, sure that paranoia was at play, and had a new one from Missy.

Made it home finally. Like at three. No thanks to you.

Penelope smiled and replied.

Glad to hear. Knew you could do it.

We have to get rid of these skunks. Do you know anybody?

Carl Jr. probably does. Ask him.

Yes! Carl Jr. can save the day. Dimwit hasn't outfoxed us yet!

Got to go. At the gym. Weird trainer lady is currently staring at me while doing squats in front of a mirror.

Why?

I took too long at the water fountain and it made her mad.

Come over and have a Bloody Mary and forget about it. Gyms are for neurotics. Love your body as it is.

Tammy's Tanning Shack?

Touché. Any hot guys I need to see? I love a sweaty man. Carl Jr. always has a faint dew.

Yes. One. But got to go. Will call later.

Fitness Megan was still squatting, still glaring, and she'd added audible grunts to her repertoire. Whatever. Theo was texting.

We're a couple of hours from camp. Dad forgot my inhaler. Can you mail it to me? Dad says like today.

Could she mail it? Of course she could. Right up James's ass.
Another text came in.

We forgot a water bottle too. Dad says overnight it and inhaler.

And now she had to pay for the express shipping?
Another text.

Dad says he will pay you back.

Damn straight he would. Mr. Proud Packer? Give her a break. You could stack the trunk to Euclidian perfection, but who cared if you forgot the inhaler? Penelope thought her mantra could be reduced to this: *Less slide rule precision, more albuterol.*

She took one final gulp of her coffee and instantly the magical elixir did its thing. Her mind cleared, and pieces of a puzzle that had been rattling around in her subconscious slowly fell into place. She imagined that James—in the driveway, staring into the void of a popped trunk with luggage all around his feet—often felt like this at the *Eureka!* moment.

To wit:

1. James was dating a trainer.

2. A person named Megan Scott made—and then mysteriously removed—a Facebook friend request.

3. The scowling woman at the fountain was wearing a *Megan* name tag.

Ergo: continued mean looks from the woman currently doing weird pirouettes at the TRX had nothing to do with fountain decorum and everything to do with a trunk-packing whiz of a Tarheel named James.

A number of thoughts passed through Penelope's head. That she'd been Facebook-stalked the night before was indisputable, as plain as the coffee she'd just spilled on her *Team Mom* T-shirt. One Megan Scott, trainer, was perusing for juicy details about a certain Penelope when a wayward finger had slipped, an unintentional friend request made, and her snooping adventure had gone briefly awry.

Penelope considered the facts and decided it was only natural when taking up with someone new to check out the former spouse. Nothing to worry about. Finding this interpretation of the Megan Scott situation agreeable, she put on her headphones, cranked some Zeppelin, and headed for any device that looked to have only one pulley.

⁓

A half hour later, she was on a leg machine advertised for the inner thighs. She was working those inner thigh muscles pretty hard when the reasonably hot guy she'd mentioned to Missy plopped down on the machine next to hers and began to exercise his outer thighs. Penelope found this awkward, his legs going in as hers went out, especially when she realized their movements were synchronized. She slowed her pace. That it was vigorous in the first place was something of a surprise. She'd spent the prior twenty minutes roaming peaceably around Fitness Plus, trying to act like she was following a highly detailed routine like everyone else.

Deciding she would like a better angle at which to observe Mr. Outer Thigh, she twisted toward him in a show of adjusting the machine's weight. Turned this way—her nose awash in delightful Old Spice cologne—she chanced a full-on gawk.

"That one sticks sometimes."

"Ramble On" was blasting away in her earbuds, but she heard what he said anyway and jerked upright. She was looking at the reasonably attractive man now and trying to bring her legs back together. They were currently splayed as wide as her hips would allow, frozen in place by the restraining device, which seemed to be jammed. She glanced around and discovered the peg she'd been fake adjusting was now lying on the floor beside her. Apparently she'd dislodged it when the man spoke and now she was pinioned in mechanical no-man's-land. Her current pose and the machine that held her there brought back unwelcome thoughts of things she'd been latched to at the gynecologist's office. She smiled, pointed to her earbud, and said, "Huh?"

It was a complete stall move, but the best she could do under duress. And now one of her earbuds popped out. It was dangling dangerously close to the pulley that moved the weights when the machine was operational. A tangle here would complicate matters further. She swished her head sideways and swung around wantonly with her arm to corral the wayward bud, but found that her compromised position limited upward mobility as well. And now her claustrophobia kicked in a little. She was weighing how to extricate herself from the medieval stretching rack when the fairly attractive man with the no-nonsense deodorant popped out of his seat, retrieved the peg, and said, "What setting?"

Penelope had no idea. What she did know was that the recent coffee stain on her *Team Mom* T-shirt had just come to the man's attention. His wrinkled nose was fleeting but undeniable. He looked to be rather on the fastidious side. Now he seemed to be weighing the whole package before him: the splayed legs, the coffee blotch, the dangling earbud that proved that middle-aged women could still get the Led out.

"Thirty, I think," Penelope said.

"Number three setting?"

Penelope now gave in to the ridiculousness of her predicament and the notion of meeting a cute guy at the gym—in Hillsboro—when her one snappy outfit was in the dirty clothes.

"Your call," she said. "I have no idea."

He nodded in a serious manner—it was clear he was all business at Fitness Plus—and bent to position the peg. As soon as she heard the satisfying *click*, Penelope brought her legs together and stayed like that a moment, trying to decide whether to just pop up before she was imprisoned again or make a show of finishing her set. She felt the dedicated fellow beside her would appreciate the latter, and not wanting to look ungrateful, she went back to opening and closing her thighs. The guy beside her did the same, and once again Penelope noted their harmonized motion.

"Are you a new member?"

The question was accompanied by the steady clacking of metal plates. Old Spice was really going to town on his outer thighs. She surmised his peg to be set at fifteen by the Fitness Plus accounting system.

"I am, actually," said Penelope, thankful for an excuse to pause in her exertion. "How could you ever tell?"

"I've never seen you before."

"I just joined last week. I'm still trying to figure out how all this stuff works and where everything is."

"Great gym. I'm here like six days a week. Seven if I can swing it."

Penelope could believe it. He was not tall, maybe five nine, but all lithe muscle. Taking a firmer gander now while his head was once again facing forward, she realized that he was likely a little older than she was, maybe midforties. What hair he had left was shaved close and his serious brow glistened with sweat and intensity. Penelope had never dated a bald guy before but thought she could swing it if she had to. He was handsome in a stern sort of way. On his wrist was a plastic gizmo that looked like a watch but wasn't.

"If you're not using that, can I get a set in?" said a harsh female voice from the other side of her.

Penelope yanked her head around, aware that she'd breached the Fitness Plus code of conduct by sitting at the inner thigh machine without actually working the inner thighs, to find Megan Scott, trainer, looking peeved.

"Sure," said Penelope, flustered but popping up.

She was still basically midlaunch from her perch when Megan

Scott yanked a towel she'd stored somewhere on her person and made a big show of wiping the seat where, seconds before, Penelope had been resting so comfortably.

"You must be new," said Megan Scott. "You're supposed to wipe off the machines when you're done using them."

These thoughts went through Penelope's head simultaneously:

1. It was like forty degrees in Fitness Plus, so one P. Lemon wasn't sweating in the slightest.

2. She hadn't known about the towel rule, but would follow it in the future.

3. Even if she had known, she'd been too rushed off the machine to cleanse the germy, infectious body fluids seeping out of her.

4. Megan Scott was pretending not to know her, despite an evening spent as an investigative reporter.

"Hey, Brad," she said to Old Spice as she moved the peg from three to ten.

"What's up, Megan?"

What followed was a discussion of a future rock climbing event.

Penelope stayed glued to the spot, pretty sure Megan Scott had smirked while adjusting the peg. If so, it was a nervy move. She could have done more weight. A lot more. Her legs were really strong. In fact, half of her wanted to stand glaring at Megan Scott until she finished her set then hop back on the machine, peg it up to about thirteen, and show what was what when it came to inner thigh power.

The other half, however, was pretty tired and just wanted to go do a few crunches on one of those big rubber balls everyone seemed to be playing with, then get on down the road. This was the decision she made. No need to get into a goofy weight lifting contest with James's pushy new girlfriend.

She was heading out of the gym, feeling light of foot, the big rubber ball as fun as advertised. Rounding the corner, she was hailed by the sort of handsome bald guy who wore Old Spice.

"Hey," he said, jogging to catch up.

"Hey," she replied, fearful for a moment that he was going to keep jogging around her even after she'd stopped. He seemed chock-full of energy.

"I'm Brad," he said, still pacing back and forth like someone dancing the hustle, a towel around his neck.

"I'm Penelope."

"Sorry," he said, pointing at the gizmo on his wrist. "Didn't get out of the office till near midnight."

Penelope must have looked puzzled for he slowed his pacing in her vicinity to say: "Twenty thousand steps a day. Missed yesterday. Doubling up today. Gotta get forty K or no frozen yogurt for me."

Penelope had no idea what he was talking about, but the people at the check-in desk were looking at them now and Penelope wished he'd hailed her sooner—or later—when they were a bit out of public range.

"Since you're new," said Brad, "I was wondering if you might want someone to help you come up with a workout routine or something."

"You must have seen me roaming around aimlessly."

Bald Brad came to a complete stop for the briefest of moments and smiled. "Yeah, you looked like you were kind of faking it. Glad to give you a shout sometime and show you the ropes. Some of these machines are a little complicated."

Penelope considered this for a moment, giving her number to a guy she'd just met. When was the last time she'd done that? James? That karaoke night at Wet Willie's when she'd brought the house down with "Precious" by the Pretenders?

She considered, as well, her married suburban friends, who preferred her in a 24/7 macramé club.

She also thought briefly—very briefly—about Fitzwilliam. Then she forked over the digits.

8

Later that morning, Penelope was in the car, enjoying the warm satisfaction that always came after a successful voyage to and from UPS. She didn't know how UPS shops were in the rest of the country, but the Hillsboro version truly rocked. It was amazing how fast they could box, tape, address, and send a steroid inhaler screaming toward an asthmatic little adventurer in North Carolina. The fact that they had a little bowl of Dum Dums for the customers was just icing on the cake.

She was gnawing exuberantly on one of those suckers when she checked the clock on the dash. Theo should be arriving for his first camp sojourn within the hour and this would be her last chance to hear his voice for two whole weeks. She didn't know how she could miss him already, but she did. She dialed James's number, knowing that Theo would answer. No way James would face the music after his inhaler debacle. Master packer, her ass.

"Hey Mom," came Theo's reply.

"Hey honey, are you guys almost there?"

"Yeah. Dad says we're close. We're out in the middle of nowhere. I can't even get Wi-Fi. But before that, you wouldn't believe it!"

Her son now launched into a recitation of his blissful four-hour PlinkyMo day, a tale of high adventure, near misses, and heroic captures. He'd added a whole parcel of North Carolina Plinkies to his virtual menagerie. The tale, epic in scope and breadth, took about eight minutes to recite, and Penelope was pleased that—doomsayers to the contrary—the American oral tradition was alive and well.

By the time he'd finished his Homeric yarn, she was sitting in the driveway of her new place, weighing Soft Linen versus Daisy White.

"That's great, honey. And listen, I overnighted that stuff, so it should be there Monday afternoon. Try to avoid mold and feathers till then. Well, I love you. Write me lots of letters, okay?"

"Love you too."

She didn't miss the fact that he'd hung up before committing to correspondence, and had to salute his stubborn refusal to be pinned down. That was one trait he'd gotten from dear old Mom.

$\sim$

After lunch she was applying even-awesomer-than-expected turquoise to another wall and rocking out again with her good friend Beyoncé when the phone rang. She picked up to find Missy in a near panic.

"I can't get hold of Carl Junior. He's down at Dollywood and won't be back till next week. Damn it to hell, I forgot about that. He's down there eating sorghum and biscuits with Dolly and clogging the night away. Just laughing and drinking and having a party. Meanwhile, I've got an army of experimental skunks about to run me out of town. You've got to help me."

Penelope had also forgotten about Carl Jr.'s Pigeon Forge vacation with his grandkids. She thought it was likely more go-carts and water parks than a biscuit-eating hoedown with the queen of country music but decided to let it slide.

"What can I do?" she said. "I've got a date tonight."

"Don't worry, I haven't forgotten about you and Fitzpatrick McGillicuddy. Or his sweater. Personally, I can't wait to hear about his heirloom tomato garden on Monday. It should be fascinating. But listen, this is an absolute emergency."

Penelope wished now she hadn't shown Missy the LoveSynch

photo of Fitzwilliam in his cozy cardigan. She'd mentioned nothing about tomatoes, but this didn't sound too far afield, unfortunately. What had she gotten herself into?

"Again," said Penelope, "what can I do about your skunk problem? Which is one regular Hillsboro skunk, by the way. Nothing more."

"You have to know someone in this town that can get rid of varmints. I assumed half the people in Hillsboro did that for a living."

Penelope laughed and said, "Just look in the phone book."

"I did. No go. Come on, help a sister out. You know everybody in the county. What about your first ex-husband? I like the way that sounds, by the way. Like you're Liz Taylor or something. First ex-husband. Second ex-husband. Eighth ex-husband. Anyway, surely the HHR knows someone."

"I don't want to call him."

"Come on. Pretty please. You agreed to help out with Operation Dimwit."

"No I didn't."

"But it was kind of assumed you would."

"And why is that?"

"Because you always help a sister in need."

"Not this time."

"Okay, whatever. Just make one little call for me."

Penelope considered her options. If she said no to contacting the HHR, the calls and texts might continue all night and weekend. If she said yes, it would shut Missy up for a few hours and she could get some painting done.

"All right," she said. "I'll do it. But that's it. That's the end of my involvement with this skunk nonsense."

"I knew I could count on you," Missy said. "Operation Dimwit is on!"

Penelope clicked off and paced around her den for a while, inspecting the paint job. At this rate, and with some free time tomorrow, she'd be applying the trim even sooner than she hoped. And it was true.

She'd come to her final decision. Daisy White it was and would forever be. Soft Linen simply didn't have what it took.

She went to the bedroom, wondering what the HHR had in store—bear cubs he was raising as his own? A new strain of marijuana that gave him X-ray vision? It could be anything. Standing in front of her closet, she thumbed through clothes, trying to decide what to wear for her date. What she saw were the same outfits she'd been looking at for the past three years. When was the last time she bought something for herself that wasn't socks, bras, or panties? Would she always be broke? Yes, she would, if Theo's monster feet kept growing three inches a day. She'd bought three pairs of shoes for him since the last pair for herself.

Her eye landed on a nice-looking sundress that she'd had for a decade. So what if it was old? It was pale pink and bright yellow and could pass for summer casual or a tiny bit more if the word *fromage* was going to be tossed about. It was a good dress and a flattering one too. It would be fine.

While perusing her clothes, she couldn't help but notice the empty space on the highest shelf, which struck her as the perfect spot for a complicated gift—an adults-only gift—which was green and orange and christened **PENELOPE LEMON**. Her dresser was simply too much in play when Theo was on a charger rampage.

That settled things, and she snatched the item in question and—standing on tiptoes—thrust it to the farthest recesses of the closet. For good measure, she piled three sweaters on top. All but slapping her hands together in the classic *job complete* gesture, she plopped down on her bed, suddenly libidinous.

Her new erotic novel beckoned from the bedside table. She'd raced through the climax of *Carnal Liaisons* and was neither surprised nor disappointed when the young actor with the ska band got the part in the Netflix series he so desperately wanted. Anyone that hot, that good in bed, and yet that true to his Nebraska/ska values deserved all that life—or Esmeralda—had to offer. Penelope had been so pleased with the outcome, and so thrilled that she could stay up as late as she wanted on a Friday night, that she'd started right away on *Unchaste Places*. It, too, looked promising.

When she'd left off, Miranda was just about to enter the Turkish bath at that ritzy little resort Henri had taken her to. There were complications waiting in that bath. What kind, neither Miranda nor Penelope knew. But you could bet your bottom dollar that Henri had more than caviar and Prosecco on his mind. So why didn't Miranda heed the warnings of the masseuse at Spa Helvetica, the one who seemed like she was speaking from experience? Was it because some part of Miranda was drawn to the danger? Or was she simply too trusting? One thing was sure: life at tiny Meade College hadn't prepared her for a man like Henri.

But would even young, naive Miranda—fresh from grad school— be so skittish about the item on the top shelf? Penelope was alone in her own place in the middle of the day and her son was gone for two weeks. Why was she suddenly so hot and bothered? The sneaking around had something to do with it, the lure of the illicit that called to her from beneath the winter sweaters, which were more and more starting to remind her of Winston Hackler. It definitely wasn't her pending date with Fitzwilliam. Maybe it was spending the morning with bald, active Brad and the excitement of giving her number to a stranger for the first time in years. She didn't know, but any kinks that might need to be worked out could wait till after the call to the HHR.

As always, the phone rang and rang before he picked up. The HHR likely couldn't hear it over the Mötley Crüe that was blaring on the four-foot floor speakers he'd purchased at Radio Shack the same month their electricity got cut off.

Finally, he answered, hollering as he did, "Hey Weasel, turn that down. Penelope's on the line. And Shiflett, you wouldn't know Area Fifty-One if it bit you on the ass. We'll see what Penelope says. Well, hello Penelope."

"Hey. How are you?"

"Doing fine, doing fine. Just over here with a couple misinformed locals who wouldn't know their ass from a hole in the ground when it comes to extraterrestrials."

The locals being referenced were classmates of Penelope's from Hillsboro High and running buddies of the HHR going on thirty years. Weasel acted as first lieutenant on the HHR's lawn mowing crew and Shiflett worked over at the Hostess plant, making delicious confections for America's youth.

Penelope passed on well wishes to her fellow alums, which elicited shouts from the gallery to come join them. These requests were followed by the inevitable flick of a lighter, an audible *whoosh* of air being pulled violently up a plastic tube, and then an extended coughing session from the HHR.

"Shiflett and Weasel say you ought to swing by and hang out," said the HHR, his voice hoarse and scratchy sounding.

"Can't do it. I'm painting my den today."

"What color?"

"Turquoise."

"Excellent decision. I read an article about the psychology of color last week and turquoise came highly recommended. It's calming. Very good for intuition. I think you'll be pleased with it."

The HHR was a proud amateur psychologist, specializing in dream analysis as it related to sexual desire and fishing. Despite these limited qualifications, he might be on to something. She had *intuitively* picked turquoise after only four minutes in Lowe's.

"Thanks for that. But listen, I need a favor. We're having a skunk problem where I work and my boss is wondering if you know anyone who might be able to help us out. Like, this weekend."

The HHR took a contemplative puff on something smaller, likely a friendly roach being passed from the couch to the La-Z-Boy, the throne from which he worked the remote control and directed metaphysical discussions. It was an elegant sound, this puff, thoughtful and not without purpose. He was working himself into problem-solving mode, Penelope could tell.

"You're over at Rolling Acres," he said, exhaling with Laurence Olivier panache. "Why don't you get Uncle Carl Junior on it?"

"He's at Dollywood and won't be back for a week. My boss is completely freaking out and can't wait till then."

"Freaking out over skunks?"

"Tell me about it."

"Buford King's your man, if you can get him. But he's particular about what cases he takes. He's an honest-to-God tracker and doesn't want to mess with getting a possum out of your trash or something. Plus, he's basically retired. But you might be able to get him, since you used to be family."

"Huh?"

"He's Momma's great-uncle by marriage. Carl Senior's youngest sister Darlene's husband. You've met him. At Thanksgiving or Christmas or something. Darlene's the one who keeps bees."

Penelope racked her brain but couldn't place Buford King or Darlene, though she did remember the clover honey. The HHR used to pile it an inch thick on his cornbread before basically putting his face in the plate to gobble it up. Lord how the HHR loved honey. Maybe that was what drew the bear cub to him in the first place.

"You don't have his number, by chance?" Penelope asked.

"Nope. But it's in the phone book. Just look up the Critter Catcher and that's your man."

"All right. And thanks. I really appreciate it. My boss has been driving me crazy worrying about these skunks."

The HHR now took another dainty drag off the roach and said in a conspiratorial whisper, "Hey, just play along with what I'm about to say to these jokers. They think you're smart as hell and this will put our little argument to bed once and for all. Is that cool?"

Penelope felt herself smiling. How often had she played the referee, the judge, the game show host during a coffee table colloquium at the HHR's?

"Sure," she said. "Have at it."

With this, the HHR hollered, "Hey dipshits, Penelope agrees that it's much more likely that Area Fifty-One is an extraterrestrial reanimation project than it is the original spot where aliens first began breeding with humans. Isn't that right, Penelope?"

Penelope agreed that it was.

"And Shiflett," the HHR hollered anew, pressing his advantage. "Penelope also says that everybody knows that alien breeding took place in Egypt thousands of years ago. That's why all their artwork has those people with pointy heads. She suggests you read a little history before you starting talking out the side of your ass."

Penelope smiled wider at this, thanked the HHR again for the name, and hung up, fighting the vaguest of urges to head over and join the ridiculous roundtable.

9

"I knew you'd come through," Missy said when Penelope got out of the car at the Rolling Acres office. "You're like the fixer in this town."

Penelope could tell she was being buttered up and offered an insincere smile in return. Where she wanted to be was in her den, taping the trim in preparation for good old Daisy White. Or getting mentally prepared for her first real date in years via a long candlelit bath and soothing music. Or just lounging on the couch, seeing how Miranda was making out at Spa Helvetica. What she didn't want to be doing, not at all, was hanging out at her workplace on a Saturday afternoon, waiting on a skunk catcher.

"So your first ex-husband came through for you, huh?" said Missy, smiling below her massive sunglasses and *Wayne's World* baseball cap and standing so near the car door that Penelope couldn't get out of the driver's seat.

"Oh, excuse me," Missy said. "Let me move my leathery ass out of your way so you can get out. I'm telling you, Tammy fried me up like a skinny little catfish yesterday."

Penelope climbed out of her car and checked her watch. It was 1:45. Cousin Buford, or Uncle Buford, or whatever he was to the HHR, was supposed to arrive in fifteen minutes. Once introductions were made, she planned on hitting the road. Was she even getting overtime for this?

"You're getting overtime, by the way," Missy said.

It was obvious Missy had picked up on her nonverbal clues and Penelope dialed back her aggressive gum chomping a notch. She was no longer quite as irritated, either, which kind of irritated her. Why couldn't she stay peeved? It was embarrassing.

"Yeah," Penelope said, smiling for the first time, "the HHR came through."

"He's just hot as hell, isn't he?" Missy said, all but licking her lips. "Country catnip for the ladies, like a young Carl Junior. But speaking of hotties, did you talk to that dude at the gym?"

"Yes."

"Did you give him your number?" Missy asked, drumming on the hood of Penelope's car in a way that suggested one too many espressos.

For some reason—Fitzwilliam maybe—she felt sheepish about responding. Her reluctance must have been telling because Missy said: "Good for you, sister. Good for you. Let's just go ahead and move on from Fitzhugh Milligan."

"Fitzwilliam Darcy."

"Exactly."

"He's not that old."

"How old?"

"Sixties. Like sixty-three probably."

"Old."

"What about Carl Junior then?"

"Are you kidding me?" Missy said, stopping her drumming in the middle of a powerful solo. "That's apples to heirlooms. That's coveralls and cardigans. Give me a break, would you? Carl Junior is probably fighting Dolly off as we speak. She's clogging her little heart out for him in her secret mountain getaway. And underneath that coat of many colors? Nothing but a rhinestone garter belt. You're out of your mind to compare Carl Junior and Fitzduncan McDuncan. That's absurd."

"No it's not."

"Listen, I guarantee you that right now, down in her gold-plated holler, Dolly and Carl Junior aren't listening to a Ted Talk while pondering tomato cross-pollination. Which is absolutely the best you can hope for tonight on Fitzgilligan's Island."

Before Penelope could respond, Missy held up a hand to stop her, a placating smile beneath the very tan drumsticks that were her hands.

"Let's venture," she said, "into more neutral waters. So, the mystery guy at the gym, what's his name?"

"Brad."

Missy nodded at this, as if her instincts had been correct. The name pleased her. "And what does slightly sweaty Brad do for a living?"

"We talked for like ninety seconds."

"What if he's a fry cook at Waffle House or something?"

"I don't know. If the guy's cool, I don't worry too much about what they do, or how much money they have."

"It's all about the sack time, huh?" Missy said, resuming her drumming in a languorous Latin beat. "Getting the freak on? Yeah, honey, I'm right there with you. At the end of the day, money comes and goes, but orgasms are forever."

Penelope felt like a few faulty assumptions had been made during Missy's spiel about the primary traits she was looking for in a man, but let it slide. The time for her date with Fitzwilliam was drawing nigh and she felt, more clearly than ever, that she'd prefer to spend the night painting and rocking out in her den. Why hadn't she suggested lunch—at a restaurant—instead?

"What about that chick at the water fountain? Did you show her who was boss?"

"No," said Penelope, "I did not show Megan the trainer who was boss. In fact, she barked at me for taking too long on a thigh machine."

"Maybe I'll go down there with you next time," Missy said, setting her tiny, tan jaw. "And bring like a seventy-two-ounce jug. And when I see her heading to the water fountain, I'll make her wait for about an hour and half while I fill it up. And the whole time, I'm just pausing now and then to take tiny little sips. I'm not joking. I could stay there forever. Till they locked up the place. Staring means nothing to me."

Penelope liked the sound of that. Confrontation wasn't her thing, but for Missy it was truly mother's milk.

"I think she might be dating James," Penelope said, grinning in anticipation of the effect this would have on the little drummer girl before her.

"No," said Missy, snapping fully alert. "First he dates your son's teacher, and now a trainer? Who does this little Romeo think he is?"

"Beats me. But I'm pretty sure this woman Facebook-stalked me last night."

"Oh, sister, she'll be hiding in the bushes if you don't get this under control. Taking photos and framing you for crimes you didn't commit. I wouldn't put anything past this wacko. Give me a little time to get a dossier going and then a plan. I've had about a thousand stalkers in my day and not a one of them came back for seconds after I got through with them, I can promise you that."

Penelope grinned, doubting this trainer thing was anything serious. Over James? Had she seen him in his karate outfit yet? Or perusing *Modern Robin Hood*, his archery magazine, and sighing over arrow quivers? Had she heard him use the word *opus* about one of his longer-is-better favorite books? If not, she would soon enough, and from that day forward stalking in his honor would be laughable indeed.

But now Missy was yanking her *Wayne's World* cap in all directions, like someone afraid of being snuck up on.

"Do you smell something?" she asked, twitching everywhichway.

"Yes," Penelope said, loudly sniffing the air. "I smell an army of trained skunks."

"You're being sarcastic."

"You think?"

"You weren't here for Skunk Armageddon. If you were, you wouldn't be quite so smug, I'll tell you that much."

So saying, she turned and stared up the hill at Dimwit's trailer.

Penelope couldn't tell if the look was meant to be more forlorn or more determined, only that it was super dramatic, like a cowboy about to take a stand against long odds. You could hear the lonesome prairie whistling in her eyes.

"One skunk," Penelope said. "One normal, regular Hillsboro skunk."

"I'm just telling you that there is no way that funk came from one skunk. And I'm telling you, further, that they maneuvered themselves such that I was all but rounded up there at the bottom of Dimwit's hill. And further still, that they surrounded the office perimeter after I'd surrendered the hill. For all practical purposes, I was a prisoner of war until my daring escape. No thanks to you, by the way."

"Did you see a skunk?"

"No," Missy said, head still swiveling side to side, tan, worried nose stabbing the air.

"I'm telling you, it was just one. Their smell—even from really far away—is super strong. And it lasts for a really long time. That's just how Hillsboro smells in the summer."

"Listen, I have no idea how Hillsboro smells at night, other than the inside of Applebee's, which smells like fried onions and love. But this was a skunk army."

Penelope was not going to give in. Her country girl common sense was being challenged, as was her knowledge of local wildlife. Had one of Missy's ex-husbands rescued a bear cub and spent the night in a tree? She thought not.

"All right, listen," Missy said. "When he gets here, you do the talking at first. You're magic with these yokels. They all think I'm a satanist or a Yankee or something. I'm just not naturally good with them."

Penelope felt this went without saying, but before she could offer a smart retort, a pickup truck ever so gently drove through the trailer park entrance.

10

The truck was an older Chevy, very old but well maintained, and it paused at the entrance to admire the curvy, fancy lettering that spelled out *Rolling Acres* on the brick sign in the median. The truck stayed where it was, idling softly, for fifteen seconds, thirty, a full minute. A thin wisp of smoke wafted from the open window, a leisurely, satisfied plume, as if the occupant of the vehicle was pleased by the neatness of the sign, and the median so meticulously tended by Carl Jr., and the whole of the Rolling Acres Estates. It was pipe smoke, a smell Penelope had always liked, and she wondered if Missy with her psychosomatically injured nose could smell it as well.

When the truck was again in motion, it made its languid way toward the office before pausing again to watch two squirrels chasing each around a Bradford pear tree. Even after the squirrels frolicked out of sight, the vehicle stayed where it was, as if contemplating the memory of fluffy tails madcapping like Shriners in their funny little cars. Penelope wondered how long it would take the pickup to make the full one-hundred-yard drive to the office, and whether it ever would. She could read the sign on the door, painted in an elegant royal blue script: *The Critter Catcher.*

For reasons she couldn't explain, the unhurried truck and the placidly spiraling smoke that emanated from its window held her rapt. She and Missy and the modular office were all plainly in sight. Why would anyone drive that slowly or pause that often when the goal of the journey was so clearly in sight? And who in this day and age had so little regard for time, its measurement, and its passage?

"It's the skunk man," Missy whispered.

Penelope nodded but didn't reply.

A large, rectangular compartment ran horizontally behind the cab. Penelope assumed this was where captured critters were kept.

Eventually, impatience got the best of Missy. She waved her arms and shouted, "Hey there! Hey! Hey! We're over here."

The driver gazed for a bit longer at the spot where the squirrels had played, then turned slowly to face the woman hailing him. Penelope could see him now, his trim, white beard and the same weathered, rugged look as Carl Jr. He was capless, an odd sight in this town considering his line of work, and his white hair was longish and came past the collar of his denim work shirt. He smiled now at Missy, and nodded, then did the same to Penelope. Still the truck didn't move.

"Is he stoned or something?" Missy whispered out of the side of her mouth. "Why's he just sitting there looking at us?"

"He's not stoned," Penelope whispered back. "He's just not in a hurry."

"He looks like an Old Testament prophet," Missy said quietly, while still waving her arms in a beckoning motion and smiling idiotically. "What if he's here to make me repent for my ways? Or to smite me for my wickedness? I've got a bad burning bush feeling about this."

"Maybe he's just letting you think about your transgressions for a while. Like harassing your employees with texts all night and making them come in for harebrained jobs on the weekend."

"I've done a lot worse things than that. And this skunk man can tell. Look at him. He's staring right into my soul. He's reading me like the dirty little book that I am."

This made Penelope laugh and in response the Critter Catcher laughed as well, pleased that his presence was bringing such mirth. Or perhaps it was the squirrels' mirth. Or the mirth of the day. Anyway, he was mirthful, and once again in motion.

Pulling into the lot, he nodded and beamed again at both of them, then took about three minutes backing in—and then out—and then in again. That there were no other cars in the seven available spots affected his precision not at all. He paused once to adjust the mirror on the passenger side for a better look at a painted line. And twice to take casual puffs on his pipe. Penelope felt like she might as well have been watching the HHR tie his intricate fishing lures, a process that could only be done perfectly and exactly and with a plethora of smoke inhalation.

Parked, with eighteen inches from the lines to spare on each side, he smiled warmly to himself at the notion of equidistance, then rooted in his glove box for several moments, engine idling softly, farm report reciting bushel prices on the radio. Penelope could feel Missy squirming with impatience and nervous energy behind her but refused to indulge her with a wink or eye roll, as Missy doubtlessly was beseeching her to do. The trapper could take his sweet time as far as Penelope was concerned.

Her boss was making a strange, dry sound beside her, as if trying to clear a throat that didn't need clearing. She was dying to talk, Penelope knew, but now the skunk man had paused in his door opening to give full attention to the farm report. Beef cattle were bringing eleven hundred dollars a head and this news elicited an appreciative whistle. He seemed to find it a tidy sum.

Then he stirred. First he switched off the radio. Then the truck. Then he closed the glove compartment, several times actually, as it didn't seem to want to shut with as soft a touch as Buford King was applying. Three, four, five times he cautiously and tenderly pushed the door closed until it caught. Giving the glove compartment a friendly pat and a nod, he placed a felt Stetson on his head and exited the truck. The hat was grey and well worn, and he looked like a sheriff of yore. He stood before the women and extended a business card to each.

"You're Penelope," he said. "The one who likes honey."

Penelope did like honey, but just in the normal way. Then she caught on. "I think you're talking about my ex-husband."

"That's right, that's right," the Critter Catcher said, chuckling. "Hagi. He ate it like a bear. I remember it now. Used to tickle Darlene when he did that. More honey than cornbread. Well, I'm Buford. Buford King. Good to see you again, Penelope. And this must be your friend who's worried about the skunks."

He turned his fond gaze on Missy, who was making a show of studying the business card in her hand. Summoned, Missy snapped up her chin and set eyes a-gleaming. Her mouth was twisted at the pending release of extended speech after the long drought of silence. Penelope could see the flood of words building in her face and knew her twitchy tumult would soon come to an end. Just then, Buford King noticed something in the nearby woods behind the office, some fifty yards away, and started a crisp trek in that direction. En route, he pulled a small implement from his belt and wiped it once on the multipocketed legs of his Dickies. Beside her, Missy let out a faint groan and Penelope looked for the first time at the business card she held.

The Critter Catcher

Wildlife Removal Expert: Skunks, Raccoons, Rodents, Snakes, Opossums, Coyotes. Hedgehogs, Moles, Voles, Squirrels, Flying Squirrels, Bobcats, Muskrats, Beaver, Other

Professional Forager: Ramp, persimmons, mushrooms, wild honey, mountain pears, dandelion greens, assorted nuts, natural teas (black birch, sassafras, ginseng), chaga, cloudberries, purple dead nettle

Penelope noted the inclusion of both kinds of squirrels, not sure if she'd ever seen one of the flying variety. She'd also never seen a bobcat in the wild, or a muskrat. Nor had she heard of cloudberries, which sounded delicious, or purple dead nettle, which sounded painful. Maybe she wasn't quite the country girl she supposed.

In the woods, the Critter Catcher was down on one knee, digging around some unidentifiable vegetation, before pulling it up in a bunch. He shook dirt from the roots then reached into one of his many pockets for a handkerchief, which he used to sort and clean what now appeared to be individual stalks and not just a clump. He wiped off his tool, restored it to the belt, and walked back toward the parking lot, peeling the stalks as he came.

During all this, Missy had circled twice around Penelope, bugging her eyes and mouthing words that Penelope couldn't make out even if she wanted to. The silent words and the circling were both occurring too swiftly for any sort of deciphering to occur. Penelope had seen caged monkeys act similarly at the zoo in Richmond, though they were perhaps not quite this frenzied.

"Ramp," said the Critter Catcher when he stood before them again. He took a bite of his recently discovered treat. "I bet you didn't know you had ramp back there, did you?"

"No," said Missy, reluctantly taking what Buford King had just peeled and handed her. "I didn't know that."

Penelope watched this exchange with barely concealed glee. As far as she knew, Missy's tastes in foods were limited to Captain Crunch, nachos, and Italian submarine sandwiches minus the lettuce. Penelope had never seen her eat an actual vegetable, fruit, nut, or herb, other than the lime that came with her after-work margarita. Her spice of choice was salt.

"Try you a little bite," Buford King said. "Spring onions is what some people call them, but that name is technically incorrect. They are similar species, but not the same. That there is ramp. *Allium tricoccum.* It's like if an onion and some garlic had a pretty little delicate child."

While Missy hemmed and hawed about not wanting to ruin her supper, and how she'd add the ramp to her daily salad later that evening, Penelope allowed herself to smile openly and freely at the stream of lies coming from her boss's mouth. Deceit, evasion, and treachery—Missy's stock-in-trade—were nothing in the face of an earnest Hillsborian offering his largesse. She might as well be refusing to sample a tasty bud while lounging on the HHR's beanbag chair. Or an Iris her mother thought should be transplanted to her front flower bed. A gift offered by a Hillsborian simply could not be refused.

"Just one little bite," said Buford King with an encouraging smile. "Just to be sociable. You can save the rest for that special salad later tonight. You'll like it. I just know you will."

"Just one little bite," said Penelope, nodding insincerely. She knew Missy was paranoid about giving offense to the working people of Hillsboro, the ones who kept the AC units going at Rolling Acres and the septic lines clear. And the working man before her was going to be asked to do the most important task she'd ever asked anyone: taming Dimwit's skunk army.

Scratching her nose with a tan and very obvious middle finger, she grinned at Penelope and shoved the ramp bulb. Penelope was pretty sure she'd just swallowed it whole, but Missy made a good show of chewing and murmuring sweet nothings as the Critter Catcher grinned his approval.

"I told you," he said. "And plenty more where that came from. I'll round up a good sackload for you before I head out. But now I reckon you'd like to talk a bit about our striped, odiferous friends of the wild."

"Yes," said Missy, though casually gagging. "I do. We have a skunk problem. A big one. And I need someone to get rid of them as quickly as possible."

The Critter Catcher smiled with his eyes only and said: "How big is *big*?"

"Like a skunk army. They surrounded me the other night while I was out making my nightly rounds and forced me back into the office. They've basically got the run of the place."

"Is that right?" said the Critter Catcher. "Is that right?"

"I told her it was probably just one skunk," said Penelope.

Buford King now turned to Penelope and offered her a candid assessment. "Just one, you say. Just one?"

"Yes," said Penelope, as Missy again scratched her nose with a flicking middle finger. "Maybe a mother with some babies. But definitely not a skunk horde stalking her like a pack of coyotes."

"A skunk horde? I like that," said the Critter Catcher. "It has a nice ring to it."

"They were organized," Missy said, moving around so that she was side by side with Penelope. "I think the guy in that trailer on the hill is training them."

"*Trained* skunks," said Penelope in a sneering tone. "Really? Did you see them?"

"No, but I smelled them. And I felt them, too. Their presence. It was like they were moving down the hill in a calculated fashion. Mr. King, that's possible, isn't it?"

Penelope let fly her choicest scoff. The Critter Catcher looked from one to the other of them, smiling a bit, then up to the sky, and then to the woods where the delicious wild ramp grew, the cloudberries and purple dead nettle. He seemed to realize he was being called upon not just as a resident wildlife expert but as an umpire in an ongoing dispute. A lone cloud crossed the sun, and the day grew dark and momentous. Then a crow cawed in three short bursts from the woods and the Critter Catcher nodded as if that was the signal he was waiting for.

"The skunk," he said, "is a very unusual animal . . . a sensitive animal . . . an intelligent animal. One might say, a very intelligent animal."

Penelope could feel Missy smiling beside her but refused to give her the satisfaction of looking. Her boss spoke up perkily now.

"So they could organize and work as a pack? And they could be trained?"

"Oh yes, they can be trained. Yes ma'am, indeed. I've trained a fair number myself."

"I knew it," said Missy with a smug nod of her *Wayne's World* cap.

Penelope did not really know as much about skunks as she'd led Missy to believe, but she threw caution to the wind. "Do they travel in organized packs?"

"The skunk," said the skunk man, "is generally a solitary creature."

"I thought so," said Penelope.

"But very intelligent, as you said," offered Missy. "And trainable."

"Yes, that's true."

"Is it fair to ask, then," said Missy, placing her tan hands behind her denim cutoffs and pacing around a bit, "if a trained, domesticated skunk would act in the same way as a wild one?"

"That is fair to ask," said the Critter Catcher. "And a very interesting question."

"I thought so," said Missy.

Her employer was trying not to gloat in front of an earnest local whose help she desperately wanted, but Penelope thought she was doing a poor job of it. She'd swished her ponytail there at the end, which was about as sassy as it got.

"Do you recall," said the Critter Catcher, "what time of day this skunk encounter occurred?"

"Around midnight was the approximate time of my initial encounter," said Missy. "They are nocturnal creatures primarily, if I'm not mistaken."

The Critter Catcher looked off in the distance for a moment, eyeing a redbud in full bloom. He took a bit of ramp from his pocket and helped himself to a nibble. Then he pulled his pipe from another pocket and tapped it thoughtfully against the side of his knee. He was deep in skunk reverie now.

"Well, that's a bit like the ramp and spring onion debate. Most people would call the skunk nocturnal. Most scientists even. But in truth, the skunk is crepuscular. Which means he likes to do his wanderings during twilight. Just before dawn. And just after dusk."

"That's fascinating," said Penelope.

"It is, isn't it?"

Penelope could tell this crepuscular news had thrown Missy for a loop and smiled sympathetically at her.

"Are they never out except for those hours?" Missy blurted.

"A good solid moon might have them out around midnight," said the Critter Catcher. "Or other, less explainable factors."

The skunk man had said this bit about *less explainable factors* with the faintest hint of a mysterious air. Penelope heard it and knew Missy had too. She'd perked up considerably since the crepuscular setback and fairly sang out, "So, Mr. King, in your professional opinion, could we rule out the possibility that I saw a skunk at midnight?"

"No we could not."

"Or the possibility that I saw more than one, and perhaps many of them?"

"That would be unusual, yes. But females do often share a den in cold weather. It's a cooperative thing when den space is scarce."

"Cooperative," said Missy. "Cooperative."

"He said in the winter," Penelope piped in. "It was seventy degrees last night."

Missy waved this off with a dismissive flick of the wrist.

"So," she said, eyeing Penelope the way Penelope was eyeing her. "So, in your opinion, can we absolutely, positively rule out the possibility that I not only saw a multitude of skunks but that I may have also been surrounded and menaced by that same multitude?"

"Well," said the Critter Catcher. "Well, well, well. Are you asking for my professional opinion? Or my personal one?"

Saying this, the skunk man looked directly into Missy's eyes. He stood equidistant from them, as proportionate as his truck in the parking space, ramp hanging loose from one pocket, his pouch of tobacco poking out of another. He was smiling wryly to himself, as if aware he was the arbiter of a great ontological debate about not just skunks, but the whole of nature's mysteries. The day was quiet except for the distant steady tapping of a woodpecker. Now the Critter Catcher focused his smile on Penelope, seeing if she was reading the table correctly. His answer—which could only please one of the women before him—would depend on Missy's response. That was what the smile was saying, Hillsborian to Hillsborian, and Penelope knew she'd just been given fair warning.

Missy paced around a spell, and squished her tongue around in her mouth, as if in search of ramp residue. She was highly agitated and her eyes never left Penelope's. If she guessed wrong, Penelope could walk away from Operation Dimwit without a backwards glance. They both knew this. Those were the implied stakes. They'd both been intractable and now here they were. Penelope kept her face as straight as she could and looked neither at her boss nor at the skunk man. The woodpecker's thumping was louder now, steady and eternal, and Penelope tried with all her might to concentrate on that sound.

"Personal," Missy said.

Penelope nearly groaned, but didn't. Had she blinked? Did she have a tell?

Mr. King looked wistfully at Penelope before replying. They'd once been family, after all.

"These are unusual skunks," said the Critter Catcher in a warm soft whisper that spoke of bourbon barrels and the light winds of Valhalla. "Unusual indeed. Special skunks, even. And in my personal opinion—which is what you asked for—my intuitive personal opinion is that you absolutely cannot rule anything out. The skunk is one of the Creator's most fascinating and mysterious creatures."

11

A few hours after engaging in brinksmanship with Missy—and losing—Penelope was en route to her date with Fitzwilliam. She had her windows down and was pushing her factory-issued speakers to the absolute limit. Finding Cheap Trick's powerful beat regenerative, she began to feel the evening might be better than she'd feared. It couldn't possibly be worse than haggling over cosmic skunks and stalking Dimwit.

Then again, she didn't have to do anything she didn't want to. That lucky guess at *personal* hadn't bound her to a thing. Implied consent meant nothing in a Virginia court of law.

Feeling consoled by jurisprudence, she envisioned the quiet evening before her. If her friends' conjecture was correct, she'd be home early enough to start on the second coat of turquoise. *Unchaste Places* would be whispering warmly in her ear as well. Maybe she'd get frisky and take a look at the complicated present from her friends. She was an adult with a house to herself, and a taxpaying American. What she did with her body was nobody's business but her own.

Her optimism grew with each car she sped by. Cheap Trick had that effect. She was scooting along at a fair clip, utilizing both lanes freely. Surely that nose whistle was a one-time thing.

Nearing the county line, where the landscape got wild and woolly, she thought of chiggers and bites and how many Theo had accrued in his first half day of camp. She felt itchy just thinking about it. The fact that his inhaler wouldn't arrive until Monday troubled her. Then again, it was virtually impossible to get Theo to physically exert himself, other than in his hell-for-leather pursuit of Plinkies, so maybe his lungs wouldn't be unduly taxed. At the moment, he was likely lounging on the sidelines during a kickball game, claiming some higher intellectual calling or another.

This notion made her smile and she felt better about Theo surviving until the albuterol arrived. She was dying to know his frame of mind when James dropped him off, but couldn't bring herself to call her ex to inquire. That was just asking for a trip down Camp Sycamore memory lane. Knowing her luck, he'd launch into a few heartfelt lyrics from the camp theme song:

> *Along the banks of placid lake*
> *Among the dewy dells*
> *Oh, Sycamore, Camp Sycamore*
> *Where friends I'll surely make*

As much as she'd like to keep mentally making fun of James, it was time to shift gears and focus on her night at Pemberley. She was surprised that Fitzwilliam lived so far out. This was true boondocks. She'd already driven by the road that led to the HHR's cabin—where a burn pile always smoked and tabs on the Illuminati were scrupulously kept—and the farmhouses were getting farther and farther apart.

And then she saw two pink balloons affixed to a mailbox, one reading *WELCOME*, the other *PENELOPE!* She checked to confirm that this was indeed Lambton Lane. The gravel drive wasn't what she'd expected, nor the overgrown hedge that blocked any view from the road. It looked like the entrance to a local militia outfit where men prepared for the end of days by shooting beer cans and riding four-wheelers.

She took a deep breath, upped the volume on "Surrender," and made the turn through the hedges and toward her date, with the soft clunk of rocks kicking up beneath the car. Twenty seconds elapsed and still she hadn't located the house. She passed a pond with a gazebo beside it, and now the landscape opened up to rolling hills interspersed with fruit trees of some sort, neatly separated into orchards by split rail fences. What looked like grapes grew on several of the hills and a small wooden sign said, *Slowly Now: Quail Preserve.*

She came next to a raised bridge. As the planks rattled beneath her, she looked down to see a lovely bubbly creek and benches for gazing upon it along the mossy bank. Wordsworth's "Tintern Abbey," which she remembered from Mrs. Sketchins's frighteningly effective junior English class, popped into her mind and she wondered if this was where Fitzwilliam came to indulge his literary passions. She also wondered if perhaps Fitzwilliam was on the wealthy side.

This thought was confirmed when she crested a hill and saw the manor. And make no mistake, it was a manor. Just the sort, in fact, that heroines in her erotic novels often found themselves in. Rebecca Dunmoore, the small-town computer genius from Des Moines—more book smart than street—had found herself nude and blindfolded in the wine cellar as her boss, Franz, tempted her with rich cabernets and a lot more in *Beyond Secret,* the book she'd read just before *Carnal Liaisons* and *Unchaste Places.* This thought made Penelope's heart jump a bit. She didn't want to be confined like Rebecca Dunmoore, out here in the middle of nowhere. She let her mind race for a spell, just for sport, but was reassured by the thought that if any funny business occurred, she could crack Fitzwilliam over her knee like a dry twig.

Gravel had given way to a paved drive that circled a spewing fountain, and Penelope couldn't decide whether to park here or over in front of the four-car garage. Fitzwilliam had driven a VW bug to their date at Starbucks and she couldn't imagine what other vehicles lay within. If there were more, she hoped to see the rest of his fleet. As was commonly known, she was a bit of a car junkie. She'd never had a cool car, sports or otherwise, but she'd made out in quite a few, and not just Winston Hackler's RX-7, though that had proven the gold standard for hot guy/hot car combo.

She decided to park in front of the fountain, near the main entrance, and disembarked from her twelve-year-old jalopy, smiling at herself and her car-tarty ways. While ringing the doorbell, she noticed the brickwork at her feet, which spelled *Pemberley*. Wow. He really was a Fitzwilliam.

The door opened and there he was, wearing an apron over the same cardigan he'd posed in on LoveSynch. Penelope thought it much too warm for sweaters, but perhaps the house was cool, his blood thin. He looked every bit of sixty-five. He might need compression socks for all she knew. A very fat cat peeked from behind Fitzwilliam's boat-shoe-thin ankles, flicking its tail this way and that in a haughty manner.

"Penelope," Fitzwilliam said, tilting his swooping mane of grey hair into a bow. "My dearest lemon sorbet of the Internet. Promptitude is a virtue, don't you know? And surely one of the seven holies. Frankly, I can't keep the virtues straight. The seven deadly sins, well, those I'm quite well versed in. Yes, quite familiar with those. Ha ha ha. You are right on time. Right on the sixth bell."

At this, a great chiming commenced from inside, the loudest grandfather clock Penelope had ever heard. She wondered if this thing gonged all night, and if it did, how Fitzwilliam ever got any sleep. It fairly rattled the noggin. That same head was now being kissed lightly on both cheeks in rapid succession, a greeting one didn't often encounter in Hillsboro. Penelope wasn't sure what to do. She pursed her lips, in case she was supposed to cheek-peck back, and tried to avoid swaying her head to accommodate the received kisses, lest she crack the old squire's grey head. She'd never felt less European.

"Yes, right on the sixth bell," said Fitzwilliam, after his blitzkrieg on her face was over. "Do come in, my dear TheosMom75. Come in, come in."

Fitzwilliam shut the door behind them. For a moment, it was just Penelope and the cat looking at one another. As was her way, she bent down and said, "Hello, Algernon. It's nice to meet you. Thank you for inviting me to your house."

As a reply, Algernon mouthed a silent hiss.

Fitzwilliam hadn't seen this and said: "Yes, yes. This is the great playboy bachelor about whom you've heard so much. Mr. Algernon Moncrieff the second. Esquire, raconteur, and true lord of the manor."

Algernon showed what he thought of this flattery by offering his backside to Fitzwilliam and sauntering out of sight.

"Oh ha ha," said Fitzwilliam. "Yes, yes. You just leave us, my dear bumptious boy. Pretend as if you aren't interested in our guest. Oh yes, I am sure. Places to go and people to see. We know, we know."

Fitzwilliam gave Penelope a playful wink as Algernon's fluffy tail swished out of sight, then stood beside her as she took in the surroundings. She was in the first grand parlor she'd ever seen, other than the one at the governor's mansion in Colonial Williamsburg, which she'd visited on a school trip in fifth grade and only dimly remembered. She did recall—vividly—her friend Debbie pretending to play a fife and dancing a jig in a way that was really funny. At least until they got snatched out of there by Mrs. Turnbull for disturbing the bewigged man's presentation.

She snapped to. She was no longer being rousted from a historical landmark by the elbow but standing on a white marble floor, looking at a winding staircase, a smiling older gentleman in an apron that said *Purrfectly Charming*, and the largest portrait of a woman she'd ever seen. Classical music filled the air from invisible speakers. She wouldn't admit it publicly, but violins kind of hurt her ears. She felt a long way from Cheap Trick.

She looked again at the painting, which was at least ten feet high and dominated the parlor. The woman was emerging from water and pushing her hair off her shoulder. She was tall and sinewy and wore a bemused smile, as if the swim had been both refreshing and ironic. She was also quite nude and less particular about trends in personal grooming than was generally expected from a modern woman. That area of the painting fairly jumped out at the viewer. Maybe it was just all that purple against her pale grey body. The formula for figuring the area of a triangle was somewhere in the back of Penelope's mind from tenth grade algebra, but she couldn't presently call it up. Whatever. It was quite the woolly equilateral. Like two feet worth. Maybe more.

"Ah, yes," Fitzwilliam said, with a modest sweep of his hand. "You've met Roxanne."

"It's a beautiful painting," Penelope said. She'd seen a few nudes in museums before but never in a private home, and though no expert on art, she liked the painting very much. "Who's the artist?"

"*A poor thing perhaps, but my own*, if I may borrow a phrase from the Bard. Just one of my eccentric habits. A man must have distractions, of course. The difficulty, of course, is finding models. Ones with *sangfroid*! With *joie de vivre*! Eve with the apple in hand, if I may be so bold. Oh ha ha ha ha ha!"

Penelope wasn't quite sure what to do with all these jollities, especially as Fitzwilliam literally said *Ha, ha, ha, ha, ha*, instead of just laughing like most people did, so she was glad when he offered her a drink and led her toward the kitchen. En route, Algernon Moncrieff reentered from parts unknown and sniffed disdainfully at her ankles as she walked. Maybe she should have brought a dessert or bottle of wine after all, despite Fitzwilliam's protestations. Algernon was unimpressed.

The kitchen was massive and dominated by windows, which allowed the sun to dance on the marble countertops and the gleaming copper pots and pans hanging above the island. It was a lovely room and aromatic too. Fitzwilliam commenced a vigorous stirring of a simmering pan.

"I hope you like piccata," Fitzwilliam said, smiling over his shoulder as his nose fifed a lively tune as often heard in Colonial Williamsburg. "And our first course shall be escargot. But in the meantime, a delectable to tide you over?"

He nodded to a silver tray on the kitchen table. "Next to the vase."

Penelope noted that he pronounced the receptacle as if it rhymed with *cause* and not *case*. She'd heard this pronunciation on television before and thus assumed it was correct. Still, she couldn't bring herself to say it that way. A start down fancy pronunciation road would have her saying *aunt* like it rhymed with *gaunt*. It was just too complicated.

Glass of Viognier in hand, from some region in France that Fitzwilliam had once biked across *so many years agone*, Penelope headed for the treat tray.

"The chocolates are Swiss, of course. Anything else is sacrilege. And the *fromage* is all of an international variety—French and Italian, primarily. Try them all, my dearest Lemon Sorbet. It will be a spell yet before we dine."

"They all look so good," Penelope said, beginning to speculate about Fitzwilliam and the nature of this date. He was sweet and sophisticated, but did his art indicate a still-strong sexual desire? Like, for her? Or was that unsophisticated to think? Frankly, in that apron and cardigan, he looked about as sexual as one of the copper pots hanging above him.

"Now Algernon, you stop pestering our guest or I shall have to scold you most roundly," Fitzwilliam said, removing his apron and scooping up the fur ball that had spent the last several moments scratching the chair leg nearest Penelope's foot. Algernon looked at Fitzwilliam, whiskers wafting insolently, then sprang from Fitzwilliam's apron onto her exposed calf, hissing and spitting all the way.

"Algernon! You treacherous, jealous fellow! Out you go. Yes, out out out you go."

Fitzwilliam scooped up the cat and marched him to the sliding glass door that led to the sunroom. Out he went. While Penelope chomped on the chocolate—nougat, unfortunately—and ran a hand over the scratches on her leg, Algernon Moncrieff looked at her, sneeringly, with his nose pressed against the glass, hissing still. If there was any doubt before, that doubt was vanquished. Algernon cared not for the middle class.

"Yes, Algernon, you may grump all you want to," said Fitzwilliam, crouching till he was nearly face-to-face with the cat. "And at dinner-time, too? Well, tut-tut. You'll not get your din-din till a satisfactory time-out is served. Life isn't all beer and skittles, you know."

Fitzwilliam rose nimbly—as if he did yoga—and came toward her, offering a silk pocket handkerchief as he did. "My dear Penelope, I do hope Algernon has not seriously injured you. Honestly, that fellow is incorrigible."

"I'm fine," Penelope said, taking the handkerchief and running it lightly down her legs. She was actually bleeding a little and wondered if this was karmic payback for her obsession with Theo's leg scabs and impetigo. "He just barely nicked me. I'm fine. I always had cats growing up and don't mind a little scratch or two. Algernon is just frisky."

"Algernon is a very bad boy," Fitzwilliam said, turning toward the sunroom and wagging a finger.

To Penelope's eye, Algernon looked less than chagrined. This was confirmed when he turned his backside to them and commenced a leisurely bath.

"If you'll excuse me for a moment, my dear Penelope, I need to powder my face. I absolutely reek of garlic and butter. Delightful aromas both, but not as a cologne, I'm afraid. Ha. Ha. Ha. So while I'm in the back, feel free to have a look around the house. The nearest loo is just down that hall if you need to have a closer look at those love marks from Algernon. I'm back in a jiff."

12

Penelope walked down a hall with twelve-foot ceilings toward the *loo*, feeling for the second time that day like a heroine from an erotic novel. She entered what was the nicest lavatory she'd ever seen. Classical music played in here too. Where were those invisible speakers? And why did classical music always remind her of scary movies when she was alone? *The Omen*, that's why. Even though that was more of a Gregorian chant thing than classical. Whatever. That movie was scary as hell.

She knew she was trying to freak herself out just for the fun of it. Bludgeoned by a nose-whistling cardigan? She thought not. Confirming this notion was a nude woman in pink who gave Penelope a comforting, if slightly seductive, look from above the toilet. It was another of Fitzwilliam's paintings. The pink woman was reclined on a chaise longue before a window with billowing curtains. Below her, on the piazza, the bustling and fully clothed could be seen going about their humdrum lives, oblivious to the languorous intrigue in the flat above. Her smile all but said, *Poor things.* Penelope could see why. Something was going on, or soon would be, or just had, there on that chaise longue, and Penelope felt sure that whatever it was would be A-OK with her.

True, the only chaise longue she'd ever been on was at her grandmother's house, and it had been called a *lounge*. She'd found it pretty uncomfortable to sit on and too short to fully recline in. Then again, she'd never tried it naked above a piazza. Honestly, she didn't if know that was a piazza in the painting or not. Miranda and the other characters in her naughty books were always popping in and out of piazzas and mezzanines and bistros. And getting popped in a few of them as well. Would Penelope know the difference between a piazza and a public square, for instance? It was food for thought.

A more pertinent issue: Fitzwilliam sure seemed to like naked women, or at least painting them. Next to the chaise longue woman was another glamorous nude. This one—like Roxanne of the exploding bush—was emerging from water. Penelope recalled her drive up to Pemberley and the pond with the gazebo beside. The orange woman was posed in front of just such a tableau, complete with rolling hills, neat orchards, and split rail fence in the background.

This backdrop gave Penelope pause. She assumed the artwork had come from an earlier Fitzwilliam, perhaps when he lived abroad and didn't wear aprons and cardigans. Hillsboro had been his home for only a couple of years. Which meant—if her theory was correct—that naked women had been on Pemberley grounds fairly recently. And that these same naked women had posed willingly for Fitzwilliam's canvas.

Was this a result of animal magnetism that Penelope had not yet picked up on? Or just cold hard cash? No matter which, Penelope had never seen women that looked anything like these in Hillsboro.

Penelope was pondering the maxim about covers and books when she noticed what lay beneath Fitzwilliam's painting of the woman by the pond. It sat side by side with the toilet and was of a similar porcelain construction. Penelope inferred they were to be used for similar purposes, or as a kind of one-two punch. She approached the devices and walked around the unfamiliar one, encouraged by the orange smiling eyes, which seemed to speak to her in a sisterhood of curiosity.

Penelope Lemon, lifelong Hillsborian, was looking at an honest-to-God *bidet*.

She knew it was weird to feel sophisticated in front of a lavatory, regardless how fancy or unfamiliar, but sophisticated was how she felt. She looked from the smoldering pink woman to the smiling orange one and felt a sense of community. She, Penelope Lemon, was not out of place in a bidet world. In fact, the confident, comforting nude women in the paintings seemed to say that—but for fate—she was truly to the manor born.

Give it a whirl, they seemed to say. *Bidets are just the start of it.*

She was about to try a dry run when her phone buzzed with a text. She checked, in case it was Camp Sycamore with news of the first scorpion bite in camp history. It was not Camp Sycamore but her erstwhile partner in the skunk-catching trade. Against her better judgment, she opened the message.

Have you figured out what your tell is yet? I read you like a book.

She banished the message as fast as she could, put the phone back in her purse, and resumed her communion with the bidet and Fitzwilliam's mystery women. Feeling bold, like Miranda before the brass door, she decided against a dry run. Her first bidet would be a real bidet. She slid down her panties, lifted her sundress, and assumed position. The only question was the frontward/backwards one, but logic held that front was front, as with the boring and oh-so-American toilet beside her. It was escargot versus Big Macs at this point as far as Penelope was concerned. It occurred to her that she hadn't used the bathroom, and really didn't need to, and that some less adventurous souls might consider it strange to bidet just for the heck of it.

But who cared? Who would know anyway, other than her free-spirited soul sisters in the paintings? She realized she was overthinking, and also that her legs were starting to shake from holding the squat for as long as she had. That inner thigh machine had taken more out of her than she realized. She reached behind her and turned on the leftmost and rightmost of the three faucets. She assumed that the bidet worked like a shower, only with the water firing in the opposite direction. If that theory held, then she'd just turned on the warm and cold water.

Sure enough, water gently bubbled beneath her. It would be easier to reach the faucets if facing the opposite direction so she dethroned. It was truly escargot now—squatting and facing the nude women in the paintings—and this seemed right. The only issue was how badly her nice panties were being stretched, hunkered thus, so she yanked them off and let them fall to the floor. Now it was go time. Cautiously, she turned the middle faucet to activate the nozzle, feeling as international as she ever had.

There came a roar of efficient power. Then the realization that either she'd crouched too low or that Fitzwilliam's bidet had been built for people—like the women in the paintings—with longer legs than her own. The first indication was the wet hem of her sundress. The second was the massive puddle on the floor. The third, the drenched panties now floating atop that pool.

She remained hunched where she was, panicked and drip-drying. The water had been cold. She'd rather expected a warm/gentle/comforting swish of not much. What she'd gotten instead was a frigid blast of tap water, not unlike what the HHR had applied to many a vinyl siding with his power washer. The question now was what to tell Fitzwilliam. There seemed no explanation that wouldn't make her look like a ridiculous rube. She *was* a ridiculous rube—that went without saying—but still. No need to advertise the fact twenty minutes into a dinner date.

Having dripped off as well as she could, she abdicated her ignominious throne. She snatched the panties from their watery grave and squeegeed them out as best she could in the sink. Her unmentionables were truly unmentionable now, and they'd been so pretty before. They were lilac, with tiny garlands of magenta flowers on them. Zinnias possibly. Her mother would have approved of the flowers in any Hillsborian garden. They were a standby for her—zinnias—and as close to horticultural chaos as she would allow among her formal tulips and roses.

Unfortunately, the zinnia panties were also cotton and absorbent and had taken all of what the geysering bidet had to offer. What she needed was a powerful hair dryer. She looked in the cabinet under the sink and also in the bathroom closet, opening and closing drawers and doors as quietly as she could so as not to arouse suspicion, but had no luck. And now came a steady meowing from outside the bathroom window. She went to the window and peeked around the curtain, feeling a cool breeze on her bare undercarriage as she did.

It was Algernon up on the ledge, peering in at her. His yellow eyes indicated he knew something was afoot. He offered one bored hiss then turned his gaze to the nude women above the bidet. The sight of the chaise longue woman and the one by the gazebo induced a prolonged purr that grated on Penelope more than it probably should have. She closed the curtain with a fierce flip. Standing there before the bulky outline of Algernon, she realized that the breeze she felt was coming from an air vent below her. This seemed heaven-sent and she lifted her sundress up and down in a fanning motion. With her panties squished into a twisted useless knot in the sink, she felt exposed but liberated. Also air-dried. Maybe this was why the HHR went commando all the time.

Back to the matter at hand. She strode to the sink and eyed her twisted delicate. She'd brought her tiniest, cutest purse so stuffing wet panties in there was a no go. And putting them back on was also a non-starter. She wouldn't even put on a wet bathing suit at the lake. Which left only one option: ditching them in a spot where they'd never be discovered.

She opened the closet door. Inside were towels, washcloths, and general bathroom bric-a-brac. On the top shelf was an assortment of candelabras, an antiquated heating pad, and a small basin meant for washing feet, none of which looked to have been recently used. It was the perfect spot. Before she and James split up, she'd not ventured to the top shelf of their guest bathroom in years. James could have hidden a dead body up there for all she'd have known. Or those bikini briefs he liked to slink around in on occasion before she'd banished them from her sight. If ever there was a place for contraband panties, this was it.

With a casual motion, she shot—free throw style—her scanties into the abandoned washbasin as a phantom crowd roared in her ears. The shot had been nothing but net. Then she took one hand towel from the superfluous stock and mopped up the floor with it. This too she swished into the basin. She really should have stuck with basketball in high school.

She looked around the bathroom for incriminating evidence, but none was to be found. The hem of her sundress was practically dry as well. The women in the paintings seemed to share in the surreptitious moment and to think she'd battled the bidet to an honorable draw. She winked at the women, grabbed her purse, and exited the bathroom to the *thump thump thump* of Algernon's tail on the window.

13

She was wondering what insect Theo was currently swatting when Fitzwilliam entered the kitchen wearing a strawberry-colored evening jacket, white pants, Italian loafers without socks, and a mint-green ascot. The ascot stopped her in her tracks. As did the matching pocket square, now that she noticed. Moments before, she'd been chomping away on a third Swiss confection, feeling positively right with the world, free and pantyless in a world of chocolate-covered chocolate. Now she was face-to-face with her first ascot.

"Well well, my dear Penelope. How is your Viognier holding up? Shall you require a small topper?"

"Sure," said Penelope, offering her half-full glass to the ascot in front of her.

Penelope watched Fitzwilliam go to the wine bucket on the counter and replenish her glass with a subtle, slow twist of the wrist as perfected by the butlers on *Downton Abbey*. When Penelope poured wine, she generally just plopped it all in in one quick go. Speed was generally what she was after, not craftsmanship. Then again, she'd never poured wine while wearing an ascot. With that adornment, it probably wouldn't feel right just sloshing it in.

"Oh, look at the light," said Fitzwilliam, turning to the large plate window above the sink, which afforded a view of the declining sun against the mountains. "A painter's light if ever I saw one. Shall we take a stroll about? I've left the piccata on simmer. It can't be rushed, you know. Mr. Butter, Ms. Lemon, and the little ones, the capers, need time to become a family. Ha! And sunsets spent strolling with friends is one of life's precious treasures."

"That sounds lovely," said Penelope, wondering why she'd said *lovely* instead of *good* or *nice* as she normally would. She'd only been at Pemberley for half an hour and already she was putting on airs. It was the Madonna-in-England thing all over again.

"Algernon usually accompanies me on my perambulations. He fancies himself a great hunter and stalks about like a lion on the Serengeti. It's really quite comical when he thinks he is terrorizing Mr. Squirrel and Mr. Squirrel cares not a whit. But don't let him see you laughing at the spectacle! He hates to be made sport of. Simply detests it!"

Fitzwilliam looked around for Algernon now, as if afraid he'd been eavesdropping. There at the end, he'd begun to whisper, and Penelope could tell that Algernon's truly was a fragile ego.

"But today," said Fitzwilliam, talking now as if he wanted the cat to hear, "if Algernon tries to join our promenade, he will be put inside posthaste for acting so boorishly to our guest. No hunting for Mr. Squirrel. No indeed. Now, if you'll take my arm, my dearest sorbet, I shall show you a few of Pemberley's charms."

Penelope did as requested, with a number of thoughts running through her head at once. That bit about *a painter's light* had struck home in a way she couldn't explain. Had Fitzwilliam donned the ascot as a prelude to a request for some portraiture time? For all she knew, there was a canvas waiting in the gazebo by the pond with her name on it.

On the one hand, being the subject of an elegant work of art had certain obvious attractions. How many Hillsborians had ever been asked to pose nude for a talented artist?

On the other hand, she was a mom, a churchgoer, and a generally well-regarded member of the local community. Her mother was a recent recipient of the Golden Hoe from the Hillsboro Garden Club, for crying out loud. If this got out, it would make the divorce scandal at Sally & Jeff's Floral Designs look like child's play.

To get her mind off the subject, she said, "It's fine with me if Algernon tags along. Cats are just unpredictable sometimes. I didn't take offense."

Fitzwilliam paused just past the swimming pool, next to the marble statue of Venus, and dramatically put hand to chest.

"My dear Penelope, your graciousness is what first caught my attention on our poignant little dating site. I may fetch Algernon anon, but first the temperamental boy must serve a time-out for his transgressions. He is likely spying on us at this very moment from his favorite rhododendron."

After he'd taken her hand and kissed it as a token of thanks, they continued on their stroll. It was the first time someone had unironically kissed her hand, and she didn't know what to do in response. It was a replay of the double-cheek greeting thing. Her first instinct was to wipe her hand on her dress, but this seemed déclassé and she resisted the urge. A little saliva on the hand never hurt anyone.

Fitzwilliam walked at a crisp, limber pace, his thin legs bouncing and springing on each step as if heel never touched ground. The nose whistling had picked up considerably now—a drum having been added to the powerful fife—and Penelope wondered if poor Fitzwilliam was truly meant for the great outdoors. Camp Sycamore would likely have proved a challenge. Now he was talking about various of Algernon's misadventures, favorite napping spots, and anecdotes of every feline stripe. Nude women might come and go, but none would ever take the place of Algernon Moncrieff.

"So how did you end up in Hillsboro?" Penelope asked.

"Ha! Ha!" said Fitzwilliam. "That is the million-dollar question, is it not? Shall we take a short jaunt to the gazebo? En route, I can explain how I came to be in this fair hamlet."

"Sure," said Penelope, head spinning a bit from Fitzwilliam's throat clearing articulation of *en route*. "I'd like that. It's really lovely out."

She heard herself saying *lovely* again and was glad she'd refrained from tossing a *grand* in there as well. She'd been sorely tempted. It was impossible after a while not to talk a little like Fitzwilliam. She should probably cut Madonna a little slack. And Gwyneth Paltrow, too.

"So you see," Fitzwilliam said as they began a leisurely amble, "my father was an executive with Actaeon Petroleum, so I lived all over. London, Tehran, Singapore, oh the list goes on. It was quite an education, being the new boy at school each year. During this time, books became my refuge and my joy. I meandered through several colleges in the States and abroad, flitting here and there like a wandering minstrel of old. I ultimately matriculated at Cornell to earn my PhD. Oh, I was a clam in sauce, I was. Reading, writing, pontificating! Ha! Ha! While in Ithaca, I had the honor of serving as a graduate assistant to Dr. Thomas T. Peaheavy. Dr. Peaheavy! What a character he was, with his lavender bowler and waistcoat, stalking around the room and thrusting his pipe at unsuspecting sophomores who had not yet memorized the *Rime of the Ancient Mariner.*"

At this, Fitzwilliam took Penelope's hand and sprang like an acrobat to one knee. Looking directly into her eyes he said:

> *He prayeth best, who loveth best*
> *All things both great and small;*
> *For the dear God who loveth us,*
> *He made and loveth all.*
> *The Mariner, whose eye is bright,*
> *Whose beard with age is hoar,*
> *Is gone: and now the Wedding-Guest*
> *Turned from the bridegroom's door.*
> *He went like one that hath been stunned,*
> *And is of sense forlorn:*
> *A sadder and a wiser man,*
> *He rose the morrow morn.*

He stood, smiling and offering the slightest of bows. Penelope wasn't sure if she should applaud the performance or not, but since Fitzwilliam retained possession of her hand it was a moot point. They continued down the hill.

"For the record," said Fitzwilliam, "Dr. Peaheavy was aware of the many wordplays surrounding his name and cherished them all. The first day of class he would introduce himself, procure a wrinkled paper from his waistcoat, and recite the list of puns his students had come up with over the years, commenting here and there on ones he found noteworthy. On the day of my graduation from Cornell, he gifted me with his whalebone cane. It is the finest gift I ever received. On that same day, my father gifted me with a handshake and these words: *Congratulations, dear boy, you are now the most well-educated hobo in the world! To honor this distinction and your chosen profession, I henceforth liberate you from the constrictions of my money, which no self-respecting hobo would continue to allow himself to accept. The world is your oyster! May you hop every train you desire!*

"I was still in my robe and mortarboard, don't you know, my little graduation tassel swaying innocently in the breeze from Cayuga Lake, when Father said that. His smile was genuine. His handshake firm. Ha! Ha! Talk about characters! Father thought education was a lot of pish-posh. Oh, look there! A northern goshawk! What a stroke of luck!"

Penelope looked where Fitzwilliam pointed and saw a large bird sitting on a fence post in front of the vineyard.

"Now, where was I? Playing Narcissus, that is where I was. Boring you with my prolonged glance in the self-reflecting pond."

"I'm not bored."

"Kindness, as they say, is a virtue. Of which you have many, my dear Penelope. Back to Father. He wanted me to study geophysical engineering, of all things! Imagine that, when there is Coleridge to be read! Ha! Ha! But I was my own man, don't you know? I hoboed around Europe, posing as a poet, staying, with a dewy romantic eye, in the lowest hovels to be found. Getting by with a translator job here, a tutoring position there. Lord Byron had nothing on me! Not a thing! Other than genius, of course. Genius I could not find, no matter where I searched. I thought I had acquired it for a period in Vienna and wrote like a madman, subsisting on nothing but mélange and strudel. I dashed off a letter to Dr. Peaheavy, proclaiming my masterpiece and asking only for his confirmation. His reply was succinct: *Don Quixote has been written. Try again.* Crushed, I decided to see about the money thing. And the rest, so they say, is *l'histoire.*"

Penelope wanted to know how he'd made his money but thought it impolite to ask. Fitzwilliam must have read her face, for he gave her hand a quick squeeze and said: "You would like to know how I made my fortune? I can see it in your face. And such a face. An open book and a closed one simultaneously. Remarkable.

"What I did, dear Penelope, is borrow one thousand pounds from my father, on the condition that I be self-sustaining in twelve months' time or accept his offer of employment at his sainted Actaeon Petroleum, running the Shanghai office. I had an eye for antiques and collectibles and began to buy and sell things in London. Knickyknacks, but fine ones. My first purchase was the vase you see in the foyer. I bought it, sold it, then bought it again. It is the very cornerstone of Pemberley.

"Eventually, I had my stake and began to dabble in equities. My strategy was simple: I invested in all of the things that make modern life a prison for me. That is to say, I bought stock in box stores, computers, technology of every stripe and hue! My sad genius, if you will forgive a bit of fanfaronade, is to have anticipated the world in which we currently live. I invested in nothing having to do with books, the arts, truth and beauty. Other than my heart, don't you know. The Faustian bargain I made with commerce led me to Hillsboro—which so reminded me of Derbyshire, but without the estate taxes—and this lovely walk with you, which I am on the verge of spoiling with an overlong autobiography."

Penelope had never heard anyone talk this long uninterrupted, especially while moistly holding her hand and gazing upon a northern goshawk. She felt more in the Pemberley mood now.

"I placed a bottle of wine down at the gazebo," Fitzwilliam said, "upon the chance we would happen that way. Shall we continue our journey? I see that you might need a replenisher."

Penelope nodded her assent but wondered again if things weren't starting to feel a little scripted. As if perhaps a similar Viognier—and this very same ascot—had led a certain orange woman above the bidet to so enthusiastically shed her clothes by the pond.

She was getting ahead of herself. A portrait like that would take time to compose, likely several hours. It had taken her two weeks in art class to paint that one bowl of fruit.

They had arrived now, and Penelope followed Fitzwilliam down a few steps to the gazebo. In front of her, the pond glistened and was still, save for the graceful gliding of a mother with her ducklings.

"You've got ducks," Penelope said, handing Fitzwilliam the glass he'd nodded to with an encouraging smile.

"Indeed I do. And now Mother Mallard is putting the young ones through their paces. Soon, all we shall see is their American backsides. Ha! Ha! Europeans would never dine so early in the evening!"

She took her refilled glass, smiling at the memory of young Theo at the park, firing bread crumbs at the ducks while making exploding noises with his mouth. She missed the little oddball. Yet, here she was, considering the prospect of nude modeling on the banks of Pemberley Pond. Was she an exhibitionist or something? If so, did that make her needy in some Freudian way that was sad to think of? Or did it indicate an enlightened feminist, not hung up on bourgeois American notions of nudity and the female form?

Even assuming her motives were purely artistic—the desire to be captured on canvas just as God and a few trips to the inner thigh machine had made her—shouldn't her role as mother disqualify her from entertaining such bohemian notions? Was something wrong with her? Right now, a counselor at Camp Sycamore was likely pulling hornet stingers from Theo's feet. And here she was, pantyless, with a third glass of wine in her hand, feeling artistic. That couldn't be normal for a small-town Virginia mom.

"I admired a few of your paintings in the guest bathroom earlier," Penelope blurted, before she could stop herself.

"Ah, yes. Dear Felicia and Simone. I am glad you found them worthy of consideration."

"I did. And I couldn't help noticing—now that we're down here—that one of the paintings—the woman done in orange—was posed beside a pond and a gazebo."

She paused here, so as not to give the wrong impression, though she didn't know what that would be.

"It is this very pond. You have an excellent eye. Lovely Simone. I think of her every time I'm at this spot."

Penelope felt compelled to speak but couldn't quite force the words out. She knew this compulsion stemmed from guilt regarding her naked mom status and Theo currently hyperventilating into a paper bag with huge welts under his eyes and no video game to calm his racing heart. It was ridiculous guilt. Everyone had inappropriate thoughts from time to time.

"I thought you might have brought me down here to ask me to pose too," she said all in a rush, before gulping a large sip.

Fitzwilliam walked closer and took her hand in his, his mint-green ascot catching the sun's rays just so.

"My dearest sorbet," he said, with his nose whistling a soft Spanish waltz. "Of course I should very much like to paint you, if you are ever so inclined. I've wanted to ever since I saw that enigmatic photo of TheosMom75 on our dating site. But first I must know you better, to let the mystery of you deepen and broaden. I find the longer I know someone, the more mysterious they become to me. Only when I do not understand a friend at all am I ready to paint her. Is that a very queer notion to have?"

"Not at all."

"I'm so glad to hear. Now, shall we go check on our piccata? And on poor, misguided Algernon?"

14

They were sitting in Fitzwilliam's grand dining room, enjoying escargot beneath a chandelier that wouldn't look out of place in a swanky hotel.

When she'd first been seated, Algernon had come to sniff her ankles a few times but found them, like the rest of her, uninteresting. Now he was somewhere under the table. Determined to win him over, as a good guest should, Penelope poked her head under the table and said: "Algernon. What are you doing down there?"

What he was doing was crouching in a ready-to-pounce way, his eyes fixed on Penelope's calf, the one he'd found savory earlier. He seemed to find the question about his under-the-table activities personal and mouthed a silent hiss in reply. Penelope surmised that he'd considered himself well concealed before and disliked being discovered.

Penelope smiled. "I'll just pretend I didn't see you."

"There is too much garlic in the escargot, isn't there, Algernon?" said Fitzwilliam, as the cat left the room. "Oh. Ha. Ha. Ever the culinary snob."

"I think it's delicious," Penelope said.

"You are too kind, but I fear Algernon is right. I was too liberal with the garlic. Isn't that right, Monsieur Moncrieff?"

Fitzwilliam had cocked his head to the door, cupped hand to ear, but no reply came.

Nibbling judiciously and counting the moments until the piccata came, she listened to Fitzwilliam discuss his time as a sous chef in Marseille and imagined what it would be like to live in such a house, and in such style, full time. No worries about cars breaking down or Theo's college or a retirement fund that currently sat at zero dollars. How nice it would be to not have money on the mind—the lack of it—almost constantly. Was there an age when a woman might, with a free conscience, marry for companionship and shared interests and security? Didn't old couples eventually get to that point anyway?

She could live with the ascot. In public it might prove a trial, but so be it. The nose whistle would prove a taller order. Likely there were ear, nose, and throat specialists who could see to that, and with a subtle push, perhaps Fitzwilliam would seek one out.

But what about sex? How many times would a fellow his age want it? He'd mentioned a yoga regimen earlier, which meant a number of veins had likely been opened up that should be properly occluded by now in a man of his years. Fitzwilliam might want it every night, like the HHR when they were in their twenties, or James when they had that free trial of the Western Channel on their cable package.

Her thoughts were interrupted when Fitzwilliam said: "I say, my dear sorbet. This chandelier is simply too bright for dining à deux. If you may spare me for a moment, I shall fetch the candelabra and be back in the shake of two lambs' tails!"

In a flash, Penelope was no longer imagining bad sex with a senior yogi but a bathroom closet stacked to the brim with candleholders and wet panties.

"While you're gone, I may use the restroom," she said, rising and hearing the edge in her voice. Her aim was to head Fitzwilliam off at the pass and she was well in motion before his ascot had even pushed out of the chair.

"I shall see you back here, my dear Penelope. With candles and piccata!"

She rushed toward the bathroom at full gallop. Incriminating panties were a candelabrum away and how could she explain those?

15

Only Algernon was afoot, peering around the corner of what she assumed was a guest bedroom. Or maybe he had his own room. Nothing would surprise her. He whisked his tail once as she barreled down the hall then assumed a sitting position, one eye casting a shrewd glance, the other feigning sleep. She hadn't given up hope of winning him over. Many a spoiled cat had warmed to her with time. Then again, none of those cats had their own rooms in a mansion or listened to this much classical music or had such a defined aesthetic when it came to paintings of naked ladies. Still, she felt sure that by night's end she and Algernon would fit neck and ascot.

She smiled at this image and entered the bathroom. There was nothing to worry about. The nudes on the wall confirmed this. She gazed upon them again and decided that yes, if asked, she would likely pose for Fitzwilliam's magnificent brush. This decision made, she came to another. She would not ever have sex with Fitzwilliam, nor take up with him, no matter how much easier her life would be. Her accent was wrong for French phrases and this sort of world seemed full of them. There was also the fact that she'd never once had sex with someone she wasn't attracted to and didn't plan to start now.

She realized this whole debate about settling down with Fitzwilliam, or even being intimate with him, had never been a debate at all. She just liked to speculate from time to time, to challenge herself with pretend moral dilemmas to see how her brain teased things out. For instance, if she had to kill someone, where would she dispose of the body? Or if she won the lottery, what would she do with the money? Simple hypothetical exercises when things got a little dull.

She turned away from the naked women and toward the bathroom closet. It was her luck, of course, that she'd decided to hide her contraband panties in the never-perused closet the one night it got perused. Such was life. Feeling philosophical as she pushed a footstool into place, she stood on tiptoe and retrieved the panties with a satisfied smile. She snagged the wet towel as well and placed it discreetly at the bottom of a tall stack, where it would dry naturally over the years, untraceable to her or her bidet adventures.

Now for the panties. She took another look in her purse, but no mystery portal had appeared there, as in *The Lion, the Witch, and the Wardrobe*. Her phone was blinking like a mother with texts indicating all kinds of urgent business, but she ignored it. Might she fling the panties out the window to collect later? No, it would be impossible to shake Fitzwilliam at night's close. He seemed just the sort to believe in long good-byes, with lots of cheek kissing, all the while shouting *Toodle-loo* and *Ta-ta*.

That settled the matter. It was closet or bust for the incriminating undies.

She heard Fitzwilliam walk down the hall, his nose in tune with the piccolos pipping from the invisible speakers. He was after candelabras and she had to move quick. Her piccata would get cold and she was still hungry. Those escargot had been a drop in the bucket. She could have eaten a whole can of those worms. On the closet floor was a large box containing masks and beads. If Fitzwilliam threw Mardi Gras parties she wanted to attend the next one. That promised to be a sophisticated freak show of the first order and Algernon would certainly come in costume. He looked made for baubles and feathered finery, and a mask would help him in those moments when he wished to be incognito, as earlier under the table.

Behind the box, in the deepest, darkest corner of the closet, looked a ripe spot to hide something that wouldn't be discovered for months, maybe years. Decision made, she scrunched down, scooted the box just so, and once again bid adieu to the wet panties.

Breathing a sigh of relief at the close call, she collared her purse, winked at the bidet, and returned to the dining room. She'd worked up quite the appetite.

She was back at the table, waiting for Fitzwilliam, when her phone buzzed. With Theo out of town and being eaten by red ants, there was no longer the obsessive need to keep it on at all hours of the day, so she reached to turn it off. She chanced just one quick glance.

The first text was from Missy.

> **When did team snacks become a thing? Back in my day, kids could go fifteen minutes without a protein bar. Is every single kid in America hypoglycemic?**

And the second.

> **Did you know that adult coloring is also a thing? Like with crayons? I'm at Applebee's and this couple is in a booth just going to town on a box of Crayolas.**

Penelope trashed these vigorously and with relish. She'd never erased texts so fast.

The next one was from Rachel.

> **How is The Admiral? Are you smoking cigarettes out of holders?**

Then her smartass partner in crime, Sandy.

> **Is Matlock asleep yet? Just sneak off and leave a note on the Pinochle table.**

She return-texted both of them.

> Way off, losers. He's a nude artist.

The replies came back in record time. They *were* losers. Manic-texting on a Saturday night like seventh graders? Get lives.

Rachel:

> **Are you now naked?**

Sandy:

> **The Admiral paints in the nude or he paints nudes?**

She smiled and wrote:

> He wants to paint me some day. Naked. But wants to get to know me better first.

As expected, her phone exploded then. First Sandy.

> **By getting to know you better that old fart means sex, doesn't he?**

Then Rachel,

> **Tell All.**

She was about to respond but changed her mind. Let them wait. It wasn't her job to save their boring night by supplying vicarious thrill after vicarious thrill. They could joke all they wanted about Admiral this and Admiral that, but at least her night wasn't dull as dirt. She was smiling at her adventurous self when her phone buzzed with yet another text. The number was unfamiliar.

Hey Brad here. From the gym. Good to meet you. Lunch next week if you're free?

And then Fitzwilliam came in with the candelabra and Penelope jammed her phone into her purse.

"Ah, the lighting is much better now, is it not? I am sorry for the delay but I could not find my best candelabra for the life of me. They will turn up one day, I am sure. Until then, we will have to make due with this lesser set. But I digress. Shall we dine?"

~

They were now on dessert—tiramisu and port—and as Penelope nibbled and sipped, she wondered how soon she could leave without appearing rude. She enjoyed talking to Fitzwilliam and hearing his globetrotting tales, and he'd asked about her own past as well, which she'd struggled a bit to explain. How to account for the HHR? Or James? Or her mother and best ever stepfather, George? Her bouncing in and out of the middle class for much of her life? Could a life lived completely in Hillsboro be interesting to anyone else, especially someone so sophisticated and well traveled?

She had hit a rich vein with Theo, specifically the bullying incident at school, which he'd successfully navigated on his own, and this elicited a number of *Bravos* and *Theo the Stouthearted* comments and finally a one-man standing ovation, over the top but sweet.

It was this reaction—as well as the inviting blank space over the mantel—which confirmed once and for all that she would pose for Fitzwilliam if asked. So she had a little ego. Didn't everyone? And how would Theo or the Garden Club or anyone else in Hillsboro ever find out that she was nude-model mom? With this kind of portrait, where the features weren't super specific, plausible deniability was built right in. No one even knew the identity of the *Mona Lisa*, for crying out loud, and she was the most famous model in the world. Penelope could pose nude one day and bring team snacks the next, and no one would be the wiser. And sometime down the road, a houseguest would ask about the painting above the mantel and Fitzwilliam would sigh wistfully and say, *Oh yes, lovely Penelope. My rustic beauty.* Sealing the deal with herself, she took a hearty gulp of the port and felt right with the world.

It was then that Fitzwilliam said, "Oh, Algernon. You have deigned to join us? And what have you there?"

The cat was across the room and blocked from her view by a serving table. All she could see was a fluffy swishing tail. The tail flipped to and fro in a stiff, measured way, and Penelope felt sure that Algernon had found something to entertain himself with. She'd not seen him this animated since just before he'd pounced on her leg.

"Come come, dear fellow, don't be coy. What have you there?"

At this, Algernon did a deliberate about-face. Penelope could see clearly now what Fitzwilliam was going on about, for Algernon did have something in his mouth, a toy or some small prey. It was grey, or purplish, but that was all she could tell from this distance.

Fitzwilliam turned toward her and said: "If he has caught something, it will be a first! On the one hand, I shall be mortified if he drops a wee mouse on the floor during dessert. On the other, how could I not beam like a proud papa at clever Algernon and his first trophy? Isn't that right, my boy? Aren't you indeed the king of the Serengeti?"

Algernon was being furtive, flashing the creature briefly then tucking it under his chin the next moment.

Fitzwilliam turned to Penelope and said: "Look at him. Like Hemingway with his chest all puffed up. Oh, have you brought Penelope a prize to apologize for your earlier behavior? Is it a mouse? A shrew? Why, it could be anything, couldn't it, my dear sorbet?"

Algernon had come fully into view and was indeed padding toward her with his trophy.

"Oh my," said Fitzwilliam. "Pray tell you are not skittish about this sort of thing, Penelope? I know it is abominable dinner behavior. But this is truly an historic occasion. Until now, I thought the dear boy was an avowed pacifist."

"No, I'm not skittish," Penelope said.

She had a better view of Algernon's prize now. The thing that the cat had drug in, as the saying went, was not grey as she'd first thought. Nor was it purple. The shade was a true lilac, like one sees during a particularly lovely sunset. Sprinkled here and there—as might appear in that same sunset—were little flashes of a color that looked very much like magenta. Penelope couldn't be sure, but she would have bet her last dollar that these glimpses of magenta were shaped like a certain flower, a wildish type that her mother allowed in her formal garden despite their undomesticated ways.

Fitzwilliam was out of his seat and coming toward the end of the table that she and Algernon shared. The cat looked once, casually, at the fast-approaching ascot, then turned back to her. They shared a moment both inscrutable and crystal clear. They each knew the score. Behind Algernon, out in the foyer, Penelope could just see one of Roxanne's bare, grey legs. Penelope thought of how Fitzwilliam might have made her portrait seem enigmatic as well. She thought of "Ode on a Grecian Urn" and the unnamed woman who was universally known as Mona Lisa.

And then Algernon dropped his prize at her feet.

She looked down at the twisted lilac bundle, the magenta zinnias just visible from where she sat.

Fitzwilliam was beside them now, patting Algernon on the head. "Now what have you here, my brave boy? What have you brought to our friend Penelope? Did you pounce upon it unawares? Ha. Ha. Did it put up a fight? Oh, do tell me you were merciful with the wee creature. Ha. Ha. Ha. Ha."

Penelope felt her face get hot and knew she was in full scarlet hue. Just moments before, she'd been swirling port in a snifter, imagining herself immortalized above the mantel, like a mysterious countess that

Vanity Fair wrote about every month when one baron killed another in a pique of continental jealousy. How had the cat retrieved them from behind that box? If only she'd left well enough alone. The washbasin had been the ticket all along.

Fitzwilliam tried to scoot Algernon away from his catch, but the cat was having none of it. He stayed where he was, eyeing first Penelope and then the parcel at his feet. He seemed worried that her eyesight was not up to snuff, and that she hadn't caught on to the fact that he, Algernon, had just busted her good. Then suddenly, like a proper cat with a mouse, he swiped at his prize, tossed it into the air, then rolled onto his back for the retrieval. He proceeded to gut away at the lilac/magenta with his hind claws, his motor roaring away, his tail flicking everywhichway, as Fitzwilliam murmured, "So ferocious. So strong. Aren't you, Algernon? Aren't you, my brave boy? And so active! So very, very active!"

And then, just as suddenly, Algernon sprang up, and with one fearsome swipe of his chubby paw sent the wee creature flying onto the table, where it landed with a soggy thump in front of Penelope, between her snifter and the small saucer that held the last savory bite of tiramisu.

"Oh my. I do apologize," said Fitzwilliam, reaching for Algernon's trophy before Penelope could register what had happened. "Such bad form."

Fitzwilliam stood there for a moment, looking quizzically at the wet, twisted, gutted item in his hands, which not long ago had been an innocent pair of panties beneath her sundress. Penelope could tell he was confused. He'd reached down quickly, but daintily, as if to remove the quarry by its tail as one does with small varmints. He held Algernon's trophy as if expecting it to give one last twitch before expiring. He looked down at the cat in a scolding fashion and then apologetically to Penelope. He seemed at a loss, as if his literary studies on the banks of Lake Cayuga had not prepared him for a moment like this, nor had biking the wine regions of France.

Penelope tried to speak, but managed only a sound like one attempting to clear a phlegmy throat. Below her, Algernon was giving himself a victory bath. She didn't know him well enough to feel betrayed, but she felt betrayed nonetheless. He'd never even given her a chance.

"Whatever in the world?" said Fitzwilliam, unfurling the twisted bit of lavender in his hand like an ancestral flag one finds in an old cedar chest. She'd seen James with that same look of curious awe when he'd first come across his great-great-grandfather's kilt one weekend at his parents' house in North Carolina, home of the Tarheels.

Fitzwilliam held the panties at arm's length, then drew them close to his eyes. Penelope wondered if she should leave now or take her medicine before beating a hasty retreat to her car and the life she was meant to live in a rented house. It was clear her days as a nude model were over before they'd started. Someone else would one day occupy the spot above the mantel, and she'd never get to see Algernon and Fitzwilliam at one of their costume balls.

"These are undergarments," Fitzwilliam said.

Again Penelope tried to speak, but no words came. What words were there?

"They are damp," said Fitzwilliam.

Penelope managed to nod her head to this.

"Oh, *ha, ha*. Oh *ha ha ha*," said Fitzwilliam, still enunciating his *has* rather than laughing freely but managing to convey mirth nonetheless. "Has the bidet claimed another victim, Algernon? You bad boy. You bad, bad boy. Embarrassing our guest as you have. Shame, shame, Algernon. After the episode with Roxanne, I thought you'd learned your lesson. She wouldn't talk to you for the rest of her stay. Oh, you are an incorrigible rogue, you are! A prankster of the first order! Oh my dear Lemon Sorbet, can you ever forgive Algernon for his little jape? And me, Fitzwilliam Darcy, who failed to warn you about the over-exuberant—*ha ha*—bidets here at Pemberley?"

Fitzwilliam gazed down at her with a small, sympathetic smile, her wet, lacerated panties nestled still in his hand.

What was there to do or say in such a situation? How to maintain a shred of dignity when life insisted again and again that such a commodity was not the purview of a twice-divorced working mom trying to date again in a place like Hillsboro?

And then she realized what had happened. That bidet was a well-known booby trap, one that had ensnared even enigmatic, cosmopolitan Roxanne. She smiled at the folly that is life, and then giggled, and then LOLed. Dignity, schmignity. She'd been born under an absurd star, there was no disputing that, but aren't we all in the end?

As if in response, Algernon came and rubbed himself against her leg. It had all been one of his japes. Laughing still, she reached down to pet him, but by then he'd sprung onto her lap.

Fitzwilliam said: "My dear Penelope, I do believe you are growing more mysterious by the minute."

16

After the eventful weekend, Penelope was relieved to pull into the parking lot Monday morning and find that she'd beaten Missy to work. This was usually the case, but after Sunday's fresh round of skunk texts and Dimwit nonsense, all bets were off. Missy could have built a look-out fort on the roof. Or hidden all weekend in the supply closet wearing infrared glasses. You couldn't put anything past her when she got like this.

She got out of the car, thinking that she should probably respond to Bald Brad at some point. Dating was so complicated now with all the instantaneous ways to contact people. It made stalling a lot harder to do. One thing that was no longer complicated was the nature of her relationship with Fitzwilliam. Though never explicitly stated, it was clear they were to be friends and no more. They'd parted—amid much good cheer and Algernon twirled around her legs—with the understanding that she was now to be a regular guest at Pemberley. No more was said about future works of art. Penelope would just play that as it came, if it came at all. Regardless, it felt good to have made a new friend and one who was so different from others in her social circle. She could hardly wait to see Algernon in his mask—or was it *masque?*—and cape come Mardi Gras. He would be a furry little mischief maker is what he'd be.

She unlocked the office door, surmising that most dating scenarios from here forward would end with a cordial parting of ways. So why bother? Why not just delete the Bald Brad text and stop thinking about it?

Hope, that's why. She could live without a steady man in her life, but if the right one came along, one who Theo liked, that would be okay by her. Right now, she'd just live in the present and concentrate on the things she could control, like whether to surprise Theo with a PlinkyMo mural in his room when get he got back from camp. She thought it important that the new place be as inviting as possible, stuck way out in the country as they were with no other kids nearby to play with.

Speaking of her new place—specifically its turquoise walls—her intuition had never felt keener. In fact, right now it was telling her that some surprise waited inside the door she was presently unlocking.

There was. Turquoise was working its magic already, though she wondered if this was a kind of black magic. On her desk were a walkie-talkie, a pair of binoculars, and a note from Missy.

Contact me on the Motorola. I'm making the rounds with the Critter Catcher.

Penelope put her things on the desk next to the walkie-talkie—which looked expensive but still stupid—and slid her just-purchased pack of Starburst into the top drawer. It was a tradition to treat herself to a pack of chewy tart goodness at the start of the workweek. If the day started to drag, she could count on her multicolored friends to act as a pick-me-up. They'd never let her down before.

All but patting the drawer fondly, she walked to the back window to investigate. She didn't see Missy or the Critter Catcher, though she did spot their vehicles parked in the cul-de-sac that marked the ending boundary of the trailer park domain. She took up the binoculars and scanned the adjoining field until she spotted a sticklike woman in heels. In the woman's hand was a two-way radio. Next to her, a long-haired older gentleman in a Stetson smiling affably as she gesticulated hither and yon. Between them was a steel cage about two feet high, commonly used to catch nuisance creatures.

Grinning, Penelope took out her phone, punched in Missy's number, then set the phone to Speaker mode. All the while, she maintained the binocular observation of her quarry.

The following things happened:

1. Missy's hands stopped moving suddenly and stiffly, as if she'd just been hit with the Petrificus Totalus spell in *Harry Potter*.

2. She scowled at her purse, which was atop the steel cage.

3. Shaking her head with a frustrated air, she set the walkie-talkie atop that same steel cage and fiercely yanked open the purse.

4. She removed a cellular phone from the purse.

5. She looked at the phone.

6. She held the phone far away from her face as if in disbelief.

7. She glanced toward the office, squinting in a perturbed way.

8. She turned to the Critter Catcher and shook her head scornfully.

9. She mouthed the profane phrase for a male born to a member of the canine family.

10. She angrily pushed a button on her phone and said: "Didn't you see my note?"

Still with binoculars trained on her boss and smiling as she rarely did on a Monday morning, Penelope said, "Yeah, I saw it."

"Then why didn't you use the Motorola as requested? I need to see if these things work over distance."

"Listen, you can try to make it sound not ridiculous with this *Motorola* business. But it's a walkie-talkie. And they're stupid when you have cell phones."

Missy now held the phone away from her face and looked at it frankly. She seemed to be weighing whether to speak her mind fully or take a discretionary route. She then stared back at the office with a quizzical tilting of head, as if, perhaps, she'd realized something.

"You're looking at me through the binoculars, aren't you?"

Penelope laughed. "Binoculars? I don't see any binoculars?"

With the Critter Catcher smiling away beside her, Missy scratched the entirety of her face with a flicking middle finger. She said: "Just come down here for a second."

~⊃

Penelope stood with Missy before the Critter Catcher in a field colloquially known as the east quadrant.

"So, Miss Penelope," said the Critter Catcher, "I was just explaining how the traps work to Miss Missy and where I'm going to place them. Like I told the boss, your residents will never even know they're here. I'll exercise the utmost discretion."

Despite the *Miss Missy* moniker just thrown at her, Penelope's boss now strode around the trap before them with a confident, irritating stride. Penelope could tell that she considered herself and Mr. King something of a team after the professional/personal episode, and Penelope a distinctly junior partner.

"Are you sure four traps are enough?" Missy said, fondling the cage.

The skunk man chuckled at this. "If we need more, I got more. But four should be a nice number to start with. As you know, skunks are scavengers and will eat most anything."

"Yes," said Missy in a professorial tone. "I did know that."

Penelope felt her mouth go slack at the bald-facedness of this lie.

"You've been doing your research," said the Critter Catcher. "But

I'll tell you what I've discovered: these rascals have a sweet tooth. And they will travel many a mile for a tasty marshmallow. I'll put a few of those in each trap for bait and that should do the trick. They've always been Jim Dandy before."

"Sounds good," Missy said, rattling the cage with her foot as if testing its trap-worthiness. "I think marshmallows are just what we need."

The use of the plural pronoun was not lost on Penelope, and she smiled at the novice backwoodswoman before her. What a kiss-up.

"I have a question," said Penelope. "What do you do when you catch *the* skunk? I mean, how do you keep from getting sprayed?"

At this, Missy quit her unseemly caressing of traps and sprinted to stand at Penelope's side. It was as obvious as the tan on her face that she was envious of the question just posed. This was the crux of the matter, obviously, and the sort of thing that a professional trapper would love to discuss with amateurs.

"Oh, I just talk to em a little," said the Critter Catcher.

"Talk to them?" Missy asked.

"Yeah. Just real gentle. *Hey there, Mrs. Skunk. How are you today? Nice warm weather we're having, isn't it? I see that you've gotten yourself into a little jam. Why don't we just see what we can do about that? How does that sound to you, Mrs. Skunk?* You know. Just that sort of thing to get em nice and relaxed and show em you're a friend."

"So you never get sprayed?" Missy said in one long competitive rush of words, all but jumping into the Critter Catcher's arms as she spoke.

"Oh, sure, sure," said the skunk man chuckling. "Ever now and then Mr. or Mrs. Skunk is having a bad day and they just got to take it out on you. And once in a blue moon, I'll startle em before I can gentle em up. So yes, a fellow who traps skunks has to expect to get the juice ever once in a while. That's just occupational hazard."

Missy had been eyeing her during this reply, yanking her head back and forth, trying to see if Penelope was intending to race and get the next question in before she could. Penelope grinned. What a little nut-job she was.

"And where do you take the skunks after they're caught?" Missy asked.

"I send them off to Skunky Heaven."

"Skunky Heaven?" Missy said. "Where's that? Oh, I see. I see."

"Virginia state law. Can't trap and relocate an animal. Rabies."

This aspect of the conversation seemed less pleasing to the Critter Catcher. When answering the question he'd gazed off into an uncertain middle distance, as if envisioning a Skunky Heaven with plenty of marshmallows and less sensitive human noses. The role of Grim Reaper was one he didn't relish, Penelope could tell. Even habitually tone-deaf Missy caught on to this, for she asked her next question in a measured, respectful tone.

"And how do you send them off to Skunky Heaven?"

Still with that distracted look in his eyes, the trapper went to the truck and put his hand on the long box that ran behind the cab. "This is my own little gas chamber here. Carbon monoxide. Induced narcosis. It's the most humane way. They never feel a thing."

The humaneness of his reaperdom seemed to pluck him up considerably, for he let down the tailgate and lifted out cages, whistling a jaunty tune.

"If y'all have no more questions, I'll get busy," he said, and with a cage in each hand, he set off toward the woods.

When he was out of earshot, Missy said: "Did you hear that?"

"Hear what, Trapper John? Your encyclopedic knowledge of skunks? *Yes, I did know they are scavengers.* You are such a brownnoser."

"Whatever. And before you correct me, little miss Dian Fossey, I don't care. I know you're proud of growing up where the red ferns grow and having birds eat out of your hands like everyone else in Hillsboro, but I'm not embarrassed that I know nothing about nature. Not a bit. But I do know a trained skunk when I see one. And now a professional has confirmed that fact."

"That wasn't his professional opinion. It was his personal one. I still can't believe you guessed that right."

"Totally clutch," Missy said, putting her hands together over her head and shaking them like a prizefighter who's just been declared winner. "I read you like a book. Don't ever play poker. That's all I can say. And don't be jealous just because the Skunk Whisperer agrees with me."

"The what?"

"The Skunk Whisperer. You heard what he said. He talks to the skunks to relax them so they don't spray him. It's animal hypnosis. Oh, I've got Dimwit right where I want him now, and it's winner take all for the fate of Rolling Acres!"

"You're getting distracted by skunks. Or *skunk,* singular. If your goal is to get rid of Dimwit, focus on proving he's a thief, not on some crackpot theory."

"Listen, Ellie Mae. Until the Whisperer puts a dent in the skunk army, we can't breach the hill to Dimwit's place. It's a two-part plan. This is phase one. The binoculars and walkie-talkies are for phase two, the stakeout and entering of Dimwit's sarcophagus proper. I don't see why this is so complicated to you."

Penelope rolled her eyes and walked toward the office. She had actual work to do.

17

Penelope entered the office to find the bathroom door shut, which meant Dimwit had snuck in while she was away. He was definitely spying on them—she'd barely been gone twenty minutes.

As always, Penelope found it hard to focus on the tasks at hand when Dimwit was on the premises and going about his intimate business. And now, distracted, she worried about Theo. He'd be starting his second full day at camp and she'd have no idea how he was doing till Tuesday or Wednesday, and then only if he'd taken the time to write. If he'd been bitten by a rabid raccoon, surely she would have heard something. Right now, he was either placidly canoeing bucolic Lake Sycamore or being tied to an anthill like the fat kid in *Lord of the Flies*. There were other options, mostly involving injury and ointments, but these were the two that battled most fiercely in her imagination. Why did she think it would be relaxing to have him gone? Yes, she had freedom of movement. But freedom of mind? Not at all.

Feeling that a Starburst might be just the soothing tonic she needed, she reached in her desk drawer, hoping that the top piece would be strawberry or orange, anything but lemon, though as consolation prizes went, not a bad one.

Her reconciliation to a lemon Starburst proved theoretical, as there were no Starbursts of any hue to be found. The whole, shiny pack was missing. With the drawer yanked almost completely out, she paused in her mad shuffling of paper clips and pens to consider if she was losing her mind. Maybe, in her walkie-talkie discombobulation, she'd placed the pack in the drawer then removed it immediately after, wanting to keep them handy in case this skunk business demanded instant sugar countering.

The toilet flushed and she heard the squeak of Dimwit's boots on tile. Leaping up, she raced to the reception area before Dimwit could make his getaway.

Dimwit exited and looked first toward the desk and then back toward Missy's office. He didn't spot Penelope, sitting alertly in the chair before the front door, until he'd clomped halfway across the room in his dirty boots.

"Hey Dewitt," she said, as she did every day when he left. She couldn't help herself. George had told her when she was a young girl that nice people say hello to everybody and she'd never been able to break the habit.

Dewitt's typical response after being greeted was a stopping in tracks; a gaping of mouth; a bug-eyed perusal of her feet, legs, and all the rest; a second go at the feet; and, finally, a curt tipping of Yosemite Sam. These first four steps he now executed. He was en route to step five, when Penelope said, "Dewitt, do you have any gum on you?"

Yosemite Sam was stopped midnod by this, though he did continue to fire his gun and offer his middle digit to the world. Penelope was getting flipped off all over the place. Dewitt's gape grew gapier.

"I have a bad taste in my mouth from breakfast," Penelope continued, "and I'm completely out of gum."

Dewitt shook Yosemite Sam side to side as a response.

"What about candy?" Penelope asked, standing up now and blocking the door. "Like a mint or something."

Dewitt said "Naw" and made a tentative step to go around her. With a smile, Penelope mirrored his movement. They were four feet apart and looking eye to eye. Dewitt was a touch taller, but scrawny. His nose began to twitch as a rabbit's does. He dug for a moment in his ear. He could be smelled from this distance. A spasm started in his cheek, just above the stubble. The hand that was in the ear moved to the curly chest hair that leaped from the top of his coveralls. He lingered here, curling and uncurling individual members of his hirsute tribe in a manner that looked comforting.

"Nothing at all?" said Penelope. "Not even a Starburst or something?"

This was the longest Dewitt had ever been detained in the office and his eyes went involuntarily to the windows, then to Missy's office, as if searching for alternative means of escape.

"I ain't got nothing like that."

In the worst way possible, Penelope wanted to demand that he empty his pockets. Or better yet to frisk him herself if she could quickly find rubber gloves and one of those outfits that nuclear plant workers wear to prevent contamination. Even without the gear, she was sorely tempted. A half-empty pack of gum here, an individually wrapped peppermint there. Even the cute little yellow socks. She could live with the pilfering of those. But a Monday morning pack of Starburst? That was a bridge too far.

"I got to go," Dewitt said.

"Where to?" Penelope said, fake-smiling in a way she hoped was obvious.

"I got some things to do up at my place."

"You don't have any candy up there, do you? I don't want to make another trip to Seven-Eleven."

She thought Dewitt blinked more than usual at the use of *another* but couldn't be sure. An unmoored chest hair could have briefly gotten into his eye.

"I don't truck with gum or candy. That stuff's bad for your teeth."

Penelope let that comment linger in the air for a while and continued to match the minuscule movements of Dewitt, left, then right. She thought by now he should have worked in a head fake and a quick counterstep to get the angle on her, but the extended human interaction seemed to have dulled his native survival skills.

"Surely you've got something in your house?"

"Nope."

"Your car?"

"Naw."

Penelope broadened her smile and stepped aside to let Dewitt pass. He opened the door and she peeked her head out behind him. "It's such a beautiful day," she said. "I may walk up to your place with you just to stretch my legs. You don't mind, do you?"

Dimwit appeared to take this as the rhetorical question it was and headed down the steps. Penelope followed, her eyes scanning his multipocketed coveralls. One of those grimy zippers held the purloined Starburst.

Down the office steps, across the small parking lot, across Rolling Acres Way, and then they were at the foot of Dimwit's gravel drive. Dimwit walked quickly, then sluggishly, then started up again in a burst, as if trying to get Penelope to walk either more in front of him or more behind, rather than right beside as she was. He seemed skittish about human proximity not of his own choosing. Luckily, Penelope was wearing her summer flats and was able to manage his changes of pace with no problem. She felt keen.

"Did you ever have actual feeders on these?" she asked, as they walked past the soiled Confederate flag and the *Don't Tread on Me* banner.

"Momma did. Don't care for birds. Too messy. Too noisy."

"Where'd you get your flags?

"Internet."

"Do you buy a lot of things on the Internet?"

Dimwit seemed to view this question as a touch intimate and offered no response. Penelope wasn't sure exactly what her aim was, now that they were halfway up the drive, but she'd decided to see him to the door, come hell or high water. If Dimwit felt a little violated by her presence, then good. Turnabout was fair play.

They walked in silence, shoes crunching gravel. The air was still and the day had grown warm and close feeling. Behind them and to either side, lush greenery and things in bloom. But up here, only a few sad weeds and red clay. The riddle of the lunar landscape around his trailer was one for the ages. Maybe it was a septic issue and a million biological hazards lurked beneath her pretty tan flats. A rusty tire rim rose up out of the wasteland, looking as if it had started rolling down to freedom before losing all will to live. It was a lonely-looking tire. Her mind raced now, thinking of lip gloss and yellow socks that were likely in the run-down trailer they approached. Also dead bodies.

Dimwit stopped abruptly when they'd crested the hill. He said: "I ain't got no candy for you. You're wasting your time."

His back was to the front door, which was padlocked, and he'd fished out a massive key ring from one of his inscrutable pockets. He held the ring tightly, as if afraid she might try to swipe it. She realized she was casing the joint.

"You're not going to invite me in?" Penelope said, stepping toward the door.

"Ain't got time to socialize."

"Okay Dewitt. I'll see you later."

They stood there atop the hill, with Rolling Acres below, the mountains to the east, downtown Hillsboro to the west. She could see the bank building from here. Maybe that was why he'd cut down the trees. The view was pretty spectacular, as long as you didn't actually look at his property. Dimwit didn't turn toward his door and Penelope didn't start down the hill. They were face-to-grim-face under the hot sun. He was not big on eye contact and Penelope knew she was making him uncomfortable. He rocked back and forth in his brogans and switched his keys to the other hand. Behind him was an ancient cement flowerpot filled with Sun Drop cans, some of which had spilled over the side and begun to pile all around it.

"We have recycling you know," Penelope said.

Dimwit blinked three times but didn't reply. The sun was in his face, not hers, and now his eyes began to water. A bead of sweat dripped from beneath the bird finger of Yosemite Sam, and Dewitt let it run across his forehead, along his sideburn, until it disappeared in the murky growth on his face.

"How's the view on the back side of your place?" Penelope asked. As she did, she made a quick movement around him toward the far corner of his home. She was past the bathroom window before he could recover, and the propane tank lying on its side, and the uncovered charcoal grill and plastic lawn chair, and the binoculars that lay beside it. She nearly asked if the binoculars were for bird watching but decided against it.

"View's same back there as out front," said Dimwit, rushing past her with keys jangling.

She was behind the trailer now, where he parked his old Nova. From his hilltop redoubt, he could see 360 degrees around him. If he was home, sneaking up was out of the question. And even if he was out on his mystery midnight errands, the place looked impenetrable. The back door was padlocked like the front and every window painted shut. The whole time she was appraising the place, Dimwit kept himself between her and the trailer. He seemed to fear a sudden attempt at forced entry.

"I've already said I ain't got no sweet things for you. And look there, your boss just got back. Why don't you go see if she's got a goody and let me go about my business?"

Missy was indeed pulling into the office parking lot, and doing so with tires squealing. They watched her spring out of the car, slam the door, and stomp up the stairs to the office, already talking.

Penelope faced her adversary and said, "You can see everything that goes on from up here, can't you, Dewitt?"

Dimwit shrugged. "Not much to see, other than old people and grass. I haven't given it much thought."

With as sweet a voice as she could muster, she said: "Okay Dewitt. I guess I better get back to work. If you come across any candy, please let me know."

Dimwit gave a noncommittal nod and took a step toward the direction she was heading, hoping to prompt her to quicker movement she surmised. When he moved, Penelope noticed something she'd missed in her earlier assessment, a door with a flap on it, like a small animal would use to come and go as it pleased.

She took a hard, long look at that flap, trying to commit its measurements to memory. It looked like a cat door, if anything, or maybe something for a dachshund or other small dog. No way on earth she could squeeze through there. But someone smaller and skinny and really tan?

Maybe.

She smiled and nodded good-bye then started down the hill, concentrating as she did on walking as nonchalantly as possible, though she very much wanted to run.

18

She burst through the office door in Missy-esque fashion and shouted, "Dimwit just stole my brand-new pack of Starburst!"

The head honcho was pacing the reception area, anxious and distracted. She said: "I'm all confused. That meeting with the tax assessor isn't till tomorrow. I missed a day somewhere. I'm not getting enough sleep. Dimwit is in my head."

Penelope approached her employer and put hands on both shoulders in an attempt to stop the rambling. It was tempting to pretend that—for her own good—slapping her silly was the only way to go. Penelope looked into her eyes and said, very slowly: "Did you hear what I said? Dimwit stole a pack of Starburst right under my nose."

Missy nodded dumbly.

"I was just up at his place. I'm pissed now. This is the last straw."

"Huh? You did what?"

"I went up to his place on the pretext of wanting to bum some candy. But once I was up there, I cased the joint pretty good."

Missy nodded at the detective jargon and her right eye blinked quickly for several seconds in a row. It looked as if she were reentering the world she normally inhabited after a brief foray into doubt and inertia. Her visage cleared and she was once again the ferocious tan dachshund that Penelope knew so well.

"Oh yes, oh hell yes," she said, wiggling her shoulders out of Penelope's clutches and sprinting to the desk recently rifled by Dewitt. She opened every drawer at once and said, "Do they make home fingerprint sets?"

"I don't know, but it wouldn't matter. You just touched every surface over there."

Missy waved a dismissive hand and circled the desk several times, as if looking for a damning chest hair follicle or mislaid Yosemite Sam cap. The search proved fruitless so she plopped down in Penelope's chair with a sigh.

"Dimwit's gone full klepto," she said. "He's definitely keeping totems from his victims. It's like every serial killer movie ever. Cute little socks turned into puppets one day, Starburst the next. I wonder what he does with those little sticky squares."

Penelope shook her head in disgust.

"He could literally wedge them anywhere," Missy said.

"You can't gross me out more than I already am."

Missy cackled. "I bet I could. But what exactly did you mean when you said *This is the last straw?*"

"I'm over Dimwit. I'm on a mission to take him down."

"Now, my friend, you are talking. I still like Operation Dimwit better, but Mission Dim-possible isn't bad either."

"I'm not calling it Mission Dim-possible."

"*P* is for *Pendetta?*"

"What?"

"*P* as in *Penelope.*"

"No."

"Operation Dimwit it is."

"I probably won't call it that either. But anyway, like I said, I got a pretty good look at what we're up against. His place is a fortress. Windows painted, padlocked doors."

"But?" said Missy, tilting her head.

Penelope smiled. Without realizing it, she had done that thing they do in buddy movies, where the kicker line is left off in order to build drama. Missy was playing her part perfectly.

"But I did notice a flap at the bottom of the back door. A cat door. Or maybe a doggie door. But it would have to be a pretty small dog."

"Cats and dogs, my ass. That's a skunk door!"

"You keep getting sidetracked. Stop obsessing on nonsense and focus on proving Dimwit's a thief."

Penelope watched Missy take a deep breath, all but counting to ten before speaking. It was an admirable show of discipline.

Gritting her teeth, Missy said, "How small?"

"Very. Are you flexible?"

As an answer, Missy dove on the floor, rounded herself into a tiny tan ball, and rolled under the desk where Penelope's chair usually sat. "How's that for flexible? And if you need further proof, I've got a list of guys you can call who can vouch for me. I'm practically double-jointed. I could roll through that skunk door and into Dimwit's dungeon, no questions asked."

"The door's shorter than that."

"G.I. Joe," Missy said, flopping down on her belly and sliding like a brown snake from under the desk. She then crawled ten feet across the carpet, her high heels flopping behind her.

"I think you're still too wide," Penelope said, smiling. At this point she was just putting her boss through the paces. "Can you scrunch up your shoulders a little more?"

Grunting, Missy tried to kick off her heels. Her dress was hiked up nearly to her waist and a run in her hose was making its way all the way around one thigh. Penelope took out her phone and snapped several photos. Missy was impossible to incriminate, but Penelope thought she'd enjoy looking at them from time to time when feeling a little down. Shoes finally off, Missy hunched her neck and shoulders down and scooted awkwardly forward on her elbows. She looked like a cross between a turtle and an uncoordinated inchworm.

"Like this?"

"I don't know. Keep going for a little while."

"I've got rug burns like a mother, but okay."

Penelope started to laugh.

Missy looked over one hunched shoulder and said, "Damn it to hell, can I get in that door like this or not?"

"I don't know."

"But maybe?"

"It'll be close."

Missy stood up and dusted lint balls from her dress, face, and hair. Her eyes were bugged and she panted freely. "You enjoyed that, didn't you?"

Penelope smiled and nodded.

"How big is the door? Show me with your hands."

Penelope made an imaginary box with her hands approximately eighteen inches by eighteen inches.

Missy offered two thumbs up. "Piece of cake."

"It's a tight squeeze."

Missy shooed this skepticism as one does a slow-moving fly. She came closer now, hand extended, and said: "But you're really on the team now? Operation Dimwit? One for all and all for one?"

Penelope shook the offered hand.

"You wanna try out the walkie-talkies?" Missy asked.

"Are you a rank amateur? I saw binoculars up at Dimwit's. He's watching us nonstop. I've already tipped our hand by going up there. We can't give anything else away."

"Oh man, oh man. I knew he was spying. Well listen, country girl, I know you aren't worried about skunks, and likely rode one to school when you was but a young'un. But I am. And I won't be breaking into Dimwit's until we show those skunks who's boss. So if you'll excuse me, I'm going to check the Whisperer's traps."

Penelope had planned to go to the gym after work but couldn't quite talk herself into it. She was now walking up the front stoop of her house, mail in hand—all of it bills—when she saw the note stuck in the screen door. The lavender stationery was the first clue that the note was from her mother, the sprawling, elegant script that swirled the last *E* of her name the second. Standards might come and go, but her mother was not one to skimp on style, no matter how small the occasion. Penelope snatched the note with a grin.

Just dropped by to take a look at the walkway. I think I took a photo with my phone but can't be sure. These new phones are more trouble than they're worth.

I have a good mental picture regardless and know just what I'll do to pretty up the place. Tell me a good day to drop by and discuss. I can't wait to get my hands in your dirt (or red clay as is likely the case). Call me.

Love Mom.

PS: Have you heard from Theo yet? I'm sure he's made plenty of friends and is having a great time. Stop worrying.

Penelope tucked the note under her arm, threw the bills on the counter with a disdainful flourish, and reached for the cold bottle of wine that had been calling her name since she'd left Rolling Acres. She reminded herself again that it was only Monday and that the absolute earliest she'd get a note from Theo would be Wednesday.

She stepped onto the screened-in porch and sat on the glider she'd been gifted from George, the one she'd grown up swinging on. She took the first sip of wine and it did not disappoint.

Seated, she realized how tired she was. Other than the hour she'd wasted on Dimwit, skunks, and Starburst, she'd gone nonstop. Still, maybe she should have worked out. Was she really that beat, or was she just trying to avoid a trainer named Megan? If so, that was weak. Yes, she was nonconfrontational by nature. Her kindergarten teacher had sent a note home, worried because she smiled all day long at school. She couldn't help it if she was naturally happy and didn't like getting into tiffs. She was a grown woman now, not a five-year-old insanely grinning during Duck, Duck, Goose.

To heck with James's new girlfriend. She was not going to be intimated by her or anybody else. She'd go to the gym tomorrow and every other day this week. Doing so would likely mean an encounter with Bald Brad, whom she'd yet to reply to. And why hadn't she? Was it the bald thing? She wasn't twenty anymore and couldn't expect every man to have hair like Eddie Van Halen, as sad as that notion was. And even thinking of him as Bald Brad seemed shallow and immature. Why not just Brad? No, he was too active for a single syllable. Active Brad. That was better, more positive. It wasn't his fault he was bald.

Then again, he did have a good body and looked like he might know his way around a Penelope Lemon. She tried to imagine having sex with Active Brad but could only conjure a flushed pink dome, workout clothes, and a Fitbit. Even if she could picture him in a conjugal state, she wouldn't know the full scope of things. According to her erotic novels, all sorts of individualistic things were going on below the belt. Having been married for the better part of the last two decades, she'd thankfully escaped most of that.

There was that one overzealous foray by James. This was either just before or just after his brief journey into the world of competitive Ping-Pong. The timing was fuzzy. What wasn't fuzzy was James. All she knew was that when he dropped the shorty robe for the first time after slashing away with razor, scissors, and possibly tweezers, it looked exactly like a pink salamander recently startled from the deepest underbrush. She hadn't known where to look. He hadn't warned her, and then there it was, the frightened albino salamander. On closer inspection, it might have looked more like plucked chicken under Saran wrap at the grocery store, but that was splitting hairs that were no longer evident.

That was five years ago, at least. Who knew what was current now? It could be crop circles for all she knew. It could be little Hitler moustaches. She truly had no idea, only that she'd find out one of these days, and maybe with Active Brad.

The thought of having sex again put her, fittingly, in the mood for it. Maybe later—after a dose of *Unchaste Places*—she'd check out Sandy and Rachel's special present.

It dawned on her that she'd never called the gift by any of its widely used monikers, even in her own head. They just all sounded so stupid. That's what it was. She couldn't get past the names. *Implement* was about the least embarrassing, though she still wanted to put the word *farm* before it. Plus, her own name was emblazoned on the thing, which kind of drove home the point that—no matter how strong her imagination—**PENELOPE LEMON** would be doing Penelope Lemon.

This realization was both funny and sad and she turned back to her glass of wine, laughing to herself about the strangeness of sex, of desire, and of good ole Penelope Lemon, alone on a screened-in porch, looking out lustfully over the farmland and the rolling hills before her.

19

It was Thursday after work and Penelope was trying not to fret that she'd yet to hear from Camp Sycamore. She was currently in the front row of a rocking Dance Fusion class at Fitness Plus. The day before she'd made the mistake of being in the last row and had felt distinctly like a backup dancer to the women up front. Not only that, but her view of the instructor was often blocked and she'd missed or been late on several snappy moves. Lesson learned. Today, wearing her fuchsia spandex and her best sleeveless workout top, she was dead center, mirroring Cheryl, the twentysomething dance leader. The music was a mix of hip-hop, techno, and old-school funk, and she was shaking her groove thing like nobody's business. In the mirror she could see *her* backup dancers behind her and didn't fight the notion that she and Cheryl were basically co-teaching the class.

While she stepped, boogied, shook, thrust, and spun, she forced herself not to think of skunks after five full days of hearing nothing but at work. The Critter Catcher had yet to snare anything and Missy had spent most of the day on the Internet researching skunk bait. She was doubting the marshmallows and doubting them hard.

Okay, maybe she was thinking about skunks, and Dimwit too, and now she'd been late on that fun little knee-kick and spin thing. The old lady beside her, every bit of seventy-five, smiled and said: "Don't worry, honey, you're doing great. You'll get the hang of it soon enough."

Penelope smiled and was back in the groove now. She watched the old woman in the mirror and had to admit she was shaking it, not faking it, in her white leotard and pink tights. She was kicking her legs up nearly as high as Penelope and not even breathing hard. Wow. First springy Fitzwilliam and now Fusion Granny.

She'd done a good job during this last song of not looking at herself too much in the mirror despite how awesome she was dancing, but as they segued to "Hey Ya!," she couldn't resist a quick peek. The fuchsia spandex was absolutely the bomb, one of her all-time best investments. She was admiring her sparkly, shiny self when she noticed someone outside the class staring in. The dividing wall was clear, and men on the track often slowed to rubberneck as they passed. But she'd never seen anyone just set up shop out there. It was strange. Dancing bodies were moving back and forth in front of the Plexiglas wall, so Penelope couldn't be sure at first who the brazen onlooker was.

And then she was sure. It was James's new love, the dragon trainer herself, and she was staring intently at the reflection of Penelope Lemon. And even when they caught eyes in the mirror, she didn't look away. Distracted, Penelope twirled a half beat behind Cheryl. Okay, whatever. Now she was back on time. Then the door opened and people with surprised looks were making room for a very late arrival.

Baffled and discomfited, Penelope watched as someone darted and weaved through rows of dancers.

"Can I squeeze in *please?*"

Penelope was still hoofing it, though she was hopelessly lost in her steps. She surveyed the lay of the land in the mirror. There was no room to be had on the front row, or really any row. The class was jammed. Without waiting for a response, Trainer Megan danced into the narrow gap between Penelope and Fusion Granny.

"Hope it's okay, Cheryl, that I just popped in," Megan said, while swaying her shoulders in a way that made Penelope move three feet to the left. This forced eviction left Penelope crammed into the woman in green shorts. Penelope mumbled an apology and the woman responded with an irritated shrug, whether at her or Megan, she couldn't tell.

Cheryl smiled and gave a big thumbs-up to the trainer.

"And how are you today, Mimi?" the shoulder-throwing Megan asked the funky old lady.

"Still here, baby. Still kicking."

Penelope continued with the routine, but her heart had gone out of it. Had her personal space ever been so overtly invaded by someone not named Dimwit? No, it hadn't. She couldn't fully extend her kicks anymore or spin properly. Who barged into a class—half an hour late—and muscled her way to the front? Common courtesy for late arrivals was to stand near the door and make themselves small.

She was sorely tempted to execute a proper kick to the back of Megan's head. Such a Chuck Norris stunt would be ironic after all the fun she'd made of Karate James, but who cared? This was intimidation pure and simple.

Before she could do something rash, the music stopped and Cheryl said: "Last break. Get water if you need it. We're going to sweat it out these last fifteen."

Penelope stalked to her water bottle—the one with the straw that Orca Boy had chewed to a nub—which she'd placed against the side wall. She stood there gulping and staring at this very rude person. Was she mental? The object of her scorn was talking to Mimi. There were several women around Grandma Newton John, all of them chatting and smiling away as they sipped from their own water bottles. It was clear Mimi was the Fonz of the class and that everyone wanted a piece of the fountain of youth she was swigging from. Seeing Penelope standing alone, the older woman hailed her with a "Come on over and meet the gals, honey."

This invitation disarmed Penelope a bit and she strode over wondering if she'd overreacted to the stalker-trainer thing. Maybe being at the front was a Fitness Plus employee bonus. The women around Mimi were around Penelope's age or younger and they smiled and welcomed her, got her name, and gave theirs. All except Megan.

"This new girl here caught on quick," Mimi said, placing her hand on Penelope's shoulder. "She might give Cheryl a run for her money."

The dance leader was fiddling with the CD player but apparently overheard this, for she said, "Tell me about it. She's like Mimi junior up there."

Penelope's irritation vanished at the news that she had been dancing as diva-fantastic as she thought. She knew she was smiling too much and should have begged off with a bit of self-deprecation but before she could speak, Trainer Megan said, "So Mimi, what are you doing this weekend?"

This turned the conversation away from the newest ass-kicking member of the dance team and back onto the jazzy senior, just—Penelope suspected—as Megan had intended. The trainer was turned so that her back was to Penelope, much like one basketball player boxing out another. When the music started again, Mimi winked and said, "Get back over here next to me, Penelope. Megan won't mind."

Though Megan obviously did mind, she said otherwise. It was clear no one wanted to look uncool in front of Mimi. Penelope was back in her former spot but had no more room to work with. Trainer Megan was now giving the lady in green a wide berth and crowding the hell out of her from the left. She decided to just tough it out and ride that Mimi wink to the end of class. One day soon, she hoped, she and the older woman would be gym besties.

When class was over, Penelope was planning to talk outside the studio with Mimi, then maybe try out some new machines. She was standing next to the indoor track, waiting for the group of admirers around the geriatric marvel to disperse, when she was tapped brusquely on the shoulder. She turned to find Trainer Megan standing before her.

"I hear Brad asked you out."

Penelope said, "What?"

"Brad said he asked you out, but you didn't reply."

Penelope felt no compulsion to verify this.

"Well, he's a really good friend of mine. We're in the same rock climbing group. Do you climb?"

Penelope gave her best indulgent smile and said, "Not at all."

"I figured. He's really into outdoor adventure kind of stuff. Mountain biking, rappelling, that sort of thing. I think he's looking for someone who's into extreme sports as well. Just a heads up."

As she took all this in, Penelope noticed someone race across the training area, checking his watch as he did, stomp up the stairs to the cycling zone, and hop astride a stationary bike. Megan saw this and Penelope's mystified look as well, and said: "He's training for a triathlon next month."

"That's cool," Penelope said. "I ran the Boston Marathon last year."

"What was your time?"

Penelope realized this woman thought she was lying, and not just being an old-fashioned smartass.

"I don't like to brag, but it was a personal best. Boston wasn't nearly as tough as I thought it would be. I didn't even train that much. It's totally overrated."

"Oh, come on. What was your time? I can look it up online, you know."

Penelope was annoyed now and refused to give in. She could keep this going as long as it took. Unfortunately, she had no idea if a fast marathon runner should take two or four or sixteen hours. She walked plenty but couldn't remember the last time she'd run. Probably that time at the park when Theo got chased by the ducks.

"I really hate to brag. It was a personal best though. By a lot."

"You should sign up for the Hillsboro mini tri next month. Brad and I are both doing it. Let me get you a registration form from the front desk."

Fine, thought Penelope. *Knock yourself out. I'll be there bright and early at never o'clock.*

She was heading toward the free weights when Brad hopped off his stationary bike and dashed toward the track. He didn't slow at all as he ran past her but did say, "Did you get my message?"

Penelope shouted at his sweaty back that she had. He sprinted past her twice more as she trekked over to the weights. She was moving more gingerly than usual because her butt and thighs were starting to hurt. She feared immobility in the morning as the price for showing off in class, but thought the pain well worth it. Brad seemed especially active and was dashing past seniors in the walking lane and shouting *On your right!* every three seconds. As he ran he would check his watch and then his Fitbit. The devices were on opposite wrists so as he swung them up toward his face he looked very much like a windup toy soldier on speed. It was quite the spectacle.

She'd already decided that she would agree to meet him for lunch or coffee. Maybe even a drink after work. But did agreeing to that—alcohol in the PM—imply that hanky-panky was in play?

She went to a machine with a single bar hanging down. Who cared how it looked? She was a grown woman. She could have a drink whenever she wanted. It didn't imply anything. Who'd brainwashed her to be so priggish about form? She sat down on the seat, unsure which way to face. It was the bidet dilemma all over again. Luckily, Mimi walked by and said, "If you want to work your shoulders, face away. If you want to work your triceps, face forward. It took me forever to figure out how all these work."

"Thanks," Penelope said.

"Don't think a thing about it. I'm glad to have a smiley new gal in the gym. Too many grumps in here."

Mimi gave a dramatic eye roll and a smile then went toward the free weights. After she was gone, Brad jogged over, checking his watch as he did.

"Hey," he said, with sweat streaming off his gleaming dome. "How's it going?"

"Good. I'm not working nearly as hard as you."

"Yeah," he said, starting a series of vigorous squats. "I'm racing around like a madman, trying out this total body circuit training. I get bored if I do the same thing over and over, so I'm always looking for new workouts. With this one, you do ten stations—or circuits—for three minutes each. Mix of strength, endurance, and fitness. It's pretty fun. You should try it sometime. I've got burpees next."

Penelope wasn't sure what a burpee was but the name alone gave her indigestion.

"I'm just going to do a few machines then head out. Maybe some other time."

"Sure," he said, standing up and checking his watch before launching into another set. "No worries. And still glad to help you with a workout routine if you like. I can tailor it however you want."

"That would be great. Maybe during a weekend sometime. Or after work? Then we could grab coffee or a drink afterwards?"

"Awesome," he replied midsquat. It wasn't the most attractive thing she'd ever seen while making a date but she supposed there were different rules in a gym. "Would Saturday work? And then maybe lunch?"

"I think so, but let me check my schedule. I can text you and let you know."

"Sounds good. We'll keep it casual."

He paused at the top of his squat and looked over her shoulder with a furrowed brow. Penelope turned to find the obsessed trainer coming their way, brusquely waving a piece of paper.

"Hey Brad," she said. "I was just getting a registration form for our new member. She says she's really into marathons, so I thought she'd be interested in our little tri."

Brad checked his watch. The burpee portion of his day was growing nigh.

"Really?" said Brad, looking at Penelope.

"She says she ran the Boston Marathon last year and it wasn't that hard. Isn't that right?"

Brad checked his watch again, and Penelope decided to stall.

"Well here's the form," Megan said, thrusting it toward her.

"You say it's a mini triathlon?"

Penelope said this with a sour-pickle face to show that she found such an event beneath her talent and training.

"Yes," said Megan. "So it should be a piece of cake. I think she should sign up, don't you, Brad?"

"Sure. We could all train together. What do you say, Penelope?"

Penelope could tell she was on the verge of committing to something just to call a bluff but resisted. "I don't know. I'm really busy with this situation at work, but I'll have a look."

"Great," said Brad. "We can talk about it later. I've got to jet. Text me."

And with that he was booking across the gym, heeding the siren call of a hundred burpees.

Megan said, "The form's right there."

"Thanks so much," Penelope said, offering her most insincere smile.

Then she was pulling at the bar in a way that was supposed to work either her shoulders or triceps. She had no idea.

20

Penelope was back home after dodging triathlons at Fitness Plus. She'd gone to the mailbox first thing and discovered the usual heaping helping of bills. Visa, Verizon, and Hillsboro Utility all wanted her to pay up pronto. It would be tight, very tight, until her next paycheck, but if nothing unexpected came up, she could swing it.

There was also a letter from Theo.

Walking down her gravel drive, she reminded herself that the trash would come tomorrow and that she shouldn't push it out to the road until in the morning. She'd received a call that morning from Chad, her landlord, warning of roaming dogs in the area who'd been tipping garbage cans. Thoughts of dogs made her wish for one.

A nice pet might keep Theo from getting lonely in his new house.

She entered the kitchen, fiddling with the letter, which, now that she examined it, looked as if had been used to scoop up salamanders. It was smudged all over with grimy fingerprints, dirt, and possibly peanut butter. Too anxious to open the envelope that would either alleviate her worries or expand them exponentially, she thought again of the feasibility of a dog. They had the perfect spot for a one if the landlords were cool with it. Of course there was the whole pet dander issue, yet another Bubble Boy trait Theo had gotten from his father.

She was thinking about dogs and bills and her ex-husband's Anglo-

Saxon frailties as a way to distract herself from the seven hundred dollars her creditors were requesting and from Theo's lonely missive from camp. Able to stand the tension no longer, she flung the bills—fuckers—onto the kitchen table and ripped into the soiled envelope. In slanted print, the height of the letters varying from word to word as if it had been composed in the bowels of a rolling ship, Theo wrote:

Dear Mom,

Camp is okay. We fish and hike a lot. It's hot. I lost my compass when I tipped over in the canoe. Don't worry, I had a life jacket on. They are ringing the dinner bell so I have to go. Kids yell if you make your cabin line up late. First cabin gets to eat first.

Love,
Theo

Penelope didn't like that part about kids yelling. Theo hadn't mentioned that he was the tardy cabin member, but she'd bet money he'd screwed up the line at least once. It was virtually impossible to get him to move without vigorous prompting, unless continued video gaming power was involved.

Penelope let out a long breath she didn't know she was holding. There was no overt bad news. Theo was fine. She should stop worrying.

She decided on a quick, light supper, a glass of wine, and a long, unhurried, candlelit bath. Then she'd finish the night with a healthy stretch of *Unchaste Places*. She'd reply to Brad, as well, but suggest lunch without the workout. Or just straight-up drinks and supper. Yes, that sounded better. She didn't have to live vicariously through Miranda her whole life.

~

She awoke Friday morning from a dream that had begun auspiciously, with her entering a room with a brass door and discovering that what lay within was a sumptuous sauna that bore a close resemblance to Spa Helvetica. She was in the bubbly warm water with a man who was speaking French and offering her champagne. At some point, right when drink flutes had been flung without repercussions over her and the Frenchy's shoulders and they were moving in for their first erotic embrace, the sauna had turned into her own bathroom and Henri had morphed into Active Brad. He seemed nude but Penelope couldn't be sure. Two sweaty wrists, a watch, and Fitbit were clear but the rest hazy. Still, this was promising.

Unfortunately, Active Brad then turned into Theo. He was looking for his missing compass and had stumbled upon the complicated present hidden in her bedroom closet. His face was scrunched up and he was turning the green cylinder in his hand as if trying to get it to point due north. He said, "Why is your name on this, Mom?" And then her mother was there, too, though now they were in her high school bedroom. Theo handed the item to his grandmother with a puzzled look, but she shook her head and said, "No, Theo, this isn't the trowel. Don't you know your garden implements?"

This is when Penelope woke with a start. It took her a while to extricate herself from her knotted and sweat-soaked sheets and she cursed herself for forgetting to turn down the air before turning in. Sleeping in a hot room always gave her crazy dreams. Head clearing, she recalled the specifics of the nightmare. The HHR would have a field day interpreting this one, but the dullest blade in the drawer could trace the source of this angst back to the gift in the closet. Having just freed herself from the fetters of her sheets, she bounded from bed feeling both embarrassingly Puritanical and firmly resolute. Sexual liberation or no, the inscribed implement would have to go.

She threw on her robe and slippers and procured the item in question, perplexed again by the color combination. The green was the color of Fitzwilliam's ascot and the orange that of a plastic jack-o'-

lantern. They didn't match at all. And the font that spelled her name couldn't have been less romantic, all blockish and techno looking. It was a sex toy for a computer. Sex toy. What a truly stupid name. And perverse too. Why did they have to invoke childhood? She associated sex toys with weird guys in sheds. Was the oxymoron supposed to be funny? It sure wasn't enticing. Dildo? Dildo was a clown with a nose that honked and a lapel flower that squirted water.

Whether it was the unfortunate names associated with the gift or her worry that Theo would stumble upon it in a mad search for battery chargers that made her decide it had to go, she wasn't sure. But go it did. Straight to the trash can under the sink in the kitchen.

There. It was done. Maybe one of these days when Theo was out of the house permanently she could be a bit more adventurous as a soloist. Besides, she'd managed fine in the alone-time department since her teenage years. Back then, all she'd needed was a shirtless Jim Morrison poster to get the ball rolling. Now, it was the occasional erotic novel. She wasn't prudish, just weird about stupid names and answering questions from a nine-year-old boy about her private affairs. It was completely understandable.

Out the window, the sun was just peeking over the trees. It looked to be a hot day. She hoped Theo would remember to put on sunscreen and wondered if he was peeling yet. He usually lost several layers of epidermis during the course of a summer and his shoulders were always a flaky mess. She started her coffee and placed a bagel in the toaster oven then took the bag from the trash can, tied it, and took it to the big bin in the carport. She could see the garish green through the thin white bag as she walked and make out the orange **PENELOPE LEMON** as well. On her way back to the house, she heard a dog bark from over the hill and recalled the landlord's warning about marauding, trash-tipping canines. What if they got to her bin before the trashmen did? Her refuse would be all over the lawn where anyone could see. She couldn't risk it.

Feeling paranoid and moronic but also cagey, she opened the big bin, untied the top trash bag, and removed **PENELOPE LEMON**. She shook off a few coffee grounds that had attached themselves to it then stuck the device in the pocket of her robe. She glanced furtively once toward the landlord's house in search of witnesses and felt silly for doing so. The recycling guys came to Rolling Acres today. It was a safer way to go, and more environmentally friendly, too.

21

She got to the office fifteen minutes early on the off chance that Missy would show up before nine. The personal item was in her purse and wrapped in a cloth napkin. She wished now that she'd put it inside some other recyclable object as a better cover, but the napkin had been the first thing to pop in her mind.

Hillsboro Waste Management picked up behind the office, near Carl Jr.'s tool shed, so all she had to do was sneak the pleasure device into some empty vessel she found lying around the office. She went to the front window to ensure that no one was about, then to the back window, where she visually swept the street before settling on Dimwit's trailer. Studying this for a good while, looking for a glint of sun off of binoculars, she satisfied herself that nothing was obviously amiss and went back to her purse. With her back to the far window and spreading herself as broadly as she could, she sank slowly and subtly into a semisquat, removed the personal hardware from her purse, and thrust it—still wrapped in the napkin—into the farthest corner of her bottommost drawer. She shut the drawer as quietly as possible, then resumed a standing position.

Penelope realized she was acting like a paranoiac and that she'd been holding her breath during the entirety of this cloak-and-dagger mission. She also realized that she'd flattened all the cardboard boxes the day before and disposed of them. She was SOL in the container department. Her best chance for ditching **PENELOPE LEMON** without alerting witnesses would be to pop it in the recycling bin for plastics when she heard the truck rumble through the gate later this morning. It was a plan that would require timing, execution, and nerves of steel. She couldn't have that thing just plop out of the bin where Roy and Steve, the recycling guys, would see it. Talk about embarrassing. Adrenaline was now coursing through her. Subterfuge of this sort would be good practice for the eventual breaching of Dimwit's lair.

Satisfied with her plan, she sat down at her desk to write Theo a quick letter before beginning her workday. As she pulled out pen and paper, the Camp Sycamore theme song, specifically the line *Where friends I'll surely make,* popped into her head. It was a hopeful line, she guessed, but wasn't there also a hint of desperation? Friendship was plausible, even likely, but not a surefire guarantee. Then again, James, the know-it-all dinosaur boy of scowling childhood photos, had apparently made enough friends to have fond memories of the place. This thought appeased her and she closed her letter on an upbeat note, taunting her son by signing herself #UndisputedMarioKartDominator.

If this goading didn't elicit a speedy reply, then she'd know for sure that he was duct taped to a canoe floating in a forgotten cove of Lake Sycamore.

She'd just put the stamp on the envelope when Missy dashed into the office and said, "When did *Of course* become the new *You're welcome*?"

Penelope smiled and shrugged, though she'd recently noted the same trend.

Flinging her purse ten feet to the couch in the reception area, Missy ran a theatrical hand through her hair and began her laps around Penelope's desk.

"Seriously," she said, "I was just in Kroger's, getting team snacks for the one millionth time for Damien's godforsaken baseball team, and when I said thanks to the checkout guy, he said, *Of course.* I hear it everywhere now. It's out of control. Did some Kardashian start this or something?"

Thank you for giving me your kidney.
Of course.
Thank you for solving world hunger.
Of course.
Thank you for killing Dimwit for me.
Of course.

She was standing now in the waiting area and did a backwards swoon onto the couch, her arm draped dramatically over her head like a silent movie heroine fainting away. "This travel baseball is killing me."

Penelope laughed and finished her text to Active Brad, suggesting drinks or an early dinner the following night. If he was free, that would be two Saturday nights in a row with a date. Pretty cool.

"Travel baseball. Give me a break," Missy said with her arm still covering her eyes. "With their matching bat bags and fourteen different uniforms, most of them white, which are impossible to get clean. Do I look like a charwoman who wants to spend every night of her life Spray and Washing grass stains? And the e-mails. Like five hundred a day. *Tomorrow will be hot, be sure and have the boys hydrate.* I can't take it."

The monologue seemed to have exhausted her. She was breathing heavily, mouth open. Carl Jr. couldn't get back in town fast enough. He had a calming influence that no one else could replace.

To cheer her up, Penelope said, "So it looks like I might be stuck doing a mini triathlon."

"What?" said Missy, rising up stiffly like Dracula after a long night in the tanning bed coffin. "Are you insane?"

"Apparently." She then gave an overview of the previous afternoon at Fitness Plus.

"Are bicycle seats any softer than they used to be?" Missy asked. "Because my uterus couldn't stand all that jostling. Anyway, you've obviously got to do it. You can't let this woman get the best of you. Give her an inch and she'll take a mile, mark my word."

"Should I start with swimming or biking or running first?"

Missy started to respond but, seeing the grin on Penelope's, face reconsidered. "Did you at least get things going with the sweaty hunk?"

"Just texted him about a date tomorrow."

"So dinner first? Or just straight to the sack?"

"Maybe you should check your skunk cages."

Missy popped up at this suggestion and raced to the window, shouting over her shoulder as she ran, "Did you spot one with the binoculars? Were you saving this for a surprise?"

Missy was twitching at the window, her binoculars scanning this way and that. "Is that one? I think I see something, but I can't be sure."

"You should go check," Penelope said, hoping for a little more time to perfectly map out her recycling bin strategy and the disposal of compromising household utensils in her possession before settling down to a scrumptious PB and J.

Setting the glasses down, Missy raced across the room, seized her purse, and, fairly panting, said, "With the skunks taken care of, we can move on to Dimwit!"

Then she was gone, slamming the door behind her.

A little while after viewing Missy through the binoculars as she stomped around looking at empty cages—a most enjoyable five minutes—Penelope received a call from someone in the parking lot about renting one of the empty units. She checked the clock. Missy had gone straight from checking skunk cages to Walmart for yet another pair of socks for her son's baseball team, but should be back soon. Showings usually lasted about thirty minutes. She could take the personal item down now but might risk running into Mr. Burke with a load of Perrier bottles. Best to stick to the original plan and book ass just when the recycling truck rumbled through the gates. She still had plenty of time. Last week they'd arrived around 11:00 and it was just now 9:45. The only sticking point was that Dimwit had yet to make his appearance. Leaving him alone with her personal item was a high-risk scenario. She texted Missy:

> When are you going to be back? Someone wants to see #4 and
> Dimwit hasn't made his visit yet.

**Riffling socks as we speak and wishing I'd brought gloves. FYI, the
cages were empty. Marshmallows my ass. We need to put some
live bait in there. Like a big pot of grubs. Why don't you call the
local bait shop and see what they have?**

> I'll get right on that. Seriously, when are you back?

Be there in fifteen.

> Thanks.

Of course.

Penelope smiled at this then checked the time. Everything was still on schedule. Even Dimwit couldn't do all he'd want or need in fifteen minutes and Walmart was like two minutes away. Once she got back to the office, she'd send Missy on another wild skunk chase and dispose of the evidence in peaceful solitude. It would be a snap. She grabbed her purse and—like the true paranoiac she was—checked that her implement had not disappeared into thin air. She tipped her figurative hat to its gently slumbering form and left the office.

~

The couple interested in the unit, recent retirees from Minnesota, proved quite the talkers. Penelope had always thought that Midwesterners were taciturn, but not Horace and JoJo. If there was a tidbit about Mankato they failed to share, it was hard to imagine what that might be. They'd miss steak night at the American Legion, karaoke at the Parkers' house, and the deep-dish pizza at Eduardo's.

What they wouldn't miss were the taxes. That—the tax rate—city, state, and federal—had been the main topic of conversation. Horace had made his money fair and square and thought he should be able to keep it. While inspecting the kitchen, JoJo concurred on all points. It was plain to her that the Mankato city council was bound and determined to bleed every last citizen dry, and also that the dishwasher was noisier than she hoped but not a deal breaker. They'd be back tomorrow to sign the papers.

Coming up the steps to the office, Penelope thought that she might have a knack for real estate, especially if a large component of that was just letting people get their yak on.

Real estate dollar signs were floating before her eyes when it registered that Missy's car wasn't in the lot. With apprehension building, she entered the office to find the same unrifled pile of mail she'd left on the desk for her boss. And nary a correspondence had been flung on the floor in anger. It was crystal clear that Missy had not returned in fifteen minutes as promised, and that the *Of course* was offered on fraudulent terms. Penelope checked the time. 10:45. The office had been unmanned for an hour. She glanced quickly at the bathroom door, which was open.

She was processing this turn of events when she heard the recycling truck rumble onto the property. Damn it, they were early. Heart thumping but maintaining her cool, she rushed to her bottom drawer. All the contents she expected to see were there, save the one item bearing her name. She went to the bathroom and peered in. There was no sign of Dimwit, and the toilet lid was decorously closed. Now the recycling truck was beeping in reverse. She went to her desk and yanked the drawer all the way out. Still nothing. Maybe she'd hallucinated and put it somewhere else. She checked them all. Nada.

It was then that Missy burst into the office and said, "I just got a speeding ticket in the Walmart parking lot. How is that even possible? What cop puts up a speed trap at Walmart? Isn't there a murder at Dollar General to investigate or something? Some vandalism down at the Olive Garden? My God, this is a one-horse town."

"Dimwit stole something of mine again," Penelope said. "I was worried about that, and that's why I checked to see when you were getting back. That speeding ticket really did me in."

Missy pumped her head up and down eagerly, crumpled the citation into a ball, and gave it a resolute kick across the room. Following it while still in flight, she waited impatiently for its landing, then stomped it several times for good measure. It was good and dead now.

"There's no way I was going forty. They've got like three speed bumps. It's totally bogus. Plus they didn't have those stupid socks I needed. Why can't Damien just play the cello or something? You buy one thing and you're done with it. I swear to God, I'm this close to shoving about forty pairs of socks up that coach's ass."

Outside, Penelope heard the recycling guys getting the first of the bins and glass rattling and breaking as it was dumped into the truck.

"Anyway, what did that inbred freak nab this time? Your Pixy Stix? Sprees? Reese's Pieces? Next time you get on me about tanning, let's have a little chat about dental hygiene."

"He didn't take something small this time. It was more like a personal item."

This got Missy's attention and she abruptly stopped kicking the crumpled ticket and raced back to Penelope's desk.

"Personal item? What kind of personal item? When I hear that term, I know where my mind goes, and it's not toward sugary snacks."

"Just something of mine he shouldn't have taken," Penelope said, fiddling with her computer mouse to keep from meeting Missy's cheeky smile.

Missy sat down at her favorite spot on the desk and said: "How personal?"

"Well, my name's inscribed on it."

"Really?" Missy said, popping off the desk for one more go at the crumpled ball in the doorway to her office. With one vicious soccer-style kick, she sent it sailing over her own desk and out of sight.

"This could be the break we've been waiting for," she said. "It would be tough to prove Dimwit stole candy or a pair of socks. But something with your name on it? In his very own crypt? We'd have him dead to rights. So what is it exactly, this monogrammed personal thing of yours?"

"I'm not saying."

"You have to or we can't file a police report."

"There is zero chance I'm telling the cops about this."

Missy approached the desk, frowning speculatively as if trying to suss out the nature of the pilfered item.

"Well," she said, "if it's something you're too embarrassed to confide to the authorities, and you insist on calling it *personal*, then I'm guessing I can figure it out. Quick game of Twenty Questions?"

"I don't think so."

"Is it monogrammed panties from Fitzdilbert?"

"I said I'm not playing."

"Novelty handcuffs? No, that's not your style. I'm guessing it's something you've recently gotten and then decided to get rid of. But you didn't want to dispose of it at home so you brought it to the office."

Missy was pacing in the waiting area where Penelope couldn't help but see her, stroking her chin like a detective getting closer and closer to solving the riddle. How she could be so good at this sort of analysis and so hapless about skunks, Dimwit, and everything else was a question for the ages.

She stopped suddenly, turned on her tiny heel, and said, "Dimwit swiped your dildo."

22

Penelope feigned looking for something in her purse to avoid Missy's smirk.

"I told you about your poker face already," Missy said. "You might as well admit I'm right."

"It was a gag gift from Sandy and Rachel. At my housewarming."

Missy nodded in what was meant to be an understanding fashion, trying her best not to smile but having little success. "Wrong size?"

"What? I don't know. I didn't even try it. It was green and had my name on it, for God's sake."

Missy continued her inquisition, but Penelope wasn't listening. All she could hear was the banging rattle of the recycling truck pulling out of Rolling Acres and onto the highway. She was regretting a number of things, but mostly her extended virtual tour of the Land of 10,000 Lakes.

"We have to get Dimwit," Penelope said.

"Oh, I agree, I agree. As soon as we take out the skunk army."

Penelope bit her tongue on this, feeling vulnerable after the discovery of her personal apparatus.

"Listen," said Missy, "I know you want to bypass phase one of the operation and storm Dimwit's hovel tonight, but I'm firm on the skunk thing. Our only other option is to call the police, report a burglary, and let them handle it. If they find something with your name on, like a massive green dildo, for instance, then Dimwit gets arrested and the issue is settled. So let's call the cops and file a report. Easy-peasy."

"I'm not calling the cops and letting them find that thing up there. That would be all over town in five minutes."

"I could call Gary and ask him to investigate it off the books. He's still obsessed with me. It's my own fault. I broke his spirit. Word to the wise: save the professional moves for professionals. Otherwise you ruin a man for other women. It's sad, really."

Missy was nodding somberly, trying not to grin. Penelope had met Gary once earlier in the summer and had to admit he was the lovelorn policeman Missy described.

"We're not calling the cops until I get my stuff back," Penelope said. "Maybe he stole something else we can prove is ours, besides my whatchamacallit."

"Please use your big-girl words. We say *penis* and *vagina* in this family. Also *dildo*. Try it. *Dil-do.*"

"No thanks."

"Pleasure pole? Stiffy in a jiffy?"

"No."

Missy cackled at this exchange then went casually to the back window. Lazily, habitually, she picked up the binoculars to check the skunk cages for the umpteenth time that week.

"Even if we can get in, and we do see our stuff," Penelope said, "we still can't call the police. We'd have to admit breaking and entering."

"That sounds like an urban legend, but let's worry about that when the time comes."

So saying, she resumed her halfhearted vigil at the window. Then her head jerked sideways and binoculars banged roughly against glass. This was followed by weird squeaking sounds emanating from her throat. She was on tiptoes, craning her head far to the left and twitching in an unsightly manner.

"Get me a chair, quick! I think I see something in the east quadrant!"

Despite herself, Penelope caught the rapidly spreading skunk fever and dashed to the window with a chair from reception. Missy hopped up, breathing hard, and again banged the binoculars into the window. "Ow! Damn it. I just gave myself two black eyes, but whatever. That's a skunk if I ever saw one. In fact, it looks like the leader of the horde. It is! I remember that white stripe."

"You admitted you didn't see any skunks. And they all have all stripes."

"I did see one, I'm pretty sure. And each skunk has unique patterning. Ask the Whisperer if they don't. Speaking of which, get his ass on the phone. We've made our first dent in Dimwit's army! Yee-hi!"

The skunk facts were about to start coming fast and furious, so Penelope sprinted to the phone before Missy could spring any more research on her. She pulled the Critter Catcher's card from her desk as Missy narrated from across the room:

"Ooh, he's mad, just look at him. He's snarling and pacing like a caged tiger. Now he's doing something weird with his snout. It is a snout, right? Or is that just pigs? What if he's signaling the rest of the corps? They could be streaming through Dimwit's skunk door as we speak. Hurry! I need you to take the walkie-talkie and survey the hill to make sure they don't surround me again before the Whisperer gets here."

The Critter Catcher answered the phone thusly: "Hellllo, Buford King speaking. What can I do for you this bright, lovely day?"

"We caught one!" Penelope said, giving in to the excitement of the occasion at last. Who was kidding who? She'd never doubted the marshmallows, and now her faith had been rewarded. Live bait? What a city slicker.

"Did we now?" said the Critter Catcher.

"Tell him I think it's the skunk king," said Missy.

Penelope frowned and pretended not to hear.

"Tell him it's pacing like a mother and looking highly agitated," Missy said. "Tell him he's going to have to whisper his ass off to calm this fucker down."

Penelope put a finger in her unoccupied ear to drown out the noise. Buford King was explaining in loving detail his plans to head their way as soon as he made stops at the hardware store, and the feed store, and his grandbaby's house to drop off a little play-pretty that he picked up at the flea market over the weekend. He was spoiling her rotten, but you couldn't blame him. Cutest little thing you ever saw. Spitting image of Darlene, right down to the little button nose. In sum, he'd be there directly.

Penelope said that would be fine and hung up.

"What did he say?" Missy asked.

"He'll be here in a little while."

"That's it? Did he go over his plan? What are the details?"

"He didn't say."

"What was he talking about for five minutes, then?"

"This and that. He's coming. Stop sweating it."

"Stop sweating it? We've trapped the skunk overlord. And right now his kinfolks are streaming out of that flappy door at Dimwit's. Snag a walkie-talkie and go check. I'll man the lookout window."

Penelope left the office, shaking her cell phone over her shoulder for Missy's benefit. She knew there was nothing to see but thought she'd clear her head a bit outside before the Critter Catcher's arrival. She'd been outside for approximately three seconds when her phone rang.

"Do you see anything?"

Penelope walked around to the back and stole a glance at Missy. She was frowning over her binoculars and jerking her head all over the place.

Crouching out of her employer's field of vision, she crabwalked until she was just beneath the window. Into her phone she said, "I think there might be one out back. I smell it for sure. And now I hear rustling!"

Then she rattled the hell out of the pane with her fist.

When she stood upright, she could no longer see her boss. She said, "*Did you hear that? What was it?*"

"They're coming! I told you. I'm up on your desk. Get back inside quick!"

Worried about heart attacks, panic attacks, and injuries resulting from falls from on high, any of which would end with her having to drive to the emergency room, Penelope called off the dogs. She signaled this by standing up, looking inside, and rapping the theme from *The Lone Ranger* on the glass.

Missy let the binoculars hang limply around her neck and gifted her with a double-bird salute. Penelope smiled and bowed. As she did, the breeze picked up and she noted for the first time the faint aroma of skunk. She glanced up the hill toward Dimwit's place. If she played her cards right with the captured skunk and the Critter Catcher, phase two of Operation Dimwit could get started that very night.

23

Ninety minutes later, Penelope stood in the parking lot, watching the Critter Catcher make his ambling way into Rolling Acres Estates, pipe smoke trailing from the window, small animals capering before him.

It took about fifteen minutes to get the truck parked to his exacting specifications, excluding the time he spent stopping to wave, smile, nod, and reconfigure his rearview mirror. Seeing the pickup finally come to a full stop and the engine turned off, Penelope poked her head in the office and said, "Buford King's here. It's safe to come out."

"Thank God," said Missy, bouncing past her down the steps and into the lot where the trapper was disembarking from the Critter Mobile and whistling a merry rendition of "Santa Claus Is Coming to Town."

"Well, we did it," Missy said, approaching the trapper with high five at the ready and binoculars swinging freely about her neck. "We caught the king. Or queen. Or whatever. It's the leader. I remember that distinctive stripe from the night they swarmed me. Those marshmallows did the trick, all right!"

The bewildered trapper stood frozen in place, staring at the proffered palm, unsure of its meaning or purpose. Dropping her hand from on high, Missy pulled the binoculars from her neck and said, "Here, have a look. See if it's not the leader of the pack."

This was a gesture easily deciphered, and Buford King took the field glasses and aimed them in the direction indicated by Missy's pointing finger.

First he whistled in a low, appreciative way. Then he clucked and clicked his tongue in further expressions of awe. Following this was a softly rendered slam poem consisting solely of the word *well*. About nine stanzas, all told.

Having fully appraised the captive on the east quadrant, his poem took a surprising free verse turn: "Look at Miss Pretty. Oh me. Oh my. That is, Miss Missy, a distinctive white stripe. Most distinctive indeed. Oh, she is a beauty. Pepé Le Pew should be along any minute now, any minute. I am almost positive she is female. So that would be the queen, and not the king, who is now kicking up a fuss. And spitting. And stomping them feet. That, my friends, is what is known as a deimatic display. It is meant to warn off predators who might be getting peculiar ideas about their next meal. Well, I best go check on our friend and see what's ailing her."

Smiling and clucking and whistling still, he handed the glasses to Missy, nodded to Penelope, and hopped back into his truck.

Missy looked puzzled as the engine on the Critter Mobile started up, and she turned both palms up to Penelope in a *What gives?* gesture. Buford King had closed the door and had his hand on the gearshift when Missy knocked lightly on the half-open window.

"Aren't we going with you? I thought you might need a little backup. Penelope and I would love to help."

"No we wouldn't," Penelope said.

Missy shot her a look and Penelope repeated her earlier statement.

"I appreciate that," said the Critter Catcher, chuckling. "Really, I do. I usually work alone, but if you want to tag along, I've no objection. Just follow me down in one of your cars and we'll see what we can see."

After several aborted attempts, the Critter Catcher managed to back his truck out, and the caravan was under way. He drove slowly, despite Missy's tailgating, and slower still as he navigated the three-inch curb that abutted the field. *Gentle* was a not gentle enough word for his negotiation of this obstacle. Once he'd nudged over it and Missy had rip-assed over that same boundary, they bounced a quarter mile or so over the vacant lot. Eventually, the Critter Mobile came to an easy stop, twenty feet from the east quadrant cage. This was much closer than Penelope would have advised, but she was not a professional tracker. She parked behind the CC, then, reconsidering, backed up a hundred feet or so.

"What are you doing?" Missy said, dropping her binoculars with no little drama. "Go on up there with the Whisperer. I'm wearing heels, for God's sake."

"I think I'm fine here. You're the one who gets so freaked out by skunks. I'm admitting a healthy respect when I actually see one, not when I think there's a phantom horde after me like some people I know."

Missy weighed this. She picked up the binoculars for a closer look. Mr. King was making his initial foray into opening the truck door. Next—in quite a lot more than a wink—he'd debark. Time was not of the essence. Missy put the glasses down. She gave Penelope one long, dramatic stare then shoved a walkie-talkie across the seat toward her.

"Because I'm the coolest boss ever, I'm going to let you hear the Whisperer work his magic even though you're too chicken to get up close. Watch and learn, country girl. These aren't ordinary skunks, but me and the Whisperer aren't ordinary experts either."

She hopped out and approached the trapper, who was still fiddling with something in the cab of the truck. Penelope assumed some sort of gear or equipment must be needed to handle an angry skunk. She wondered about the transit from cage to truck to gas chamber. It seemed like a lot of steps before the voyage to Skunky Heaven. Missy was engaged in conversation with him. She nodded, brow furrowed, a number of times and seemed to be agreeing with the proposed course of action. Eventually the Critter Catcher emerged. Penelope had been expecting some sort of intricate outfit, perhaps like a beekeeper would wear, but the only thing new was a lit long-handled pipe, which he was now peaceably smoking, and a bag of marshmallows in one hand.

The walkie-talkie crackled to life and Missy said, "Check, one, two. Check, one, two."

She gave Penelope her most determined face, eyes squinted and all, and Penelope said, "Ten-four, good buddy. I got my ears on. You can put the pedal to the metal."

Missy shook her head in a sad way, as one does when serious matters are put before the unserious. The Critter Catcher was opening his knife and deciding which of the multitude of blades to use to open the marshmallow bag when Missy said, "So Mr. King, what's the plan?"

She was holding the walkie-talkie at arm's length, so Penelope could hear both ends of the conversation. She had the air of an arty documentarian.

"Well, Miss Missy," said Buford King, as he finally settled on the right blade and commenced slicing. "The first thing I'll do is have me a little conversation with Miss America yonder. I'll start here in a bit, so she gets used to the sound of my voice. That's before I ever make my approach."

Missy nodded and said to Penelope: "Did you hear that? He's going to use voice hypnosis initially to relax the animal."

"Affirmative," said Penelope. "I copy."

When Missy shot her a look this time, Penelope gave a grinning thumbs-up. She'd grown up yakking away to truckers on George's CB and it felt good to be using the vernacular again.

Missy shifted weight back and forth in her high heels and swatted at a bug with her free hand. Glancing at her palm, she seemed pleased with the results. That hand was now wiped on the hem of her Gucci dress. "What's step two?"

"Step two, little lady, is a very slow approach, so I don't startle our friend. I'll be walking behind that towel you see on the front seat. Once I've done my calming, I'll drape that towel over the cage, nice and easy, and Mrs. Skunk will think it's nighttime. She'll get real settled then and we'll be home free. I usually toss in a few marshmallows as a kind of last meal. Just to say *No hard feelings.*"

Through a little radio static, Missy said: "And then?"

"And then I'll very gently walk the trap over to my truck and place it in that chamber right there to induce narcosis. I won't dispose of the remains until I'm home and can do it properly."

Both Missy and the CC liked the medical sound of that and nodded to each other agreeably. Missy said: "And what can I do to help?"

The trapper tipped his Stetson to the sky and took a puff on the pipe. A turkey buzzard was flying overhead, riding the wind, and it held him rapt for a spell with its long-winged aerobatics. Missy looked nervously back and forth from the Critter Catcher to the car, as if she feared being shut out of the process at this very late date and the subsequent mockery of her skeptical coworker.

"Well," said Buford King, after the bird had flown from sight, "I used to have a junior partner. But between you and me, he lacked the patience for trapping. He's now working down at Ace Hardware. Good young fellow but better off selling nails, if you know what I mean. Anyhow, I used to let him handle the towel. I'd sidle up to the trap, doing my gentling, and he'd sneak round from the back. It generally worked real nice. I guess you could handle the towel if you want to."

"Oh, I want to," Missy said. "I'm really interested in hearing your voice hypnosis. And if this skunk is as smart as we think it is, a two-man operation seems like the safest way to go. You still think it's possibly trained, right?"

"I have ruled nothing out at this juncture. That much I can tell you."

Saying this, he shot the briefest of glances toward Penelope, as if to affirm, again, his truly impartial stance. Whether this was a special skunk or just a run-of-the-mill one was still to be determined.

The Critter Catcher knocked his pipe against his pants leg, then set it lovingly above the dashboard, as if he wanted easy access to it after the job was through. He grabbed the towel and handed it to Missy.

"Sneak around the other side of the truck," he said. "And wait there till I give you the signal."

Missy took the towel and said, "Got you. What's the signal?"

"When I say *Are you sleepy, Mrs. Skunk?* you make your approach. Real quiet. Real gentle. There's no need in the world to hurry. Our skunk friend isn't going anywhere and neither are we. When you're right behind it, I'll say *Good night, Mrs. Skunk. I hope you sleep well.* And then you lay the towel all the way over the cage. She'll be half asleep by the time I'm done talking and will never even know you're back there. Easy as pie."

The Skunk Whisperer motioned with his head for Missy to take her position, then indicated with his finger that he was heading toward the cage. Just before he departed, he pumped both palms down in a slow fashion in the classic *Easy now* gesture.

Missy put the walkie-talkie to her mouth and said, "We're going in."

Penelope said: "I got your back door, Rubber Duck. Put the hammer down."

"What?"

"Affirmative. Ten-four. I copy, good neighbor."

Her boss shook her head again in that disappointed way, then walked to the back of the truck, where she crouched like an infantryman waiting for the signal to charge.

24

From where Penelope was parked she could view all three participants in the unfolding drama. She observed the Critter Catcher mosey toward the trap, smiling and talking. The skunk had noticed him and stopped pacing. Motionless, it watched the approaching man. Missy was squatting awkwardly in her heels behind the Critter Mobile, teetering on her skinny, tan legs. Her dress was hiked up well above her thighs but she seemed to give this no thought. Glancing back to Penelope, she put walkie-talkie to mouth and whispered: "I'm going to let you hear the Skunk Whisperer work his magic. He's the real deal. I'm getting sleepy just listening to him. Check it out."

So saying, she waddled a few paces along the side of the truck, walkie-talkie held aloft, towel draped round her neck like a scarf worn by a World War I airman. The voice on the other end sounded like it came from a tunnel but Penelope could hear Mr. King clearly: "Well, hey there, pretty girl. Ain't you a sight for sore eyes? And that stripe. I've never seen one quite so white, nor wide. Why, you've got white-wall tires, is what you got. And hey now, I got you a little treat. Would you like that? Would you like yourself a goodie?"

Missy now whispered into the mouthpiece: "Do you copy?"

"Affirmative, Rubber Duck."

Missy shot Penelope a disgusted look to indicate that now was not the time. Penelope smiled but said no more. She felt the tension of the moment.

During the CC's monologue the skunk had very sluggishly lain down. It rested now like a sleepy cat, head nestled on front paws. Penelope wouldn't have believed it if she hadn't just seen it with her own eyes. The cornered skunk looked not just docile, but asleep. Was she truly witnessing animal hypnosis?

Out of nowhere goose bumps appeared on her neck. She thought this resulted from the wonders of nature, then realized she felt as if she were being watched. Turning slowly in her seat, back toward Rolling Acres proper, and hiding her face as best she could with the headrest, she saw a small, hatted figure on the hill. It was Dimwit with his binoculars, watching the whole shooting match below. She thought of the Starbursts, and how one right now would make her feel like she was at the movies. Then the walkie-talkie crackled and she heard Missy say, "The Whisperer has worked his magic. That skunk is sawing logs. Listen."

The skunk lifted its sleepy head and turned at the sound of the radio static. Missy froze with her walkie-talkie arm in air, as if she'd just been touched in freeze tag. Then, ever so purposefully, she switched hands and held the radio close to her body, trying to be discreet.

The Critter Catcher said: "Now, Mrs. Skunk, don't you worry yourself about that little lady over yonder. She's my friend. And your friend too."

The skunk took the trapper at his word and placed head back on paws. Her eyes were closed and Penelope could see her body rising and falling in a slow, steady rhythm. Missy turned to wink at Penelope. Then she added a thumbs-up as well, which seemed like overkill. She again stretched the radio in front of her, chest high, just as the Critter Catcher said: "Are you sleepy, Mrs. Skunk?"

This question was accompanied by a significant look for Missy, who stood, wobbled for a moment, and then was erect. Penelope thought she should put the radio down and concentrate on the job at hand, but Missy felt otherwise. Perhaps she wanted audio proof of her first live capture. She unwrapped the towel from her neck, tripped on it and nearly went down, then gingerly approached skunk and Whisperer. The Critter Catcher waited a yard from the cage. His voice had grown even softer, more mellifluous, as he said, "I believe you're the prettiest little ole skunk I ever saw."

Missy nodded her head sleepily at this but failed to advance toward the cage.

The trapper continued his spiel: "Yes indeed, little lady, you are uniquely unique. You just keep a-resting and I'll drop you down a few of these sweet treats. If you're not hungry, well, you just save them for later."

Penelope felt a little badly for the skunk, as there wasn't going to be much of a *later* for her, but soon gave up this existential line of thinking. Missy was lumbering mummy style toward the action.

In a wheezing, fearful voice she spoke into the walkie-talkie: "Did you see the skunk move?"

"Negatory, good buddy," Penelope whispered. "You're still in the rocking chair. Keep the pedal down."

"I'm pretty sure I saw it look at me."

"Negatory. Quit talking. You'll wake it up."

Missy nodded stiffly to this and advanced a few tentative steps. She was now within eight feet of the cage. The Talk button remained engaged, for Penelope heard the Critter Catcher say: "Here's them marshmallows we were talking about. Mm-mm good."

As he cooed this, he very lightly tossed two or three of the morsels to the side of the captive's head. The skunk ever so briefly looked at them then resumed her relaxed posture of before. Things were going as smoothly as advertised and again the Critter Catcher nodded significantly at Missy. It was towel time. The signaling phrase was imminent. Penelope smiled. It was like watching *The Crocodile Hunter* but up close and personal. Missy was behind the skunk, off its left haunch, a mere two feet away.

"I saw it twitch," Missy whispered hoarsely over the radio.

"What?" replied Penelope. "No it didn't. Get the towel."

The Critter Catcher nodded and smiled brightly to Missy. Then he said: "Good night, Mrs. Skunk. I hope you sleep well."

Missy put the mouthpiece in front of her face and whispered: "It knows I'm here. I can tell. And I'm in the direct line of fire."

Staring intently at the tableau before her and whispering as quietly as she could, Penelope said, "Please quit talking."

The Critter Catcher was still smiling but now looked directly at Missy and repeated: "Good night, Mrs. Skunk. I hope you sleep well."

Missy said: "Dimwit trained them to recognize my scent, likely from stolen undergarments I didn't know he took."

Penelope whispered: "Put down the walkie-talkie."

"I throw my panties all over the place. He probably has a whole stack of them that I didn't know about. Look, I told you. She's turning toward me."

Penelope realized she was witnessing a severe case of logorrhea. How else to explain the chatterbox performance before her? The skunk stirred and swiveled its head toward Missy. It snarled, but the gesture seemed perfunctory.

The Critter Catcher said, very quietly, very soothingly: "Now don't go and get yourself worked up, Mrs. Skunk. That's just my friend, Miss Missy. Say *Hey*, Miss Missy, to our new friend here, Mrs. Skunk. Real peaceful like."

"Hey, Mrs. Skunk," Missy said, taking a step back as she spoke.

"Easy now," said the CC. "Everybody just be easy."

Missy said into the walkie-talkie: "Skunks don't see very well but they have an acute sense of smell. Look. She knows I'm here. My scent has been imprinted on her."

The skunk stood, wobbled a bit as if its legs were asleep, and turned to face the jabberbox. In a hushed tone, Penelope said: "Don't. Say. Another. Word."

The trapped animal, uniquely beautiful as she might be, now hissed in an unladylike way and stomped her feet. Most menacing of all, she raised her tail. It was the Whisperer who was now in the line of fire.

He looked at Missy and said, "Partner, Mrs. Skunk isn't sleepy now. Be easy there. Don't look in her eyes. I can soothe her again but it's gonna take a minute. You stand as still as you can, and please don't say another word."

Missy nodded catatonically in reply, then threw the towel at—but nowhere near—the agitated skunk in the cage. Following this, she ran for dear life toward the car.

Penelope no longer had audio but she saw the following pantomime clearly: the CC moving his lips and smiling uneasily, the skunk hissing and scowling at the tan woman now in flight, a quick dance sequence of foot stomps, a raised tail quivering as if electrified, and then the Whisperer raising his arms like he was trying to avoid something.

Then—as if hit by an invisible truck—he flew backwards to the ground.

Just as he did, Missy darted into the car, slammed the door, and said, "I told you those skunks were trained."

25

Penelope spared a quick, scornful look for her boss then turned her attention to the fallen trapper. He was immobile. The signature grey hat had flown clear and now sat forlornly on the ground well behind him. The skunk was still looking toward the car and hissing, its tail up and toward Buford King. Next to it lay the recently flung towel, looking as useless and helpless as the CC's Stetson.

"Is he dead?" Missy asked.

Penelope gave her another look but didn't deign to respond. She opened the door and was pummeled by skunk musk. "Are you okay, Mr. King?" she yelled.

The Critter Catcher turned his head toward the sound of her voice but kept his hands over his face. "I'm all right. The little rascal got me in the eyes."

He offered a wry chuckle at this and Penelope said, "What can I do to help?"

"Not a thing, my friend," said the Skunk Whisperer in a faint but clear voice. "Stay in the car. This is a powerful funk and you want no part of it. I assure you of that. I'll be up in a minute."

"Are you sure?"

"Sure as sunshine. Not the first time I've taken one in the eye. Occupational hazard, don't you know? I'll be along directly."

He removed his hands from his face now and Penelope could see him squinting and trying to open his eyes. He was still flat on his back.

"Oh shit," Missy said. "Was that my fault?"

"Of course it was your fault," Penelope snapped. "What did you think would happen when you threw that towel at the skunk and took off running?"

For one of the few times in the short history of their relationship, Missy was at a loss for words. She gawped at the scene she'd just abandoned and then at the walkie-talkie she held in her hand. She shook her head side to side and said, "I thought it was just pissed at me. I never thought it would spray the Whisperer. I thought they were friends."

"She was trying to spray you, you idiot. Or she sprayed in reaction to you. Didn't you see Mr. King standing right behind the skunk?"

"I can't remember. It's all hazy. I vaguely remember him saying *Good night, Mrs. Skunk. I hope you sleep well.* But after that, it's all a blur. I may have been hypnotized too. I was right in the path of the Whisperer's charms."

"You weren't hypnotized. You panicked. Now look what you've done."

Reluctantly, Missy forced herself to gaze at the downed man in the field.

"Look," she said. "He's up. See, he's going to be okay. A little spray can't keep the Whisperer down."

It was true. The Critter Catcher had risen. One of his eyes was closed, the other opened at a squint. He seemed to be searching for his hat.

Penelope opened the car door and yelled, "Your hat is right behind you, Mr. King."

He waved in acknowledgment and located his trademark chapeau. Penelope had shut the car door as quickly as she could, but the smell had gotten in just the same. It was getting stronger by the minute. In fact, inside or outside of the car made little difference in funk magnitude. It was a miasma of the first order. Missy was holding the neck of her dress over her nose and then pinching it. Penelope thought this the first reasonable thing she'd done and followed suit. Through cloth-pinched nose, Missy said, "Look, he's going for the trap. What a total pro he is. What a professional. You have to admit he's a professional."

Penelope felt no compulsion to talk. Then, changing her mind, she picked up the walkie-talkie on the seat beside her and said, as loudly as she could: "He is. And you're a total dipshit."

Missy nodded sadly at this. In front of them, Buford King was talking to the skunk. Then he reached into his bag of marshmallows and offered a few more, though the original ones had gone uneaten. The skunk sniffed at one and glanced back and forth from the sweets to the car where Missy sat. Its interests were torn, Penelope could tell.

The Critter Catcher never stopped talking, smiling and cajoling in a placating pantomime. The skunk ate a marshmallow. And then another. It turned completely from the car, looked at the old trapper, and lay back down on its haunches. The CC nodded, then groped blindly behind the cage until he found the towel. Once it was located, he draped it delicately over the trap, gripped the cage handle through the towel, and made his stumbling approach toward the truck.

Penelope looked at the disgraced trapper-in-training beside her and said, "There's no way we're letting him drive. He's half blind."

Missy nodded in a humbled way and—grimacing—got out of the passenger door. Bravely, she released her pinched fingers and said, "Mr. King, we're going to drive you home."

Zigzagging in an erratic way toward the Critter Mobile, the CC said, "That is unnecessary, my friend. I've been dosed worse than this plenty of times. This is nothing to the skunk and her kits I had to rouse out of the Smiths' crawl space a few years back. They were on me like a pack of hornets and me with no quick way out! That was a tight one, I tell you."

Chuckling at the memory, he continued his uneven quest for the vehicle. His eyes poured water, and every few steps he paused to wipe them away with the sleeve of his Dickies shirt.

Penelope got out of the car and briefly released her pinched nose before realizing the folly of the maneuver. She repinned and said in a nasally voice, "Mr. King, it's Penelope. We insist on driving you home."

He turned his head toward the voice but never convincingly located her. He was smiling at the hood of the truck and said, "My vision should clear in an hour or so. I can just rest in the pickup till then. It's a beautiful day. I don't mind."

"We're going to drive you," Penelope said, walking toward him and motioning to her employer to do the same.

"Well, if you insist," said the Critter Catcher. "But can either of you drive a three-on-the-tree?"

Missy shook her head to this, which was absolutely predictable. She probably never worked a clutch in her life, the sad suburbanite.

"I learned to drive on one of those," Penelope said. "I got you covered."

Buford King smiled approvingly. "I'll ride in the bed of the truck with Little Miss Pretty here. It's illegal to trap and move in the Old Dominion, but I can't see what I'm doing, and I'm afraid I might gas half the county if I try it now. I reckon it will be all right and I won't lose my license."

This contravening of wildlife statutes seemed to give him pause, but by then the ladies were next to him. Penelope nodded her employer forward and said, "Missy's going to lead you to the truck."

The Critter Catcher locked arms with Missy, smiling and shuffling his feet to rebalance the cage he held in the opposite hand. The skunk was again hissing, and the sound through the towel was eerie and disarming. "Don't mind her," he said. "She won't spray again. She's just being sassy."

They were walking now, slowly, to the huffing soundtrack of a perturbed animal beside them. Missy's eyes were watering, but she soldiered on. The stench was unreal—like rotten eggs electrocuted while floating in a water treatment plant—and Penelope had a throbbing headache.

"I'm guessing the smell is pretty bad," said the Critter Catcher.

"Funny thing is, after all these years, my olfactory is shot. At least as it relates to skunks. I can't smell a thing in that department."

Missy looked at Penelope with bugged eyes and mouthed, *Oh my God.*

Penelope felt dizzy from the stench. It was like a fog of sulfur that had been run through all the doo that had ever found its way to the bottom of James's shoes plus what Theo's bag of unwashed clothes would smell like when he got home from camp. It was the worst odor she'd ever experienced and there was no second place.

"It's not that bad," Penelope said.

"I believe you are being polite, but thank you all the same," said the trapper.

By the time Missy led him to the truck, he was no longer attempting to open his eyes. He ran his free hand along the rail of the bed and said, "Home sweet home," then lifted the cage over the side and set it down. The skunk nosed the towel a few times through the bars, as if testing it out, then hissed in a halfhearted manner.

"I believe our friend has about wore herself out," said the Whisperer. "And I will enjoy resting my legs for a spell, if I say so myself."

Eyes still closed, he placed both hands over the rail and hopped over, nimble as you please. Then he felt his way over the top of the cage before positioning himself beside it. His sat down with his back against the narcosis center.

"I guess you'll have to follow me in your car, so I can get back to the office," Penelope said.

Missy nodded in her defeated way, glanced once at the silent cage, and walked to her car.

Penelope said: "Mr. King, I see the keys are in the ignition. Is there anything you need out of the cab before we take off?"

"If you could load my pipe and light it for me, I would be much obliged. It is one of life's great pleasures to ride in the back of a truck while smoking a pipe and I do not get the opportunity as often as I'd like."

Penelope retrieved the pipe, loaded it up from the pouch of Prince Albert on the seat, found the matches, and lit up in the smooth, compact style she'd learned from the HHR so many years ago. For a fleeting moment she smelled nothing but the nice oaky scent of burning tobacco. But when she pulled the pipe away, it was straight skunk once again. She wasn't sure how an aroma could be tangible, but this one was. It had weight and mass. It was in her nose and mouth and eyes and hair. She spotted Missy in her own car, with the engine running, free from the narrow confines of stinkdom she now inhabited. It seemed a little unfair.

"Thank you, my dear," said Buford King, taking his pipe. "Not everyone knows how to start one and get it lit evenly all over. It takes a little patience, don't you know. I am obliged. My house is on Monacan Lane, out past the dairy. You know your way?"

"Yes sir," Penelope said. "I know exactly where it is."

She couldn't see any part of the skunk underneath the towel but could hear its restless pacing. The trapper heard, too, for he placed his non–pipe hand atop the cage and petted it softly several times. His eyes were still closed when he said: "We're just going for a little ride, Mrs. Skunk. Nothing to fret about. Not a thing. And if you're good, you might get you another marshmallow or two."

The skunk snuffled once to this and stopped pacing. Then, with a slight, metallic creak of the cage, it lay down.

It was time to get this show on the road. Penelope hopped in, turned the ignition, and eased it—as tenderly and smoothly as the CC could have ever asked—into gear.

~

The Critter Catcher had one eye half open when they arrived at his place, a quaint little frame house that backed up to George Washington State Park. Between house and woods were a barn, custom-built work shed, and roaming menagerie. Penelope spotted chickens, a pair of dogs, a barn cat with a litter of kittens, and a three-legged goat, which was trotting toward them.

She got out to lower the tailgate and was met by a mother lode of skunk stink. Driving, the stench had been gag-inducing but mitigated. Here in the open, there was no escape. The dogs, who had started to greet them, turned tail and fled behind the barn at the first whiff of foul air. The chickens and cats scattered as well, except for one little tuxedo kitten, who pranced beside the approaching goat. They were either inured to the smell or so glad to see Mr. King they could live with it. The goat and kitten stood just beyond the truck door, appraising Penelope. With his woolly white beard and battered horns, the goat looked quite old.

"That there is Dr. Longhair, professor emeritus," said the CC as he scooted off the tailgate. "He is our resident philosopher, and also our justice of the peace. If you have any questions or concerns, he's your man. Apparently his sniffer doesn't work like it used to. Otherwise he'd have skedaddled with the rest of his gang. Isn't that right, old friend?"

Dr. Longhair knew that he was being discussed and bleated an official greeting. He turned his head when Missy's car pulled in, kicking up gravel and dust in the driveway before skidding to a stop, then cocked his head in a way that indicated displeasure. A speeding infraction had occurred, or perhaps just a disturbance of the peace. Whichever it was, he didn't approve and jogged—more easily than you'd imagine—to stand before the driver's door of Missy's car. The tiny kitten bounded along in his wake. Missy started to get out, but her path was blocked. She rolled down her window and said, "Does this thing bite?"

The CC smiled and said, "What teeth he has left would not cut butter."

Missy mustered a resigned smile and said, "Mr. King, I'm sorry I messed up back there and got you sprayed. I feel really bad about it."

The Critter Catcher held up a weathered hand to stop any further comment. "There is no need to apologize, my dear. You are not the first partner of mine to head for the hills at the sight of a raised tail. Those deimatic behaviors are not for the faint of heart. You were simply not prepared for them."

"I feel awful. How will you get rid of the smell?"

"Well, luck is on my side. Darlene's not back from the credit union, else I'd be running for my life to escape her rolling pin. I'm going to draw me a bath in the old clawfoot tub out in the barn that I keep for days like this when occupational hazard comes into play. Old-timers like me swear by a tomato juice, boiled potato, and chaga bath. Your modern scholars scoff at this home remedy, and they may have a point. But some traditions are worth keeping. Still, just to make sure Darlene will eventually let me in the house, I will also make an ointment of hydrogen peroxide, Palmolive dish soap, and baking soda. If neither of these remedies fix me up, you will find me sleeping this evening in the barn with Dr. Longhair and his friend, the curious kitten. I can't smell a lick, so I can't tell if you ladies got some residual juice or not. If you did, I'd try the scientific way first."

With one eye still shut, the Critter Catcher lifted the cage without a jostle. Setting it on the ground, he lifted one side of the towel up so that he could see the skunk. He dropped in a couple of marshmallows and said, "And how did you like your first ride in a pickup? It was quite an experience, wasn't it, Mrs. Skunk?"

Penelope assumed the next stop for the captive was a voyage to Skunky Heaven, and she didn't want to be around for that. It was time to roll.

"Good-bye, Mr. King," she said. "I guess we better get going."

"Good-bye to you, Miss Penelope. And thank you for driving me home. I did enjoy the ride. And so did our friend here, I assure you that. Halfway home, she was off to the Land of Nod."

Penelope walked toward Missy's car, and as she did, her boss rolled the window all the way down. Jamming her head out, she yelled: "Well, at least we got the leader of the posse, didn't we, Mr. King?"

"That, I cannot say. You may be right, that there are a number of skunks on your property. Or it might be just this one. But it is a special one, I assure you. It is a special skunk, indeed."

And then he was ambling toward the barn, away from the euthanasia chamber, trap in hand, Dr. Longhair and the tuxedo kitten trotting alongside.

26

They were in the office after the ride back from the Critter Ranch. Missy, tone deaf as ever, had misinterpreted Penelope's ire for fatigue and asked several times if she hadn't slept well the night before. Penelope responded that she'd slept fine and continued to stare out the passenger window. Missy's attempt to recap the exciting day and the satisfactory conclusion had been met with stony silence and vague, mumbled responses from her employee.

Now at her desk, Penelope couldn't discern if she smelled like skunk or not. Her nose was all out of whack. Checking the clock for the hundredth time since returning, she was dismayed to see that it was only four. She had an hour left with Missy, who, unbelievably, continued to revel in the whole skunk fiasco.

Penelope was responding to an e-mail from a tenant about the possibility of switching to gas from electric when her boss interrupted.

"Listen, I hate to rub it in, but you have to admit the Whisperer all but confirmed that Dimwit is training skunks up there. You could at least have the decency to admit I was right all along."

Penelope's fingers paused on the keyboard. She tried to read over what she'd just written.

"Okay, okay, don't sweat it. I know I'm right, you know I'm right, so that's good enough for me. What a day. It was too bad about the old-timer getting sprayed, but as he said, that comes with the territory.

What a pro. He took that shot like it was nothing. I don't know if it's you or me or both of us, but the office has a distinct skunk aroma to it. Frankly, I think it's you. Probably from having to ride in the truck with the skunk and the Whisperer. But whatever. I'm used to the smell now and it's a small price to pay to get the leader of the pack. Now that it's gone, the others will be lost little lambs. What a day. You get your dildo stolen and now you smell like skunk. Seriously, what a day, what a day."

Penelope swiveled in her chair and said: "I promised you six months when I took this job, and I'm not going back on my word. But after that, I'm putting in applications other places."

Missy looked confused and shook her head a few times, as if clearing cobwebs. "Huh? What?"

"I've had it with Dimwit stealing my stuff. I've had it with Rolling Acres. And I've definitely had it with you."

"Me? What did I do?"

"Let's start with skunks. I smell like one right now. I think that's a good beginning point."

"You don't smell that much. Seriously. I hardly notice it. Just faintly. Like a tiny skunk candle. Not that bad at all."

"You're obsessed. I can't take it anymore."

"You can't quit. We're a team."

Penelope turned back to the computer. Missy raced beside her and sank down on her knees, clutching her hands like one in prayer.

"Please don't quit. Please, please, please."

"Stand up. Just stand up."

Missy did so, but reluctantly. She looked ready to buckle her knees again at the slightest provocation. "Please don't quit on me. You're the first person I've worked with who gets me."

Penelope inhaled, considered, exhaled. "Listen, you did me a huge favor by hiring me. I'll always be grateful for that. I'd still be stuck in my mom's basement without you. But I can't be a receptionist my whole life. I need to make more money. You had to know I wasn't going to stay here forever. I need something with a title. And again, more money."

Missy brightened at this and started a quick lap around the desk. "Title? What do you want? Duke of Windsor? Tsarina? Pope John Paul the Second? Take your pick and it's yours."

Penelope couldn't help herself and smiled. "You're ridiculous."

"Office manager? Ooh, that has a ring to it. It might look good on a résumé when you do start looking for jobs in a few years."

"That might help," Penelope admitted.

"It's done then. I'll get you a little wooden plaque thing that says *Office Manager* with your name on it. And some fancy business cards, too, with spiffy fonts and all that jazz."

"Thanks. I appreciate it. But long term, I still need more money. I'm not trying to negotiate with you. Just, going forward, I'm going to need something that allows me to start a retirement account, for instance. I'm going to be old one of these days and I currently have zero dollars saved. And I'd prefer to own a place instead of burning money on rent for the rest of my life. And Theo will have college. I don't have cable, I never go out to eat. Theo wants an Xbox I can't afford. That last stuff is small, but a lot of women my age don't have to check their bank account when someone asks them to meet for lunch. I do. It's stressful. I'm not sure how I'm going to get all that, or if a good enough job even exists in Hillsboro for someone with my credentials. I may have to go back to college. But that costs money too. Anyway, I'm not trying to make you feel bad. This job pays well for what it is. I'm just saying that I'll fulfill the commitment I made to you, but after that, I have to look for a permanent career."

"Okay, I hear you. I had no idea how poor you were. I obviously have no clue how the other half lives. And that's on me. I probably won't change, but at least I know how one poor person lives. I've got a fifty-dollar Applebee's gift certificate that a bartender gave me in honor of my one-hundredth margarita. I want you to have it. No argument."

"Fine. Thank you."

"Of course."

Missy nearly smiled at this but didn't. She held up a hand to let it be known her largess was just beginning. "And I'll talk to my dad about getting you a raise. A big one. We've been distracted by this move across town, but if we can get that wrapped up, I could put you up for more of a corporate position. We have regional managers all over the place and I'm not sure how long I'll be in Hillsboro. I'd like to get Damien through middle school, but we'll see. Anyhow, I'll ask Daddy. He's cheaper than hell, but I'm his only child and Damien is his only grandchild, so he can kiss it."

"I appreciate the offer. I really do. But I can't commit to anything right now, even with a raise."

Once again, Missy dropped to her knees and shook prayerful hands before her. Penelope had seen people do this in movies when pleading for a life to be spared, but never in person.

"It's Dimwit, isn't it?" Missy said. "It's not really the money. Or that you smell like a skunk. It's the bathroom whacking. Day in and day out. It wears on you like Chinese water torture. Oh please please please, don't let him win. If you quit, he wins. He's beaten me again. I can't take it. I *won't* take it."

She looked now as if she was trying to muster up some tears to go along with her pleading. She was wrinkling her nose and blinking her eyes rapidly and then turning up to stare at the overhead light, all the time shaking her hands at Penelope's knees.

"Are you trying to make yourself cry?"

"Yes, but it's impossible. I have a lot more respect for actors than I did like thirty seconds ago. How do they do it?"

"Listen, you talk a good game about getting rid of Dimwit. But when it comes time for action, you make up excuses. You allow yourself to get obsessed with garbage like trained skunks instead of going about proving he's a thief."

Missy popped up like one of those snakes in a prank box of peanuts and attempted a high karate kick. She only managed to get her leg about two feet off the ground, but one of her heels went sailing across the room nonetheless. She stood lopsided now in front of Penelope, toes on her shoeless foot wiggling crazily up and down. "I'll break in tonight!"

"Tonight?"

"You heard me. Skunks or no skunks, I'll get Dimwit for you. For both of us. Then I'll get you a raise and that plaque and business cards and we can stop this nonsense of you looking for other jobs. Dimwit's the problem. Dimwit's what came between us. He's trying to break up the team, but I'm not going to let it happen! Operation Dimwit, phase two, begins now!"

"You're serious?"

"Serious as a heart attack. I'll be in that skunk door lickety-split and take pictures of all the stuff he's swiped from us. Your dildo is the main artifact we need. It's like the Ark of the Covenant of Operation Dimwit."

"If you're serious, I'm in too."

Missy responded with another karate kick, which sent the other heel flying into her office and clattering along her desk. "Yee-hi and hell yes! My new office manager is in!"

"Do you care if I leave a little early? It's looking like a long night and I'd like to try and get rid of this smell before I come back."

"Yes. Leave early. According to Carl Junior, Dimwit leaves every night at midnight. God knows what windows he's peeking in all over town after his late-night Walmart run, but I'm guessing it's yours. Why don't I pick you up about a quarter till, so we only have to worry about stashing one car?"

Penelope agreed to this plan, gathered her things, and left to destinkify.

27

The decision was made to park across the highway at Tractor Plus in case Dimwit's late-night habits had changed since Carl Jr.'s report. They were clothed all in black, Missy in an Ozzy T-shirt and Penelope donning shirtless Jim Morrison, who'd always proved lucky, under the sheets and out. They shut their cars doors as quietly as possible and walked toward the highway. Not a car was in sight and the night was overcast, moody, and still. A dog barked from behind the tractor place and Missy nearly jumped out of her skin. She clutched Penelope's arm and said, "Did you hear that?"

"Yes. Quit talking so loud. It's just a guard dog. He's fenced in."

Missy nodded and followed Penelope across the highway, holding the sleeve of her T-shirt in one hand, a large, rattling Louis Vuitton bag in the other. "Sorry. I'm jittery as hell. I couldn't sit still after work so I made a trip down to the Shack to try and relax. Tammy had the microwave set to Popcorn, or Baked Potato, or something super high. Can you hear me crunching when I walk?"

Though a lecture was due, Penelope felt the less talking the better. They passed through the Rolling Acres gate and she nodded for Missy to follow her around back of the office. A motion light went on when they neared Carl Jr.'s maintenance shed and again Missy jumped.

"Damn it to hell," she said. "That could give us away."

Penelope walked on around the building, out of the light, and Missy followed, bag clattering against her leg.

"I'm not worried about that light," Penelope said, "but you're making a racket. What's in the bag?"

Missy arched her brows several times and her eyes shone with a piratical gleam. She reached into the satchel, pulled out a heavy cop-style flashlight, and thumped it twice against her palm. "We'll need this to see, plus I can bop Dimwit's head if he catches us. It's dual purpose. Totally practical."

"Your phone has a flashlight. And you aren't bopping anybody. That would get us busted for sure."

"Safety precaution then," Missy said, not listening at all and reaching into the bag a second time. "Okay, here's your walkie-talkie."

"We have phones."

"These feel more stakeout-y. Come on. I paid like six hundred bucks for them. And with a phone, you have to dial, redial, all that crap. These stay on all the time."

Penelope took the walkie-talkie. There was no time to argue.

"Okay," said Missy, "it's straight-up midnight, the Dimwit hour. I'm going to avoid the driveway and just book it up that hill. That way, if he throws us a curveball, I can dive in the weeds. Safer route."

"You'll break an ankle. There's no telling what he's got lying around up there. Just use the driveway."

"Negatory."

"Okay, whatever. By the way, do I still stink?"

Missy, loading her junk back in the bag, said, "Not at all. I don't smell a thing."

"You answered too fast."

"You're fresh as a daisy."

"I smell like skunk. That Palmolive bath didn't work at all."

Missy slung the bag over her shoulder, took a big obnoxious sniff, and said, "Yeah, but it's the scent of the lead skunk. That should buy us some time. With you down here playing lookout, the rest of them won't be inclined to be snooping around Dimwit's. I'll have the skunk door all to myself."

"I lit every fragranced candle I had and doused myself in body spray. I'm supposed to have a date tomorrow."

"If that's the case, I'd recommend the tomato juice, baked potato, and chaga bath."

"Boiled potato."

"You say *Po-ta-do*, I say *Po-ta-toe*. The key is the chaga. That's the special sauce. Do not skimp on the chaga. Do as the Whisperer does, is what I say, and you'll be ready for Mr. Sweaty, I guarantee it. Anyway, when I get a little ways up the hill, let's test our communication system?"

"Sure."

"Should we do a breakdown or something before I head out?"

"What?"

"You know, like when everybody on a team puts their hands in a pile, and you say *One, two, three, Operation Dimwit!*"

"I'm not doing that."

"Suit yourself," Missy said, offering a high five and a cocky grin. "Operation Dimwit is on!"

Penelope met the offered palm with an unenergetic one of her own, then Missy was trudging in her tights and Chuck Taylors across the parking lot toward Dewitt's, Louis Vuitton bag banging to wake the dead. Penelope decamped to a spot at the corner of the shed, where she could simultaneously watch the entrance and Missy's jaunt up the hill.

Penelope was more excited than she'd anticipated and was reminded of times rolling the yards of smartass boys with a gaggle of friends. Now that she was alone and the plan in motion, it seemed riskier and less planned out than it should have been. They really had no idea about Dimwit's night owl habits, other than months-old intelligence from Carl Jr. Glancing across the road to Tractor Plus, she tried to calculate the best escape route should they need to scram. She had little doubt of her own wiliness under such circumstances, but clanking-bag Ozzy might prove another story.

The radio crackled and Missy said, "Breaker one nine. Breaker. Testing. Trucker lingo, et cetera."

"I can hear you clearly without the walkie-talkie. Please shut up. You're going to wake the trailer park up."

Much quieter, Missy said: "These old farts took their hearing aids out four hours ago and are dreaming sweet dreams of Doris Day. But, yes, affirmative."

"I can see you too. You're walking right where the light is shining from Dimwit's front door. Scoot over five feet."

Penelope now watched a small figure hunch down and spider-walk toward the shadows, head twitching itchily everywhichway. Then suddenly, she was gone. Penelope squinted but could make out nothing but high weeds. The radio popped again and several wheezing profanities followed.

"What happened?"

A flashlight popped on and then off.

"Some inbred hayseed left a rusted tire up here and I busted my ass on it, that's what happened."

Penelope saw a small shadow rise, look down, and then kick. This was followed by more oaths.

"I think I just broke my toe. The Chuck Taylors were a bad idea. And I'm itching like a mother."

Limping, she moved into the darkened area that constituted approximately ninety-five percent of Dimwit's domain. How she'd managed to walk in the one lit area boggled the mind and Penelope had her first real concerns about the plausibility of this mission and the woman she'd partnered with to pull it off. The idea of arrest also entered her mind and the likelihood that she might supplant the HHR on the front page of the *Hillsboro Daily Record*.

A minute passed, then Missy strolled directly under the light of the front door. She paused—plainly visible—and crouched as if inspecting something low on the door. Penelope looked around quickly, saw the coast was still clear, and spoke into the walkie-talkie: "The doggie door is in the back. I told you that five hundred times."

Missy stood up, glanced around jerkily, and—unbelievably—responded: "Oh yeah. I forgot. Ten-four."

"Get out of the light!"

Nodding down the hill several idiotic times, she whispered "Affirmative" and slipped around the back of the trailer.

A moment later her voice came over the radio. "I am currently looking at the skunk door. Speaking of which, you haven't seen any, have you?"

"Shh! You're screaming."

A little quieter: "Have you?"

"No."

"They feel safe with their leader's scent down there. Us splitting up was a good plan."

"Get a move on."

"Putting the metal down now, Rubber Duck. It's a tight squeeze but I lubed up after Tammy's. I'm gonna strip down and slide right on in there."

"Don't take off your tights. You may have to run for it."

"Tights are off. I'm going in."

There was nothing for Penelope to do now but wait. This was the time when things could get hairy. She was scanning the perimeter when the walkie-talkie squawked again.

"Breaker one nine. I am currently in Dimwit's trailer and hell's bells does it stink."

"You're in already?"

"My head is. And my upper half. Still working my ass through. That cheeseburger at Sonic was a bad idea. Oh shit."

"What?"

"I dropped the stupid flashlight and it rolled off. I can't see a thing."

"Just get in there."

"My big-girl panties are holding me back. I should have gone cowgirl."

"You're stuck in the doggie door?"

"Currently."

"I'm coming up."

"Negatory, negatory. Do you read? Need your scent away from the scene."

Headlights now appeared on the highway and Penelope whispered as quietly as she could: "Don't panic, but there's a car heading this way."

"Distract them. Do you read? Distract them."

Penelope held her breath as the car neared the Rolling Acres entrance and then drove past. "Thank God," she said. "False alarm."

"Affirmative. But maintain current location. I just have to suck in my right cheek. It's always been the chunky one."

Penelope wondered what she was talking about. Missy was as buttless as they came.

"My God," Missy said. "It smells like an absolute whack factory in here. Like every pimply boy's room I knew at boarding school. Times one million."

"Are you through the door yet? If nothing else, you have to get that flashlight."

"Working on that cheek now. I should have hydrated. I'm retaining water after that dosage from Tammy."

"I'm coming up."

"Negatory, negatory."

But Penelope had already turned off the walkie-talkie and was running up the hill.

At the top of the drive she took a moment to check behind her. Rolling Acres remained quiet and dark, with only a few flickers here and there from a bedroom television. The highway was empty as well and their car in the Tractor Plus lot unmolested. If they had to make a quick getaway, the woods separating Dimwit's lot from the road would be the best option. The undergrowth was thick but not unmanageable. It would probably be safer to just fireman-carry Missy out, as the HHR had done with the bear cub. Otherwise, she was sure to get caught in barbed wire or something else improbable and get them busted. Decision made, Penelope booked to the back of the trailer.

Where she found two tan legs wiggling mightily outside a doggie door, tights and Converse kicked off in the grass, and a pile of bunched-up panties on skinny tan flanks stuck halfway in and halfway out of Dimwit's trailer.

"You tan naked?" Penelope said.

"I'm not Canadian. Of course I do. But I told you to stay down there. If we get caught, it's your fault."

"I could leave right now."

"Fair point. But listen, I think you're going to have to take off my undies for me."

"Seriously?"

"I don't know what I was thinking wearing these granny panties in the first place. They're like pantaloons. I was afraid my hiney would get cold."

Penelope took a closer look. They were indeed voluminous.

"Go ahead," Missy said. "Be a good girl and take off Granny's bloomers for her."

A harsh, cackling laugh came from inside the trailer and then half of a tiny butt began to wiggle in a dog door. Wondering how she came to be at this precise moment in time, Penelope went forward and smacked the tiny target one firm time. "Be still. We've got to get going."

The hindquarters came to a halt and Penelope put her hands on the panties and yanked. One side came down but not the other.

"It's the right cheek," Missy said. "I told you. Little Miss Chunky."

"They're really wedged in there."

"Well, I'm wedged all over the place. Anyway, just rip these bad boys right off."

"You sure?"

"Absolutely. Happens most weekends by request. Just give it the old heave-ho."

Penelope placed one foot against the side of the trailer for leverage, took a wide stance, and pulled for all she was worth. Missy's left leg flipped over the right one, and she let out a soft moan. Her left shank was free and clear of panties but the other side was stubborn. Penelope yanked harder. Matchstick brown legs were swishing this way and that but the right cheek would not budge. Penelope dropped to the ground and put both feet against the trailer, grunting with exertion.

"Pull!" Missy called. "Pull, you scurvy dog!"

Grunting fiercely one last time, like a European tennis player on match point, Penelope tugged. A ripping noise ensued and then the sound of half a body plopping onto a trailer floor. Penelope stood up, shredded panties in hand, to find Missy peeking through the curtains at her. Half naked and triumphant, she unlocked the door and said, "Come in, my dear, to Dimwit's House of Horrors."

28

Penelope entered, fearing the worst. There was no telling what macabre scene would greet her, or what an inspection of the premises might reveal about the depth of Dewitt's depravity. Daily office whacking might be small potatoes compared to what went on up here. It was pitch black and she couldn't see a thing. Any second now she'd trip over a Japanese sex doll dressed like Scarlet O'Hara.

The overhead light came on.

"Turn that thing off!" Penelope shouted.

The room went black again.

"I've got to find the flashlight," Missy said.

Penelope turned her phone light on. Recalling her boss's state of undress, she shone it purposely on Missy's face. "I brought your clothes from outside. Why don't you get dressed?"

"No can do. I'm going to torment Dimwit with my pheromones for a while. His little Confederate pecker will give him no peace once I'm done marking my territory."

Missy now manipulated her hand in a way that suggested the wafting of fumes from a waist-high fire. Finding this more demonstrative than necessary, Penelope turned off the light. "All he's going to smell is my skunky funk. Put your clothes on or I'm leaving."

Mumbling about fragile southern belles, Missy pulled on her tights and shoes.

The nudist colony expunged, Penelope again turned on her flashlight and did a slow, panning reveal.

"What in the hell?" Missy said. "It looks like my grandmother's living room. The sofa covered in plastic, the wooden bowl of fake fruit. My God, he's got glass paperweights on every side table."

"And it's spotless."

A quick survey of the adjoining kitchen revealed much the same order of decor. Another bowl of wax fruit sat on the dining table and a magnet on the refrigerator asked visitors to *Kiss the Cook*. The wallpaper was brown and burnt orange and showed three repeating scenes of early colonial life.

"What's that behind you?" Missy asked.

Penelope aimed the light where Missy pointed. On the wall was a framed cross-stitch of twining vines and purple flowers around a daintily lettered aphorism:

The Hurrier I Go
The Behinder I Get

"There's not jack in here," Missy said, "unless he's stashed your dildo in that cabinet with the silver and china. But I'll bet you one thousand dollars that through that door right there we find the mummified corpse of Mother Dimwit."

"Don't even joke about that."

"It's that or the skunk kennel, guaranteed. Ooh, I bet he's got little bunk beds for his children of the night and everything."

"Yeah, let's check that one, but we've got to hurry. Dimwit could be back any minute."

Missy waved off this concern and placed her hand on the doorknob of the mystery room, smiling devilishly. "I like to call this the mausoleum."

Side by side they entered. Once inside, Penelope commenced a slow reveal of the room, which, it turned out, was not a repository for human remains. Nor was it a bunkhouse for trained crepuscular creatures.

"Dear Jesus, Joseph, and Mary," Missy said. "Am I hallucinating?"

"No."

"A craft room? Seriously? Who is this freak? Look at all that yarn. It's like a Michael's catalog in here. He's making a scarf? He's worn the same clothes every day since I've known him. What in God's name would he do with a scarf?"

"I have no idea. But I do know what he does with those binoculars sitting by the window."

"Do you know what this means?" Missy asked. "Dimwit is crocheting while he spies on us and tickles his little Stonewall."

Penelope didn't know about the scenario Missy envisioned, but Dimwit was, indeed, a crocheter. And a knitter. And likely a seamster, too, unless that sewing machine was just for show. This was just the sort of room Sandy and Rachel would love to stick her in for the next decade to keep her from dating. Now that she smelled permanently of skunk, perhaps she should consider it.

"Okay," Missy said. "This room is officially freaking me out. I had a bad experience in art class one time after I made a papier-mâché ding-dong and the teacher made me sit in the supply closet for like two hours. Art teachers do not fuck around. I've got to get out of here."

They crossed the hall and entered the bathroom. Here they found a sink upon which sat an antique perfume bottle with a variety of dried flowers sticking out of it; a toilet with a wicker basket atop holding extra rolls of paper; a trilevel rack with matching towels of various sizes, all in baby blue, affixed to the door.

The lone objet d'art was an embroidered poem above the toilet.

IF YOU SPRINKLE
WHEN YOU TINKLE
BE A SWEETIE
AND WIPE THE SEATIE
♥ ♥ ♥

"Does he even use this bathroom?" Missy said. "It's an old lady museum in here. Where's all the weird stuff?"

So saying, she ripped open the medicine cabinet. Here, lined up in three neat rows were an assortment of lotions, oils, and butters in shea, coconut, almond, and lemon sage. Also a toothbrush.

"Ah-ha!" Missy shouted. "A full-service Jiffy Lube! Now this, my friend, is par for the Dimwit course. I'm not nearly as freaked out as I was. But there's nothing in here of ours. You ready for the bedroom?"

Penelope nodded and followed her employer a few feet down the hall to the last unexamined space in the trailer. They opened the door to find a bedroom with blue-green walls. It wasn't quite turquoise, but very close. The trim was assuredly Daisy White. This gave Penelope pause, her paint combination dovetailing so closely with Dimwit's. This moment of consternation soon passed. The room smelled nervous and sweaty. It reeked of epic solitary battle.

Trying to breathe only through her mouth, Penelope took in the ambience of Dimwit's private quarters. The single bed had been made starchy-tight, military style. The Spartan effect was mitigated by the homemade quilt folded neatly at the foot. The colors matched the walls. A bedside table held a lamp and a fancy, long-stemmed candy dish, the sort found filled with peppermints in every single old lady's house in the world. Something in the dish caught her eye. There it was—the shiny, unopened pack of Starbursts. She nabbed it and was about to open a long delayed treat when Missy seized her hand.

"He'll know we were here."

"These are my Starbursts."

Missy pried the candy from her closed fist and placed it back in the dish.

"I know you're upset now," Missy said, "so I'm a little hesitant to point out the slippers under the bed."

Penelope looked down. Tucked halfway under the bed and facing out—ready to be slipped into on a chilly morning—was a small pair of furry, fluffy mules, quite similar to the type that she herself wore on a winter's day. Two tee-tiny yellow socks, cute as can be, were tucked into the slippers as if they'd been recently worn and would be again, first thing in the morn.

"Those are the socks that were in my desk!"

Missy shook her head sadly, as if the eternal Innocence versus Knowledge conundrum was being played out before her eyes.

Missy took a photo of them and said, "I know they are. Your toes and Dimwit's toes are basically married now. Sad but true. And I peeked in the closet too. There's all kinds of candy and gum in there. Like individual pieces of Dentyne. And half a pack of Tic Tacs."

"Orange?"

Missy replied again with forlorn nodding. "And those watermelon Jolly Ranchers you like. There's a pair of my hose. And about forty Chapsticks and lip glosses. I think he's got Doris's retainer case too. Poor lisping retainer Doris. I don't think she fully embraced the Rolling Acres experience. Anyway, I took photos of all that junk even though there's no way to prove it's ours. We need to find your pleasure pole PDQ, or this is all a big waste of time."

Without knowing she was doing it, Penelope had avoided looking at the floor-to-ceiling shelves on the far side of the room. She'd always been good about trusting her intuition in tense moments like this, most of which involved minor transgressions of the legal code as a youth. Her intuition would say "Time to run," and she did. Or "That tree is a good place to hide." She and her intuition had a good thing going— they both seemed to care a lot about sparing a certain someone from lengthy interactions with the local constable and unpleasantness of every hue. But she could delay looking no longer.

"Get a load of Dimwit's collection over there," Missy said, wide-eyed and grinning. "What kind of freak collects back scratchers?"

Penelope took in the collection, which was vast and varied. There were wooden ones and plastic ones and ones that looked like the long metal fork George used when grilling tenderloin. Some were antique and more rounded. One was an octopus, another stamped "Louisville

Slugger." Dimwit was not a strict archivist, for he'd included a metal head tickler, a feather duster, and a little car with rounded spikes for wheels, which she assumed was meant to be rolled like a Hot Wheel on body parts needing relief.

There was one item, however, that stretched the integrity of the collection to its breaking point. It had been placed in the corner of the top shelf. This scratcher was plastic, with a green cylindrical shape. It bore the name of one of the women in the room.

Missy's mouth dropped wide. "It's your Steely Dan!"

"Yep."

"Quick, take a photo and let's get out of here."

"That won't help us. We're going to have to act like we just chanced to see it. We were up here on some pretext and happened to glance in the window. If I take a picture of it here, we'd have to admit breaking in. No way the cops would get a warrant for that."

"You're like Cagney and Lacey all wrapped into one!"

"I think I can get a clear shot from outside that window if you pull the curtain back. Just crack it enough where it would look reasonable that we saw it from outside. I'll give you a thumbs-up when I get the shot, then you pull the curtain back where it was. Got it?"

"Yeah, yeah. But listen, really zoom in. If we can't see the John Hancock on your substitute penis, we've wasted our time."

"I'll get the shot. Afterwards, you lock up like we found it and squeeze back through the doggie door again. And be quick. You think you can manage?"

"I'll strip down and be out in jiff. My butt feels smaller already."

Penelope nodded then sprinted back through the Museum of Maiden Aunts, feeling the mad rush of borrowed time.

Outside, she peeked around the back of the trailer to make sure no Dimwits were about, then raced to the bedroom window. She lined up the shot and zoomed in until the implement took up almost the entire frame. Then she backed it up a bit, so that more of the back scratchers could be seen and it would be clear where exactly in Hillsboro her dildo now resided. She double-checked that the **PENELOPE LEMON** inscription was visible. It was, and she snapped.

She was ready to give the thumbs-up to Missy when she saw lights from the highway flash through the trees. She banged on the window and said, "Get out now!"

Heart pounding, she beat around back to find the upper torso of a woman squirming through a pet flap. And then the lower half emerged, skinny flanks flashing in the moon. Missy popped up smiling with her bag of useless instruments in one hand and a purloined ball of yarn in the other. Headlights flashed on Rolling Acres Way and then those same lights pivoted slowly, as if the driver was making a careful survey of the hill before ascending.

"Dimwit's back," Missy said.

"*Shh!*"

Missy smiled and wiggled her eyebrows. She tossed the yarn in the air, nearly fumbled it, but held on. She seemed pleased with herself and sat down to put on her tights and shoes.

"No time," Penelope whispered as the headlights crept up the drive. They couldn't be seen from where they stood, so as long as they stayed still, they'd be okay.

Penelope whispered: "When we hear Dimwit open the front door, follow me. Don't move before that."

Missy gave two thumbs up then wound the tights around her head like a bandanna. "Bret Michaels from Poison. I'd scratch his back."

She was truly the worst whisperer of all time and Penelope put a stern finger to lips and bugged her eyes. Missy made the motion of locking her lips, zipping them, and throwing away the key. She was truly an idiot.

They waited in silence for a car door to open, but there was only the *chirr* of crickets and wind through leaves. Suddenly Missy perked up her nose. Then her eyes grew wide. A skunk was in the vicinity. Whether half a mile away or a hundred yards was impossible to tell.

Missy pointed at Penelope and finally whispered properly: "They smell their leader up here. Dimwit's sent the signal. I told you to wait down there."

"Be quiet."

"I'm not letting them surround me again. They know I captured their queen and won't let me out alive. I'm booking."

"No. You'll get caught."

But it was too late. Missy had begun a tenderfooted run down the hill. From the looks of things, she rarely went shoeless, other than in tanning booths, for every other step her leg shot up as if she were treading on hot coals. Penelope waited still to hear the car door open. It was every woman for herself now. She sincerely hoped that Missy didn't run directly to either the office or the car, which would get them caught for sure. Briefly, her boss passed through the illuminated section of the hill, a naked, tanner-than-normal backside, the legs on her tights swishing around her head, and then Penelope could see her no more.

The smell of skunk was stronger now, and she wondered if this would increase her personal stink. She waited, then waited some more. What was Dimwit doing in his car all this time? Trying out new scratchers? Crocheting? It could be anything.

Eventually a car door squeaked and then thunked softly shut.

Boots on gravel. A key put into a lock and clicked. A screen door squeak. And then the main door, shutting.

Penelope, on soft feet, made her silent exit.

29

Twenty minutes later they were pulling stealthily out of Tractor Supply.

In the interim, Penelope had maneuvered down Dimwit's hill, cautious and sure, only to have the wits scared out of her by a pantsless woman who announced her presence by flying out from the lowest branch of Mr. Burke's well-loved maple. Once she'd recovered from the shock, Penelope led Missy down the road via corners of houses and tree cover toward the cul-de-sac, where they crossed over Rolling Acres Way and sprinted down backyards till they were behind the office. From there, it had been a dash across the darkest portion of the highway, a leap over a ditch, which Missy nearly cleared, several moments of Penelope fetching her boss out of that wet and weedy culvert, and a final skulk, tractor to tractor, to the waiting car.

The pilfered ball of yarn, worse for wear after its arduous journey over hill and dale, rested on the seat between them, as did the massacred granny panties. Missy drove with tights bandannaed still around her head. That she was half naked, muddy, scraped, and itching away at her legs and other parts unknown seemed apt and right.

"Well, that was easy," Missy said.

Penelope glanced over, noted the angry rash running down her leg, and looked away.

"I have one question for you," Missy said. "Did you or did you not smell skunks tonight?"

"I smelled a skunk."

"I rest my case."

"I'm not arguing this again."

"No need. We've reached consensus."

Missy whistled for a while and tapped her grubby hands jollily on the steering wheel. All was right with her world.

"And you got the shot we need, right? The close-up of the P. Lemon Special?"

"I got it."

"You can see your full name, right? Because it would be just like that wily Dimwit to claim it belonged to another Penelope."

"Full name."

"Fantastic. Hey, do me a favor and text it to our old cop buddy, Gary. We can get the ball rolling on Dimwit's future incarceration."

What had once been theoretical was now all too real. A personal adult item named **PENELOPE LEMON** was about to be state's evidence. Would this evidence also find its way to the local paper? Would she have to testify in court—in front of people she knew—that a twice-divorced woman living out in the country still had needs, man or no man?

"Go ahead and send that bad boy off to Gary," Missy said. "He's so in love with me, he'll probably get a warrant tonight."

She chuckled at this, her hold over a six-foot-three local policeman.

"Listen," Penelope said, "I know I agreed, but now that official people are actually going to see it, I'm having second thoughts."

Missy turned to face her, the legs of her tights swishing briefly in front of her face as she did. "What? This is the moment we've been waiting for. We've got him dead to rights. After this, we can move to our new spot and be rid of Yosemite Sam forever."

"This is what *you've* been waiting for. A few months from now, I may not even be working for Rolling Acres."

Missy slammed on the brakes. In front of them was Skatetown, where Penelope had once roller-discoed in knee-high rainbow socks and white-trimmed gym shorts with her best friend Debbie. It looked run-down, antiquated. Was this really as far as she'd traveled since those carefree, skate-stomping, "We Will Rock You" days?

"What are you talking about?" Missy asked. "Is it the title thing again? I told you, you're vice-regent of the office."

Penelope frowned but didn't reply.

"Archbishop then. Brigadier general. Have your pick."

"I'm not talking about a title."

"If it's your salary, I've already e-mailed Daddy about a raise. I should know something by Monday. Tuesday at the latest."

"Listen, I appreciate it, I really do. It's just the job isn't exactly what I had in mind."

"Too boring? Answering the phone, showing units, et cetera."

Penelope looked at her disbelievingly. "No. The opposite in fact."

Missy waved her hand as if shooing a not very pesky fly, and again was driving. "You mean this little caper? Pshaw."

"I smell like skunk. We just broke and entered. You're not wearing pants. It's quite possible someone saw you running down the hill—in the light—and called the cops, who are looking for us right now. I could go on."

"It's me," Missy said dramatically. "You're quitting because you don't want to work with me. I'm too much for some people. I get a little wound up. When I was a baby I was always sticking stuff in the electric socket. It's nature, not nurture, I tell you. But please don't quit. Forget the photo. Forget the personalized dildo. I'd rather stay with Dimwit than lose my best friend and best-ever employee."

Best friend, what?

"Let's just go home," Penelope said. "I'm tired and irritable. I made a deal and I'll stick to it, so you'll get your photo. Dimwit is a pervert and a thief and shouldn't be able to get away with it. You can send it to Gary, but I can't do it myself."

"I'm not sending it to anybody."

"Listen, I said I'd do it, and I'm not backing out now, after what we just went through. If you don't send the photo, I'll quit. Monday, in fact. The cops should know about Dimwit. He needs to be on their radar. But I do have one request. Can you make sure they ask someone other than Judge Wyatt to sign off on the search warrant? My step-father is one of his best friends." She gave Missy a look that said she meant what she'd just said. "Send the photo."

Missy nodded, the pigtail tights bouncing lightly over Ozzy's maniacal face, then they drove the rest of the way home in silence.

30

All through the night Penelope dreamed of sirens and the banging of authorities' fists on her door. Missy had called her from jail for unknown reasons, but she hadn't gone to pick her up. At one point, Theo was running down a hill at Camp Sycamore with no pants on and a group of mean boys were throwing balls of yarn at him. Then she was with Active Brad at the gym and he was twitching his nose as if at a sour odor and tapping his Fitbit. It had stopped working and he seemed to associate the funk with his failing health gadget. Then she was running in a marathon but was hopelessly lost and so far behind everyone else she had no idea where the other racers had gone. Megan's voice was the one coming over the race loudspeaker, announcing where the awards ceremony would be held. Earlier, both Mimi and Fitzwilliam had jetted past her. They'd been encouraging and she was glad they were now friends. It was the only thing in the whole day that sort of made sense.

Dragging herself out of bed Saturday morning after the exhausting dream, she sniffed her arms and then the sheets, but couldn't tell anything. Maybe her entire house no longer smelled of fresh paint but exactly like Dimwit's Army of the Night. She had no idea about anything aromatic these days and recalled the Critter Catcher's permanently compromised olfactory. She'd have to cancel with Active Brad. She stood now at the kitchen sink, downing an instant yogurt and trying not to imagine the many giggling eyes that had seen photos of her personal item at the police station.

If Missy stuck to the story they'd concocted, she would suffer personal embarrassment but not incarceration. They'd been working late when a tenant called about possible smoke coming from Dimwit's trailer. They'd investigated—like good landlords and Samaritans—and spotted the stolen dildo in their innocent quest to keep Dimwit safe. He could argue that he never left his curtains open, but so what? They had photographic proof of theft. Basically, either she and Missy would receive an unfriendly visit from the cops today or Dimwit would. Who the accused was depended solely on Missy sticking to the script.

This notion gave Penelope little peace of mind, so she went to the fridge, grabbed the orange juice, and swigged from the carton. Theo would get scolded for such a move, but she was an outlaw now and could do as she pleased. Speaking of Theo, she was due for another letter from him. The more she thought of his last note, the more convinced she was that Camp Sycamore was a bad fit for a quirky boy. His cabin was probably eating last every single meal because of his slow-moving ways and group derision would be his reward. It would be the school bus bullying situation all over again.

Her next point of worry was what excuse to offer Active Brad for the last-minute cancellation. She needed one that let it be known she was still interested and would like to reschedule soon. She pulled out her phone, but before she could send a text, she received one.

Hey. How would you feel about postponing our get together till early next week? A guy in my kayaking club has a race this afternoon but his partner tore a rotator cuff rappelling yesterday. He's asked me to fill in.

Then a second one.

**I don't have to go. No pressure. This dude is trying to qualify for
the Wilderness X Games and I feel sorry him. He can get someone
else though.**

Penelope had never typed faster.

That's fine. I had something come up as well. I'm free all next week.
Have fun.

They traded smiley face icons like middle schoolers and that
wrapped things up. Wow. What a break. She could stink the day away
now and not have to sweat it. Dancing a little to "We Are the Champions," which had just popped into her head, she went to douse herself
with perfume and then head to the gym.

~⌒

She was pumping away on a sitting leg press, trying to exert herself to
the point that she'd no longer feel a nagging, unwarranted guilt about
being a bad friend to Missy. But who else on God's green earth could
stand a job like the one she had? Who else could live—day in and day
out—with a boss like Missy?

It was the *best friend* comment that was causing the guilt, but she'd
learn to live with it. She couldn't spend the rest of her life playing
javelin catcher for a madwoman. She needed a real job, a respectable
one. That would probably mean going back to college at some point to
finish her degree.

She was smiling at the thought of bebopping around a college cam-
pus in middle age, with ivy on the buildings and youngsters all about,
and enjoying the quietude of the gym on a Saturday afternoon. She'd
not seen Mimi, but otherwise things were A-OK. Her playlist, heavy
on Queen, couldn't have been better. And what a stroke of luck with

the rappelling fellow and his rotator cuff. The poor guy would probably need surgery, but he'd saved her bacon. She could stink in peace now and not worry about it.

She felt a tap on her shoulder and pulled out her earbuds. She regretted this decision immediately when she saw Trainer Megan standing there.

"Hey, I brought you another flyer for that triathlon we talked about. You left the other one. You're still interested right?"

That same flyer was being stuck in her face, basically blocking her vision, and she had no option but to snag it. Megan wasn't wearing her Fitness Plus uniform or name tag and Penelope wondered again why she would be at work on her off day. Shouldn't she be singing "Oklahoma!" in an Annie Oakley outfit in James's bedroom right now?

"Thanks," Penelope said, taking the flyer and sticking it under her spandexed butt where it belonged.

"Do you smell something?" Megan said, twitching her nose. "Like skunk maybe?"

Penelope made a show of turning up her nose and testing the air. "No, can't say that I do."

"Definitely skunk. But anyway, so you're in?"

"Oh yeah. I just haven't had time to sign up yet. I can do it online, right?"

"Or you can just fill this out and give it to me."

"That's really kind of you, but I'll do it at home. I'm planning on biking up Wistar's Knob later today. Just got my new wheels."

"You're biking Wistar? That's like a twenty-degree incline. Ten miles."

"Oh, I know. I just wish there was something steeper around here. I'm used to Telluride and places like that. If you want real biking, you have to go to the Rockies."

Megan squinted at Penelope's leg press, then sat down at the adjoining one. Placing the peg at thirty, or exactly double what Penelope was currently screwing around with, she got to grunting work.

Penelope smiled to herself. She'd pulled that Telluride thing out of her you-know-what. The lead article in *People* a while back had discussed Brad Pitt's fondness for biking in that quaint Colorado town. Others might doubt its journalistic quality, but for her, *People* had always come through.

"What about the swimming then?" Megan asked, straining beside her. "That's usually what gives people the most trouble."

"I swam breaststroke at USC. I probably won't even practice for that. What is it, like a mile and a half or something? I can do that while smoking a cigarette."

Megan nodded but didn't reply. The weight seemed like it might be a bit much for her, but she soldiered on nonetheless. Penelope put her earbuds back in, grinning at the thought of race day. Megan would be searching for her at the starting line, little guessing that she'd be sleeping soundly in her comfy bed, dreaming sweet dreams of not running, not swimming, and definitely not biking. The issue felt settled. Every gym had a Megan or two. There was no need to fall for their lame attempts at bullying. Life was too short.

Feeling a little sad for the competitive woman beside her, she turned up "Bohemian Rhapsody" and continued her casual pushing of metal.

31

She'd felt revitalized while telling triathlon lies to Trainer Megan, but now that she was back home, dread and doubt—about Theo, her career, and money, always money—crept back in. She walked to Theo's room and again weighed whether to surprise him with a mural. One day he'd outgrow his PlinkyMo obsession and be stuck with a little kid's wall. Would it be a waste of cash?

She was thinking of penury and Xboxes and how to entertain Theo way out here in the country and how lonely he probably was at camp, when she heard a horn honk in the driveway. She went to the kitchen window, expecting to find her stepfather, George—he was an inveterate horn-greeter—and was surprised to see the Critter Mobile instead.

The trapper spotted her in the window and tooted a little song as a greeting. Smiling, Penelope bounded out the door and down the front stoop.

"Well hey there, Mr. King. What brings you way out here on a Saturday afternoon?"

"Howdy, howdy, Miss Penelope. I hope I'm not interrupting."

"Not a thing. Can I invite you in?"

"I would, I would. But I got a little job I'm heading to. Some folks in Greasy Cove have discovered squirrels in their attic. Chewed through half the wires and starting in on the insulation. I best not tarry. Your partner over there at Rolling Acres called me this morning and said you might need a little home remedy for your—if I may be so bold—aromatic situation."

Penelope laughed at this phrasing and at the Critter Catcher's sly delivery of it. He was doing the country thing of pretending like he wasn't trying to be funny when he obviously was. It was a favored trick of local old-timers.

"Mr. King, I can use all the help I can get. I'm a little skunky."

He got out of the truck now with a paper towel in his hand. "I'm guessing you tried the dishwashing recipe on that Internet, but not the tomato juice, potato bath?"

"That's right," Penelope said, walking toward him. "It just seemed like so much trouble. And tomato juice isn't cheap."

"Oh I know, I know. Anyhow, I brought you a little chaga. It's the real secret ingredient. I think you can do without the tomato juice and just add this to the Palmolive and be right as rain afterwards."

Penelope took the proffered gift. "Thank you, Mr. King. I really appreciate you coming all the way out here to deliver it."

"Don't think a thing about it. And to be honest, I have an ulterior motive for my visit. I got something in the truck that I just don't know what to do with. I thought you might have an idea or two."

He said this with an especially twinkly eye, winked, then returned to the Critter Mobile. Penelope felt herself smile at the presentation—at the show—as he reached through the open truck window. She felt sure some homegrown vegetables or a Mason jar of Darlene's clover honey was forthcoming. Anyone who'd ever lived in Hillsboro had seen this ritual before.

After procuring the item and cupping it in two hands, he slowly crawdaddy-walked toward her, sneaking smiling glances as he came. When he was right in front of her, he opened his hands and revealed a small, alert-looking kitten, which he then passed over. The kitten greeted Penelope with a quiet meow, then squirmed to get free.

"She won't stay still long, that one," said the Critter Catcher. "She's bound and determined to see what the world has to offer."

"Isn't this the one you call the Curious Kitten? The one that was following your goat around?"

"Yes indeed, that is the Curious Kitten."

"She's adorable," Penelope said, setting the black and white ball of energy on the ground. The kitten sprang up the steps of the stoop and tried to launch herself onto the chair. It was too high, but she tried several times before scooting around the side of the house.

"Should we go get her?" Penelope asked.

"Oh, she'll be back directly. And then she'll shoot off again. I been studying that one for a while, yes I have. She's ready for what comes. I kind of believe you two might be birds of a feather."

Penelope considered Theo's many allergies and weighed this against his love of animals. She recalled that James's last girlfriend had a puppy that Theo loved playing with and that he'd not broken into hives afterwards. A cute, adorable kitten for him to come home to? They wouldn't even need an Xbox.

"I'd love a kitten, Mr. King. I love this kitten. And my son will too. It will be a great surprise when he gets home from camp."

"I am so glad to hear it. And this place will suit her to a tee. Just to a tee. Room to roam and places to explore."

He gave her his friendly, whimsical look, tipped his Stetson, and started for the truck. When he was seated, he handed out a package of dry cat food and then a small potted plant. "Here's you a little catnip. You can plant it over there by the fencerow and before you know it, you'll have a whole passel. That is, until that little imp eats it all up."

He chuckled and started the engine. He put the truck in gear and then back into Park. "Oh, I forgot to tell you. Our skunk friend that gave us the juice? She's still with us. Never seen one that pretty, or that smart neither, in all my years of trapping. Anyway, I reckon she's roaming around my farm these days and won't be troubling y'all no more. Let's just hope the authorities don't hear about this."

"You know I won't tell."

"Oh, I do know that. Well, I best see about the squirrels in the attic. Those rascals can go to town in a confined space."

With a wink and a finger to his hat, he backed his truck out of the driveway and was gone.

Penelope left the chaga, cat food, and catnip on the stoop and went around back to watch the new kitten. If it were up to her, the new addition would be named Curious K, which conjured thoughts of a cat rapper. Theo would probably like that handle as well, but the final call would be his. What a break this was! No matter how badly his two weeks at camp had gone, how lonely and friendless, or how infected his bites or peely his skin, he'd have a cute little fur ball waiting on his return. That would be a nice tonic for what ailed him.

Thinking of how this all came about, she realized a text was in order.

> Thanks for sending the Critter Catcher over with the chaga.
> I appreciate it.

A moment later she got a reply.

> **Hope you aren't as stinky for your date.**
> Date got postponed. Should smell like my old self, for better or worse, on Monday.
> **If you're free, come watch Dimwit get busted. Gary's got a search warrant he's serving in about an hour. NO JUDGE WYATT, FYI.**
> Tempting but the Whisperer brought me a kitten. That cute one that was following the goat around. I'm just gonna chill with her today.
> **Got you. Also, Gary promised me he didn't share the photo of you-know-what (i.e. a huge green dildo with your name on it) with anyone else. I told him if he did, he'd never have a chance at my hot tub again.**
> Thanks.

Of course. He also said that this sort of thing never goes to trial. They just plea bargain them out. Dimwit probably won't even go to jail. Somehow he has no priors. Gary will talk to the DA to make sure you don't have to testify.

Perfect. And now you can move to the new place. Congratulations. **Only downer is now I have to meet Gary for drinks at Applebee's on Tuesday.**

Penelope offered a weeping face emoticon. Then another text.

I'll see you Monday.
I'm glad to hear it. Thanks for putting up with me.
Of course.

Penelope weighed whether to send the text she wanted to or not, then decided what the heck. It would give Missy something new to worry about, now that Dimwit would soon be out of the picture.

The Critter Catcher said he didn't have to the heart to kill such a smart and unique animal, so the lead skunk is still on the loose. Hope she's not looking for revenge.

Then, laughing, she turned off her phone and went in search of the new kitten.

‿つ

Thirty minutes later, she heard the low rumbling of the mail truck and leaped from the screen porch couch, Curious K in hand, and race-walked to meet him. They exchanged greetings and he handed over what looked like a pile of bills and flyers for oil changes and grocery coupons. Walking back to the house, she set the kitten down and riffled through the daily load of junk. At the bottom of the pile was the correspondence she'd been waiting for. She tossed the irrelevant crap like so many crap Frisbees onto the stoop and ripped open the letter from her brave camper. In a racing, sloppy hand that all but told the addressee that what followed was written with a sharp guilt knife at neck, she read the following:

Dear Mom,

A counselor told ghost stories at the campfire the other night that were pretty good. Do you know the one about the hook hand ending up in the window? This one kid cried and he was in the oldest cabin. #lame. It wasn't that scary.

I have to go now. My friend Justin who is from Asheville wants to go to the pond. It's free time. He's launched like every Plinky but ten! Which is hard to believe for just a kid. We're going to catch tadpoles and then let them go. Tadpoles are #sick.

Also, you will probably get a note from the camp. I have impetigo but just on this one part of my leg. Don't say I told you so. Half the kids here have it too.

Love
Theo

Ps: Do you think there was anyone with the last name English who couldn't speak English? I bet Justin there was.

She read the letter over, and then once again. Theo had a friend! Good old Justin from Asheville, a PlinkyMo-launching, tadpole-loving wonder of a boy who talked about ridiculous stuff like people named English who didn't speak English.

Granted, the deployment of hashtags and the word *sick* to mean *cool*—the stupidest usage of any word in the history of the English lexicon—was all but a declaration of war. What a little smarty he was.

Well, two could play that game. Her return post would be chock-full of smiley faces, LOLs, OMGs, and maybe even some throwback lingo like #totally awesome. Or #gnarly. She might even throw a #stoked in there, which was popular during her two years of college among the richer kids who went snow skiing.

She plopped down in the recliner and breathed in the warm summer air. Theo had a camp friend. What was a little bacterial infection on the leg when you had true-blue Justin from Asheville around? The lyrics of the nightly campfire song popped into her head and she tried, but failed, to picture Theo earnestly singing them by the light of a toasting marshmallow.

> *Along the banks of placid lake*
> *Among the dewy dells*
> *Oh, Sycamore, Camp Sycamore*
> *Where friends I'll surely make*

Curious K now came snuggling and purring against her ankles. It occurred to her that she still had a week in the house by herself and that she could do whatever she pleased the rest of today and Sunday. She had to run to the store for cat supplies and while she was out, she might as well get that mural. Theo's PlinkyMo fixation wasn't going anywhere soon. She could hear the credit card whimpering from her purse, its flimsy back about to be broken by the heavy load, but so what? A decent raise was likely coming her way. And if not, she'd find something else. Definitely.

She nodded to this and smiled at Curious K who was leaping after a moth well overhead. Then she texted Sandy and Rachel.

> Home girls. I have a free house and a new kitten. About to load up on wine. Dump the kids with your fellows and hang out over here tonight. Want to show you what I've done with the place. Also, Dimwit stole the dildo you gave me, and I met a new guy. Fitzwilliam's

mansion had a bidet, which I used ineffectively. Dimwit has a craft room like the one you wish I had. I discovered it when Missy and I broke in last night. Come over if you want to hear the juicy details.

If that didn't entice them, she didn't know her married friends.

She smiled at how easy the suburban gals were to titillate, then picked up her new kitten, her letter from Theo, and went inside to run herself a long chaga bath.

ACKNOWLEDGMENTS

As they say, it takes a village to raise a writer. And mine is, and has always been, a village full of kind, wonderful people.

The first word of thanks goes to the man to whom this book is dedicated, my editor and friend, Michael Griffith, whose fine eye for the superfluous word or phrase helped implement the very lean prose style you see here. There simply aren't adequate words to describe how much Michael has meant to these books and to my career in general. He is editor nonpareil, and I'm blessed to have worked with him on these Penelope Lemon novels.

I am so very grateful for LSU Press, a first-class operation who treats writers as colleagues, partners, and friends. It's been a pleasure and a privilege to work with people like Alisa Plant, the director of the press, who had to sign off on this unusual arrangement not long after taking the reins at LSUP. It would have been an easy thing to say no to, and I appreciated the moxie and the faith to roll the dice on me and the book. Not everyone would have. James Long, the acquisitions editor, has been a stalwart and a shoulder to lean on during the long, arduous process of getting both these books off the ground, and I'm thankful for his equanimity, his encouragement, and his patience. Michelle Neustrom is the best book designer I've ever worked with, and her feel for how these Penelope Lemon novels should look has greatly enhanced the reading experience, and the comedy too. The books are funnier for her keen eye and design creativity. Neal Novak, the senior editor, has also been a joy to work with. His easy manner and understanding of how the book should be laid out on the page is the sort that every author hopes for. He and Michelle are a formidable team on the production side of things and I'm lucky to have had them as partners on this endeavor. Laura Gleason has been a friend and ally and I appreciate the many emails she answered of mine and the good advice—"be patient"—that she offered on more than one occasion. Frankly, every single person at LSUP has been a joy to work with. I've known from the start that it was my good luck to have landed with the fine folks in Baton Rouge.

My collaborator on these books is my wife, Christy. She is my sounding board for plot and character, my first reader, my best and most honest critic. If books were like movies, she'd be listed as executive producer. I couldn't have written these Penelope Lemon novels without her creativity and support, and I'm fortunate to share a house with one of the best editors in the country.

Reid Oechslin read early and very rough drafts—as he has on a number of my novels—and offered thoughtful and insightful feedback, especially as it related to big-picture issues such as heightening tension and the balance between comedy and pathos. Jason Hottel read an early version of the manuscript as well and gave the kind of encouragement that keeps a writer plowing ahead. Mark Parker and Ray Murray also chipped in by reading early pages and offering a kind word.

My brother Frank is a lifer, God bless him, when it comes to my writing career, offering kudos when things go well and an ear to bend when they don't. The impact he has had on me and my family cannot be overstated. He has kept the train on the tracks for a long time now and is the brother to top all brothers.

Thanks to the gentlemen of the Hung Jury, my fellow Charlottesville writers John Hart, John Grisham, and Corban Addison, who have been there throughout the six years it took to write and publish these

Penelope Lemon books. Their insights into the publishing business and their encouragement and advice have been invaluable, as is being able to "talk shop." I'm proud to know all of you.

The following have all helped in some way or another that I'm thankful for: Chris Vescovo, Allen McDuffie, David Jeffrey, Rose Gray, Angela Carter, Dabney Bankert, Bryan Di Salvatore, Richard Gaughran, Jean Cash, Allen Wier, Robert Stubblefield, Boris Dralyuk, Brehanu Bugg, Margaret Renkl, Wayne and Skip Carter, and Kristi Cross.

As always, my mother and stepfather, Nancy and Stan Braun, have been there for me. It's been a nearly thirty-year grind in the writing business for me now and their never-wavering support has meant the world. The same may be said for my 101-year-old grandmother, Nina Winton.

Lastly, I need to thank my kids, Tess and Maxwell, for being so sweet, so funny, and so easy. No matter how anything else is going with the writing or the career, at the end of the day I had my children to eat supper with, to laugh with, and to remind me of what really matters in life. You guys were there, along with your mom, during the dark days when I was ready to pack it in. I appreciate you all hanging in there with me. It did the trick.